Seaside Cowboy's Se

Book 1 in the Seaside Cov

By Alexa Verde

SEASIDE COWBOY'S SECOND CHANCE
Copyright © 2023 by Olga Grun writing as Alexa Verde

.

.

Editing by Deirdre Lockhart at Brilliant Cut Editing.
Cover by Julia Gussman at https://sweetlibertydesigns.com[1]

---

1. https://sweetlibertydesigns.com/

About Seaside Cowboy's Second Chance

A woman with broken dreams and promises. A cowboy with a broken—by her—heart. A stray dog with a possibly broken paw. And everyone with a dangerous secret. Even the dog.

.

When free-spirited Skylar Rafferty left her beachside hometown, she promised her high school sweetheart she'd return soon and marry him. Fifteen years later and no longer free-spirited, she returns to plan the wedding—her grandmother's. When her grandmother's fiancé goes missing, Skylar turns to her former sweetheart for help while aching for a second chance.

.

Cowboy Dallas Lawrence can't believe the woman who crushed his heart has wandered into his life again. But strange things connected to her family are happening in their quaint tourist town, and when her life is in danger, he can't walk away. But he can't get his heart broken again, either.

.

Welcome to Port Sunshine, a small coastal town where a family of cowboy brothers discover the treasures of love and uncover the mysteries of their pasts.

Prologue

He should've run.

It might be too late now.

Exhaustion had settled in Earl Lane's bones, but that wasn't the reason he'd stuck around this quaint coastal town where the locals knew each other's names and celebrated their milestones together. The place had undeniable charm, and so did Dolores Rafferty.

He squinted at the setting sun and the spectacular play of peach, gold, and blue dipping into tranquil ocean waters. How many more of these sunsets would he be able to witness? Seagulls bid him farewell as Breeze, the two-year-old golden retriever he'd recently adopted, chased them, her pink tongue lolling.

His heart contracted. Dolores was the reason he'd stayed here. Something inside him shifted. *How* did he happen to fall in love, even at his age, skeptic that he was? Not just with a place. With a woman.

Ridiculous? Yes.

Yet a rare smile tugged at his lips as he took a deep breath of the salty ocean air. The mere thought of her gave him a pleasant jolt. He never expected to become this attached to her. He'd resisted it as long as he could. It wasn't in his plans when he'd driven to this beachside gem named Port Sunshine. He'd learned the hard way he shouldn't get attached to people. It was selfish of him to propose, just as it was selfish to adopt an abandoned dog rather than take it to a local shelter.

Should he try to rehome Breeze? Leave tonight? Everything in him protested against the idea. He couldn't do it to Breeze. Couldn't leave Dolores a month before the wedding just like that, with no explanation. It all had gone way too far.

A chill having nothing to do with the ocean breeze rushed down his spine. That man had killed once. Would he hesitate to do it again?

They knew each other's secrets, and it kept them safe from one another. But some things had changed.

Premonition twisted his gut.

Breeze tired of chasing birds and darted toward him. He picked up a stick and threw it as far as he could. She leaped into the air and caught it, then brought it to him with such pride as if it were a rare treasure.

Dolores's granddaughter would be arriving soon, and he was the only one who knew she might be in danger. He winced but patted Breeze with affection. "Good job." Then he hesitated. "If something happens to me, take care of Dolores, will you?"

Shouldn't it be the other way around? Dolores hadn't even met Breeze yet. The golden retriever mix was going to be a surprise.

A breeze ruffled his hair. The evening was growing colder and darker. Goosebumps erupted on his skin. "Let's go back."

The dog kept running, refusing the suggestion. She might be getting that stubbornness from her new owner.

Exhaling, he rubbed his palms over his forearms where the shirt offered no defense against the picking-up wind and troubling thoughts. "What am I going to do with you?"

Breeze stopped running and tilted her head, staring with soulful brown eyes, but not moving closer.

"I'm going to pick up a blazer. Then we can stay outside longer, okay? I don't have fur like you do. You can stay on the porch. I'll just run inside for a moment."

The dog seemed to find his explanation logical as she trudged nearby, running forward, then returning. He couldn't walk fast any longer.

The moment he entered the small rental, he could feel something was wrong. The hairs on the back of his neck stood on end even before he heard the painfully familiar voice.

"It's about time we met again, isn't it?"

Earl flinched. He should've left today.

Chapter One

Skylar Rafferty's fingers tightened around the steering wheel as she pulled up to the gas station. She'd almost made it to her grandmother's house in Port Sunshine, but now the arrow was on empty.

That was the way she felt lately. Running on empty. Would returning to her hometown for a month refuel her?

Riiight. She chuckled without mirth as she pumped gas. Coming back here left a bittersweet taste, and she almost dulled it with the stale coffee she'd gotten before leaving. Stale. Just like her life.

What was wrong with her today? She loved her grandmother, used to love this small town and the ocean that seemed as endless as her dreams when she'd been growing up.

Then one mistake changed it all. She should've gone to the police then and there. She should have.

She winced and dropped the cup into the trash. She had to do this for her grandmother, just as she'd kept the painful secret for so long because of her. After all, Grandma had always been there for her, and Skylar hadn't really returned that favor for years.

She was about to get into her gray sedan when a low whine made her linger and glance back. A dog limped from around the pump, then sat at a distance, and lifted its paw.

"Is your paw injured?" All her hard edges softened.

The dog whined a reply and lifted her paw higher. Her long coat was dirty and matted, and who could say for sure what color it was originally? Maybe a gorgeous pale-yellow hue. A golden retriever mix? No collar and probably no microchip, either.

"Are you a stray?" Maybe Skylar should go inside the gas station and get a hamburger. "Or would you prefer a hot dog?" She had little experience with dogs, and the small gas station wouldn't likely carry kibble.

The dog stopped whining.

"I don't know why they call it a hot dog, but it's *not* made from a dog. I promise." She edged closer.

The dog whined again, favoring her paw. Skylar couldn't get a dog. Or... could she?

Years ago, she'd wanted a pet just like that, well, sans the injured paw and miserable look in its brown eyes. But she'd let that dream go, like many others. Her stomach clenched. Not the time to count her losses, especially the biggest one.

Dallas.

Her grandmother expected her by now, but how could Skylar leave an animal in need? The least she could do was take it to the vet and get some proper food. A bath wouldn't hurt, either.

She sighed. "You aren't going to bite me, are you? I'll take you to my grandma Dolores. After I take care of you, of course."

Hmm. Was it her impression, or did the dog's ears stand on alert at her grandmother's name?

"I'm not going to hurt you. I promise. I want to help you." Skylar inched even closer, half expecting the canine to take off.

Instead, she stopped whining and tilted her head, studying Skylar.

When she opened her car door, she glanced at her white blouse, too dressy for the trip, and grimaced. White blouse and charcoal-gray slacks. She used to wear bright colors. She used to be fine getting dirty, even playing in the mud.

Yup, *used to*.

"Well, it is what it is." She lifted the dog and placed her onto the car's carpeted floor that didn't have a single speck before. The canine settled near the back seat as if she belonged there.

Just like Skylar had once felt she belonged in this small coastal town. With Dallas.

Why did her thoughts keep returning to him?

Grimacing, she considered going to the bathroom to clean up her blouse, now decorated with dirty streaks. Although itching to clean up, she squeezed her teeth and slipped into the driver's seat. She'd have to carry the injured golden retriever to the veterinarian's office anyway, so her blouse would just get dirty again.

Maybe she thought about Dallas so much because she was on his turf now, in several senses.

Or was her guilty conscience speaking? Though what could she have done differently? She couldn't go back, not after... She shuddered as she took off from the gas station. But she should've talked to him instead of avoiding him every time she'd visited Grandma.

On her hands-free phone, she made a quick call to her grandmother about the delay.

Minutes later, she pulled up to the vet clinic, familiar from the times she'd visited it as a girl with Grandma's cat. The cat had seemed to weigh a ton then.

A few vehicles occupied spots in the parking lot, including a rusty navy-blue truck she'd recognize from a million others. Her heart skipped a beat, and if there was another vet clinic in town, she'd have gone there.

No. Lots of people drove such trucks. And the truck's window didn't have the usual decal with the ranch logo.

Drawing a deep breath cleansed with peach car air freshener, she parked and opened the door for the dog. "You probably won't agree, but I want that paw checked out first." Her left arm started itching. "Hmm, we'll check you for parasites, too. Then we'll get you a bath and some food at the pet store." She should've bathed her already, but she'd been too afraid to damage that paw. The awkward angle the dog held it at almost looked broken.

"That means I shouldn't let you walk, either, okay?" She'd have to kiss her pristine blouse goodbye later, but she lifted the dog and harrumphed. Office work as an accountant did nothing for her biceps.

She wobbled toward the L-shaped stucco building—one of the few buildings in town without an ocean and/or a pirate theme. Instead, a kitten and a puppy got along fabulously on its front wall. She'd painted it that way, and Dallas had helped, mostly by coloring within the lines she'd drawn. At that age, she'd sometimes had difficulty coloring within the lines. Her rib cage contracted. How very carefree and happy she'd been then. Happy with Dallas.

The puppy's once chocolate-brown floppy ears had faded in the sun, and the paint on the kitten's pink nose was peeling. But otherwise, it appeared painfully familiar, just like so many other buildings in her hometown. Nostalgia tugged at her.

Enough.

Okay, this dog didn't seem to weigh a ton, but her arms strained under the weight. She almost wished she'd encountered a stray Chihuahua instead. Or a stray kitten. Her grandmother's cat from childhood seemed light as a feather right now.

Skylar slowed and frowned at the massive front door painted to match the puppy's ears. With her hands occupied, how was she going to open the door? Okay, she'd done it with her elbow before. Then footfalls inside reached her. Or she could wait for someone to leave.

The front door opened, and she stepped aside to let them pass.

Only nobody stepped out. She looked up, and her heart started beating faster.

Seriously? Of all places on earth—okay, in their small town—why did Dallas have to end up at the clinic right this moment?

Was he... was he still angry with her? She'd broken off their engagement fifteen years ago. A long time. But it still made her heart ache, so his could be worse.

He gaped at her as if unable to believe his eyes. Well, welcome to the club.

Great. He looked great. No matter how grudgingly, she had to admit it. Outdoor labor at the family ranch sculpted muscles a black T-shirt did nothing to hide. The ranch logo stretched over his now-broad chest, and the sun had generously tanned his skin. Jeans bleached by the sun and not by chemicals hugged his trim waist and muscular legs and were tucked into cowboy boots.

His eyes, blue like the proverbial ocean, had once been open and cheerful. Half hidden under a brown Stetson, they were guarded now, and most likely, she was the reason for it. He was no longer the teenage boy she'd fallen in love with. Even promised to marry.

The dog lifted her head and growled at Dallas as if sensing animosity. Then she wiggled in Skylar's arms, awarding a clump of dirt onto Skylar's cheek. Bathing the stray seemed like a better and better idea, but then hindsight was twenty-twenty.

Always had been. But no time to think about regrets, even if her biggest one was standing in front of her. She stepped inside the building that smelled of fur and medicines.

Maybe because of the early hour the hall was empty, except for a woman in a wide-brimmed straw hat sidestepping them, holding a cat that hissed at the stray. Then another one with a turtle. Probably tourists. Though would Skylar recognize all the locals now?

Now she was alone with Dallas in the hall, and she felt it sharply.

She was the first to come out of a stupor and move forward.

But he was the first to find his tongue as he tipped his Stetson. "Hello, Skylar." Although he kept his voice neutral, a muscle twitching in his cheek gave him away. His telltale sign. Yup. He was still angry with her. "I can hold the dog for you if you'd like."

Guilt stabbed her. She'd hurt him, and he still wanted to help her.

She moved her tongue, even though it felt like a swollen log in her mouth. "Hello, Dallas. Thank you. But no thanks." She hefted the dog, her muscles straining even more. "I'm fine. We're fine."

Could be worse. She could've picked up a stray Newfoundland.

The dog let out a whine as if to say she was far from fine. Frankly, Skylar wasn't anywhere close to fine, either. But she'd done her best to appear that way for fifteen long years.

"You came back to arrange your grandmother's wedding." With the way he said it, it was a statement, not a question. News traveled fast in their small town.

Did he anticipate her appearance? Or did he dread it?

The dog wiggled in her hands, and she struggled to hold onto her. Dallas didn't have a pet in his hands, but she didn't dare ask why he was here. On the other hand, he'd always have her heart in the palm of his hand. Did that count?

Wow.

Where did that thought come from?

She should've sought him out years ago, tried to explain everything. It was too late. A proverbial ocean of hurt flowed between them now. She opened her mouth to say how sorry she was, as lame as it was by now.

He intercepted her. "Seriously, let me carry the dog."

The dog did seem to weigh a ton at this point. Skylar might drop her. Okay, she messed up this relationship so badly already, what did she have to lose?

"Well, if you don't mind the dirt..." She transferred the injured animal. The dog growled and showed teeth, and Skylar froze. But, thankfully, the stray didn't bite.

"I'm a cowboy, remember?" He nodded to his weathered cowboy boots spattered with dried mud. "We're fine with dirt."

While she'd scrubbed her life and her apartment spotlessly clean as if she could erase scary memories that had waited way too long to show up.

Dallas held the stray as if she were light as a feather. But then he was probably used to lifting calves while the heaviest things she was used to carrying were her laptop or a purse.

No, the heaviest thing she was used to carrying was *regret*.

"Yes, I do remember," she whispered. She remembered too many things.

The way his eyes crinkled when he laughed. The way her heart fluttered when he tipped her chin. The way butterflies danced in her belly when he kissed her....

"Aren't you going to follow me?" He asked over his shoulder as he strode toward the room.

"Right." This was her pet. Well, not her pet exactly, but her responsibility, and all she did was stand there, traveling down memory lane. "I need to talk to the receptionist first. I don't know if they'll accept a walk-in." She should've called first. Usually, she wasn't so scatterbrained. But being in her hometown did a number on her.

"I've got it." His tone and his words were clipped, and she didn't blame him.

He could've walked right past her, ignoring her, and she wouldn't blame him.

Before her graduation, she'd painted inside the hall here, adding more animals to the mix. Birds, turtles, chickens, and horses. The horses were for Dallas. He'd loved them.

Why hadn't they remodeled in all these years? Well, the leather furniture might be brand new, and they'd added a station for dogs to play and another one for cats. The ceiling looked different, not white but light blue like the sky, and the large, funky emerald-green tile—as if to imitate grass—on the floors didn't have cracks in it. More houseplants flourished in the corners. But the walls with her work had stayed the same, and she touched their smooth surface as if she could touch the past and relive those blissful moments.

He opened the vet's office door.

She hurried forward to protest. "We can't just barge in." It didn't work like that in her new life. Everything required an appointment and scheduling.

"We sure can." He stepped inside the office with her dog—okay, not hers yet. "Bro, I brought you a new client."

Bro?

She followed him and blinked. "Austin! What are you doing here?" Then heat rose up her neck. The white coat should've clued her in. "You became a veterinarian, and you came back to Port Sunshine."

"I sure did. I worked in the city first. But when the town's veterinarian retired seven years ago and needed someone to take his spot, I came back." Austin, one of Dallas's younger brothers and Skylar's childhood friend, raised a reddish eyebrow at her as he got up from his chair and walked over. His eyes were as shockingly blue as Dallas's, but his now neatly trimmed hair held a tint of the red Dallas didn't have. He was leaner than his brothers, and the only one she'd ever seen without a cowboy hat. "Long time no see."

After breaking up with Dallas, she couldn't bring herself to talk to his brothers, though they used to be her friends. Even with her girlfriends, she'd fallen apart. Because her girlfriends had kept asking her *why* and she couldn't answer without revealing too much. Their once-tight group of friends had continued without her.

She swallowed hard and stared at the tile, avoiding looking at Dallas and Austin. Austin and Dallas—yes, Mrs. Laurence hailed from Texas and did homage to her home state by naming two of her boys after its towns. She'd even named one of her other sons "Tex." "Things... things got messed up. Then I messed them up worse. I–I'll understand if you hate me. I–I guess I can take the dog to the city. It's only an hour's drive."

The canine barked as if to protest.

"I'll take care of you," Austin said to the dog, then shook Skylar's hand. The brothers' hands were always callused. "We don't hate you. Besides, I'd never refuse an animal in need. Welcome back."

"Thank you." She exhaled, and grateful tears prickled at the back of her eyes. "Thank you so much."

Of course, Austin had become a veterinarian. He'd always loved to help animals, from farm animals to a bird with a broken wing. And of course, he'd come back. Only three brothers had left the ranch for a long time, and two hadn't returned. The rest had stayed, calling it the call of the land.

Her heart shifted. She didn't have the call of the land, but the call of the ocean, with all the mysteries and bright hues it had to offer for inspiration. And the call of Dallas...

"Did you and Dallas...?" Austin eyed her, then Dallas, and her again. His eyebrow rose further.

Uh-oh. Flustered, she couldn't keep her hands still, and they waved in front of her almost of their own accord. Austin knew their history, and she didn't want him to think things that weren't there. "Dallas and I just met here in the building by accident. He helped me carry the dog."

"Yup." Dallas placed the pet on the examination table. He'd never talked much, while Skylar talked a mile an hour. Well, she *used to.*

The dog gave out a low growl at the medical instruments but behaved otherwise.

Was she familiar with a vet's office? Just not *this* vet's office? On a closer look, the dog appeared less like a stray and more like an abandoned pet.

Austin nodded. "Hmm. Okay. My assistant is out today, so I'm flying solo. Thankfully, we had a slow day so far. That's going to change once the tourist season starts. So what do we have here? What's her name?"

Skylar shifted her weight from one foot to another. "I, um, have no clue about the name. I found her at the gas station. So we'll need a full exam." She scratched her arm again, hoping it wasn't what she thought. Maybe she should've warned Dallas. "Um, including for parasites. And she favors her right front paw. I'm afraid it's broken."

If she could still pray, she'd ask for the paw to be okay. But she was all prayed out after... She flinched. Best not to think about it. One more reason Dallas would be better off without her. His family were all devoted Christians. Grandma had raised Skylar to have faith, as well. But that faith was nearly nonexistent now.

"You picked up a stray?" Why was there so much disbelief in Dallas's voice?

She faced the accusation in his eyes. "I'm not a cruel person."

Except for what she'd done to him.

Why do we hurt the people dear to us?

She ducked her head. Her relationship with Dallas was irreparable. She needed to concentrate on the things that could be helped. Like her grandmother's wedding or the dog's well-being. She stepped away from Dallas to Austin. "Could you also please check for a microchip? In case she wasn't always a stray?"

"Of course." With careful but confident motions, he examined the dog.

"Sorry about the mess." She waved at her ruined blouse. It looked as if she'd rolled in the mud. Her hand flew to her face and chipped some dirt. It must also look like she'd rolled in the mud.

She cringed. Why did it matter that she presented well? She couldn't get together with Dallas again. Not only because she'd broken her promise to him. But also because of her secret.

He cleared his throat. "Um, you still have some dirt on your face." He didn't step to her to remove it. He clearly didn't want to touch her. Not any longer.

"Th–thanks." Her heart sank to the tiled floor where tiny cracks were visible now, like a spiderweb that trapped her mistakes instead of flies.

And now she weirdly, ridiculously craved his touch. Though why weirdly and ridiculously? He'd been the first boy she'd kissed. He'd been the first boy she'd loved. All these years later, he'd remained the *only* man she'd ever loved.

She jerked her gaze away from his face, afraid he'd read it all in her eyes. Then she scratched her itching arm and sent him a sidelong glance. How long before he started itching, and Austin, too, for that matter? She should've bathed the dog before coming here.

She could already imagine the conversation at the Lawrence family dinner table. *"Skylar is back in town, and we wish she wasn't. She only brings bad things to us."*

"No microchip. But thankfully, no parasites, either," Austin said.

"Great!" Skylar stopped itching.

After an X-ray, Austin announced the paw wasn't broken or otherwise injured, either.

Skylar blinked. "But... but... I saw the dog lifting her paw as she walked."

Austin grinned as he brought the dog back, walking on her own, her spectacular freshly shampooed fur shining. She looked like a different creature now. "It was probably a trick to gain your compassion."

And it worked. Skylar couldn't blame the dog, unlike...

Stop it.

No use being bitter.

Besides, Austin gave her good news, and she should be grateful. "I'm glad she has no broken bones. Thank you. What about the rest? Any other injuries, cuts, or illnesses?" Even if the dog was abandoned recently, she'd survived on the street for a few days at least, and that could be rough.

"She had some cuts, likely from a cat's claws, but not deep. I treated them. Overall, she's slightly malnourished but healthy. I don't think she's been a stray for long."

"I'll put some posters in the neighborhood and post an announcement on the local social media." Her heart shifted. Weird. It was like she didn't want to let the pet go.

Austin winked at her. "Or just tell Dolores Rafferty."

The dog barked again several times as if recognizing the name. Was her owner also named Dolores?

Austin continued, "And I'll tell Mom. By tomorrow, the entire town will know you found a stray dog."

"I can ask around, too." Dallas shoved his hands in his pockets. "But it won't help if a tourist left her when their vacation ended."

Then Austin's expression turned serious. "Do you intend to keep her if that's the case? I wouldn't advise dropping her at the animal shelter. They have no open spots. Too many vacationers leave their pets." His stern tone revealed what he thought about that.

Skylar had never had any pets to leave. But she'd left her friends and family behind. And the love of her life. "I...um..."

Austin studied her. "We foster a lot of abandoned animals. Sometimes people return for them. But often not."

How could some tourist leave this beauty behind? The dog trudged to her and put her cold nose into her hand. Something inside Skylar changed.

Dallas squared his shoulders. "I'd better take the dog, then."

"No. She's going with me." Skylar spoke before she even made the decision. Thankfully, neither she nor grandmother had fur allergies, and Grandma loved animals, though she preferred cats. Then Skylar leaned to the dog who licked her hands as if understanding everything.

Dallas's eyes became less frosty.

Austin's lips tugged up. "Let's see if we can guess a name. That would be easier on the pet. I'll toss out some popular names." He listed several names, but the dog only tilted her head and didn't react.

After a while, Dallas joined in. There were always many dogs on the ranch, so he was no stranger to plenty of canine names. Still no reaction.

It seemed such a small thing to get a dog. But somehow, she could breathe easier as if she was already near the ocean with its humid, salty air. "Breathe," she told herself.

The dog ran to her and started barking as if in approval. She petted the dog.

"Huh. That would be a weird name." Austin braced his hip against the oak desk.

"I think it's like in the *breeze* of the ocean," Dallas said slowly.

"Hmm. Breeze. Breeze?" Skylar tested it, looking at the dog.

Breeze lifted her head and barked cheerfully. Then, when Skylar stooped to pet Breeze, the dog licked Skylar's face. A chuckle escaped. She scolded herself.

No attachments, remember?

"Your grandmother is going to be in for a surprise," Dallas said, and a tiny inflection of his former affection lifted the words. Everyone in town loved her grandmother.

Minutes later, they left after Austin had refused payment. Dallas opened the door, and Skylar and Breeze stepped out into much warmer air. Her gut tightened despite tender sunrays on her skin. She had so many things she wanted to tell Dallas. And even more things she couldn't tell him. "I... Thank you."

A muscle moved in his jaw again as if he expected her to say something more, but she was at a loss for words, not a regular occurrence for her.

"Take care of yourself." He marched to his truck, leaving her with a feeling of emptiness.

"Just you and me, huh?" She crouched to Breeze. "I know you must be hungry." While Austin had given Breeze a snack, it couldn't have been enough.

Her hand flew to the pendant, hidden under the smooth fabric of her blouse. Dallas had given her that pendant for their first anniversary. She'd never taken it off, no matter what. Like her memories, it was hidden by her heart but always there.

Even if the guy who'd given it to her was no longer in her life.

Her month-old sedan shone in the sun, spotless after a recent car wash. After her memories started coming back and she'd left her hometown, she'd tended to like things spotless and shiny, their colors muted, an antidote to the tumult her soul had been in then.

She pushed the ignition button on her shiny new key fob. Her car didn't start. Maybe it—and the rest of her whole shiny new life—wasn't such an antidote, after all.

Chapter Two

Dallas nearly drove away from the vet clinic parking lot. He should have. But something stopped him. He frowned.

Who was he kidding? It wasn't something. It was *somebody*.

Skylar.

He clenched his teeth as she slipped inside her silvery sedan after letting the dog in. He'd been fine without Skylar all these years. Or close to it. Was still fine.

Why now, after all this time?

Well, after this chance meeting, he'd have to do his best to avoid her. A tall order in a small town, but it shouldn't be too difficult if he stayed at the ranch. Time to go.

Her car engine sputtered, coughed, and went silent. Then again and again for several tries until it didn't even sputter.

She could get a lift from her grandmother. Or call a taxi. Unlike several of his brothers, he didn't know much about engines, so he wouldn't be able to repair whatever the issue was. Likewise, he could never repair whatever her issue was with him, because she'd never told him what it was in the first place. Just told him they should postpone their wedding. Then cancel it.

No explanation. No nothing.

Except for saying "It would be for the better." Better for whom?

When he'd called and asked to meet, she'd always found an excuse not to. Instead of coming alive with her usual chatter, their conversations had become brief, and then she'd seemed to avoid them altogether. She'd become a different person, and he couldn't understand why.

His stomach clenched, and he resisted the urge to hit the innocent steering wheel. He really should go. She'd made it clear.

He groaned and leaped out of his rusty mud-splattered truck. Then he strode toward her sparkling new sedan. She rolled down her window, her eyes wide.

He spread his arms. "I can't believe I'm doing this, either. I'm not going to look at your engine and pretend to know anything about it, so... Do you want a lift?"

"I don't understand." She blinked at him. "I bought this car recently. It shouldn't break down yet."

"Sometimes things that shouldn't get broken still do." He didn't add, *"Like the promises you gave me."*

She winced, and her once-aglow hazel eyes dimmed. Breeze barked from the back seat protectively.

Something nudged at the edges of his subconsciousness. Was this bark somewhat familiar? He struggled to place the sound but couldn't. He hadn't seen the dog before, but maybe... maybe he'd heard her?

"The car's under warranty. I can call the dealer. And a taxi." Skylar's voice was quiet while once, like her vibrant eyes, it had sparkled with many undertones.

"Aren't you tired after your trip? And it's safe to leave a car here." Why did he say those things? He wasn't looking for an opportunity to spend time with her. At all. "It'll be quicker for my brothers to look at it. It could be something simple they can fix without nullifying the warranty." Some of his brothers didn't want her even mentioned, but he'd come up with something.

She stepped out of the car. "Why are you doing this?"

A good question. "It's a small town. We help each other here."

"Thank you." Her eyes had lost their sparkle, too.

What had happened to her in those years away? *No. Don't go there. She chose to stay away. Remember?*

Away from their small town.

Away from him.

She popped the trunk, and he hefted the luggage from her car into his truck. Breeze moved herself, apparently knowing she didn't need to pretend to be injured any longer. Except for the mud on the floor Breeze had left, Skylar's car was spotless. It still had the new-car smell, along with the scent of peaches.

He took a deep breath once inside his truck. It certainly didn't smell like a new vehicle here. Between his stale coffee and the wood he'd taken to the ranch this morning, he wasn't sure what it smelled like.

He took off, doing his best to keep his focus on the road, *not* the person who'd intrigued him since he'd been a child. Why this complete change in her?

She used to love bright colors, and her vibrant sunshine-yellow and raspberry-red summer dresses still stood in front of his eyes. Now, she'd shrouded her soul with a white blouse and gray slacks, her attire as dull as her eyes.

He'd made half-hearted attempts to date after she'd broken off their engagement. But he'd never again found the same incredible feeling that pushed at the edges of his chest, the same happiness as when he'd been with her. Cliché or not, the day she'd left their small town, she'd taken his heart with her and had never returned it.

He'd never been a talker, but silence with her in a vehicle was unusual.

Finally, she said, "Could we please stop at a pet store?"

From the truck cab's backseat, Breeze voiced her support.

"Sure." Dallas nodded at a green light and turned toward the pet store.

"Thanks. I need a leash, collar, bowls, a bed, and some kibble. Anything else I should buy?"

"A few toys and a Frisbee wouldn't hurt."

Breeze voiced her support for that, as well.

Minutes later, he carried the purchases to the truck.

"Is it okay if I feed Breeze in the truck, please? She must be starving. It might create a mess, though."

When did she become so polite? The Skylar he knew did things first and asked for permission later. Well, *if* she ever asked for permission. She hadn't been rude. Just confident and straightforward, one of many things he liked about her.

On the subject of things he liked about her... His gaze slid to her doe-like eyes, then to her full lips covered in light-pink lipstick. His pulse picked up. He shouldn't be thinking about how great it had felt to kiss her.

"If it's not okay..." Her voice trailed off. "I can put things on the ground."

Right. He forgot to answer, too distracted by those lush lips and the memories they evoked. "When did I worry about the mess? Especially if an animal is starving? Please go ahead."

"I appreciate it." Skylar placed a bowl on the truck's floor and filled it with kibble.

The dog gobbled up the food fast. Compassion for the hungry dog made his rib cage contract. Once Breeze was done, Skylar cleaned up everything with napkins she'd carried in her asphalt-gray purse. "All good now. We can go."

"Okay."

They took off, but all was far from good.

The girl he'd known carried a mass of things in a worn-out purse she'd embellished with shiny crystals and turquoise fabric strips. Chipped-off crayons, colored pencils, and a wrinkled notebook had shared space with her pocket knife, bubblegum, both wrapped and unwrapped, and mint candies, again both wrapped and unwrapped. While she'd also stuffed it with dog biscuits, pins, seashells, a ribbon for seashells, and a myriad of other things.

But the only time he'd seen her carrying a napkin was because she'd drawn his portrait on it while on a date in a restaurant. She'd drawn and painted him and other people many times later, but it had been her first portrait of him. His heart moved. He'd framed that napkin. He still had it. Hidden away in a drawer after their breakup. But still there.

"How is your mom doing?" she asked, breaking the silence.

"Good." He slowed around a curve and stole a glance at her.

Her profile was unreadable while, once, emotions had clearly played out on her face. Or was it now written in a different language, one he didn't speak? "How are your brothers?"

"Good." What else could he say?

If she'd expected him to hold up his part of the conversation, she was mistaken. He'd never liked to talk much, but he'd loved to hear her talk. And she used to talk endlessly. The sound of her voice had always smoothed something inside him, especially after his father's cutting shouts. Her voice was a salve that, like the ocean waves endlessly caressing the sandy shore, could smooth out the edges of broken bottles and craft them into something to treasure. Could smooth out his sharp corners.

Until she'd left the shattered edges of heartbreak. He ground his teeth.

"Anyone married?"

He shook his head. "Nope. We're all still bachelors."

Could she care whether he was still single? But then, why would she? And her grandmother would've told her if she cared to ask.

Everything was close in a small town, and he could see Mrs. Rafferty's quirky bungalow in the distance, painted canary yellow with a white door and emerald window trim. The wall overlooking the road had seashells painted on it. Skylar had painted those. Then she'd done them again every time the house had been repainted.

His hand moved to his neck where once he'd worn a necklace strung from tiny seashells he and Skylar had gathered at the beach. She'd given him the necklace as a gift for their one-year anniversary while he'd given her a different necklace. He'd worn the seashells for many years. Then on the day she'd ended their engagement he'd ripped them off and thrown them back into the ocean. Once in a while, even after so many years, he'd forget they were no longer there and reach for them.

His heart made a strange movement as if upset Skylar would disappear from his life—again. He had so many questions to ask her. Ones she'd never answered.

Yet he didn't say a word. Neither did she, the silence sharp and crackling between them like a barbed wire fence. No, rather an electric fence. If he got too close again, he'd get electrocuted.

Even Breeze stayed quiet in the back as if feeling the tension and deciding to lay low.

"Are you doing okay?" Her voice was barely audible over the motor's throaty growl, a growl he felt like joining.

All his pent-up anger released. "Like you'd even care." He pulled up to the quirky canary-yellow cottage he used to love because he'd associated it with her—and fine, because the house and the beach used to be a haven for him and his siblings when Dad would get violent. He parked and jammed the parking brake with too much force.

This time, hurt stood clear in her hazel eyes before her expression became unreadable again.

"Of course, I care." She jumped out of the truck before he had a chance to turn off the engine and open the door for her. As if she couldn't get away from him fast enough.

Guilt stabbed him. But what did she expect?

From the truck bed, he hauled out her mouse-gray suitcase as nondescript as her clothes. "I'm okay, no thanks to you. But if anything happened to me, wouldn't you hear about it from your grandmother? If you bothered to ask?"

Her gaze lingered on him, making his treacherous heart skip a beat. "That's not what I meant. Well, never mind."

Breeze barked in his truck, probably worrying they'd forgotten her. The poor animal could already have abandonment issues, and they shouldn't be adding to them.

Though why "they"? There was no *they* or *us* when it came to Dallas and Skylar, and he'd better remember it this time. He'd been blindsided before, but now, he knew where he stood with her.

"Don't worry, Breeze." He stomped to the truck and let the dog out. He'd lift her again, but she had no issues jumping out. "I'll get it." He picked up the new dog bedding.

"I've got the rest." Skylar snatched the bags with pet supplies. She grabbed the leash, and Breeze stayed nearby.

"You can put it down," she said.

"Put down what?" He frowned.

"The luggage. It has wheels. It can roll."

"I know." Did the big-city, college-educated miss think he was a country bumpkin? "It's not heavy."

She stepped toward him. A strand of chestnut-hued hair escaped her tight bun and floated in the breeze. He had a nearly irresistible urge to tuck it behind her ear like he'd done many times before. In those times, she'd worn her curly hair strewn over her shoulders or in a flirty high ponytail instead of this strict bun so tight it pulled back the skin on her face.

The face he'd once found lovely and fascinating. A large, disobedient part of him still did.

"I'm sorry." She searched his eyes.

His heart turned over itself. Was she sorry for breaking off their engagement? For her radio silence all these years? Or for something else he didn't know about?

"Skylar! You're here!" Mrs. Rafferty stepped onto the porch, wrapped in a tawny-hued shawl.

"Hi, Grandma. Sorry for the delay. And I have a surprise."

He edged away from Skylar and hurried to her grandmother to help her on the stairs. While she still got around okay, it didn't hurt to be careful. He put down the suitcase. "Hello, Mrs. Rafferty."

She leaned on him as she walked the few steps. "Hello, stranger. Oh, good. You two reconciled?"

"No, we didn't," they said in unison.

"What a pity." She squinted at Breeze. "You have a dog?"

"I do now." Skylar walked to her grandmother and kissed her cheek. "This is the stray I told you about. The surprise. She's got no microchip or collar to track down the possible owner. Her name is Breeze. I hope it's okay I brought her here. If nobody claims her, I'll take her with me when I leave."

A knife turned in him at the word *leave*, as if he didn't already know she wouldn't stay. Why would she stay?

"Poor doggie." Mrs. Rafferty sighed. "I'll ask around, but it looks like another tourist just abandoned their pet. Strange they didn't put in a chip, though. Or maybe the dog ran away, and the tourist searched and searched for her but had to leave?" Kindhearted Dolores Rafferty always gave people the benefit of the doubt. No wonder Mom loved her so much.

"Maybe," Skylar said carefully.

"Of course, you can bring her. Let's get you and all your heavy things inside and have some tea and pastries." Mrs. Rafferty cast a glance at Breeze, who eyed her. "Except for you, cutie. Sorry, but you're getting water and dog biscuits."

Breeze rushed inside, tail swishing out her excitement about the alternative.

If Skylar had broken off the engagement because she'd wanted to stay in the city, he'd have considered moving for her. As much as he'd loved the ranch, he'd have followed her to the other side of the earth, if needed. But she'd never asked.

He brought the suitcase and the dog's bedding into the house. "Where would you like this stuff?" His voice came out gruffer than he'd intended.

Again, the hurt in Skylar's eyes at his tone cut through him as if she weren't the one who'd hurt him. The once-bright eyes where he used to know every speck and sparkle. Her lovely face where he used to know every freckle and curve.

"Just near the door is fine for now," she said. "I'll let Breeze explore her new territory."

But Breeze didn't seem to want to explore her new temporary home. She stayed near the door, then sat there, and then lifted her thankfully not-broken paw as if trying to open the door.

"Looks like she'd like to go for a walk." He petted the golden retriever, who wagged her tail as if to confirm his words.

"Oh. Yes. Right." Skylar picked up the leash.

Mrs. Rafferty turned to him, a suspicious sparkle in her eyes. "Would you mind accompanying my granddaughter? Please?"

The lady's intention was clear, but he didn't have the heart to refuse. Besides, he still had too many questions, questions to which Skylar had never provided answers. Would she ever? He opened the front door. "Sure."

Skylar's hazel eyes flashed and narrowed, and he understood. He should've refused. It would've been wise to get out now and never look back. But his thoughts scrambled when it came to her. Still did.

"Let's put you on the leash, though." Skylar snapped the collar around Breeze's neck, who didn't protest. "Good girl," Skylar crooned. "You know all about leashes, don't you?"

The dog acted mannerly, but the instant Skylar opened the door, she shot out and Skylar followed, holding the leash and nearly tumbling down the porch.

He caught up on the last step and placed his hand on her shoulder. "I can take the leash." His heart started beating erratically as he touched her, and his memory did him a disservice. It brought back all the wonderful moments when happiness was possible. When her tender lips, shiny eyes, and bright future were so near.

Her eyes widened, and her pupils dilated as if she felt something, too. But she scooted away. "It's fine. I'll manage." The same words she said when he asked her what she was going to do in the big city echoed in the emptiness inside him.

"Okay." He shrugged.

But after a sprint with a hyperactive and enthusiastic dog, Skylar was out of breath. "Do you think it's okay if I let her off the leash?"

He shrugged. "I can catch up with her if needed."

Even if he'd never be able to catch up with Skylar. Why wasn't he asking those important questions? He'd imagined their meeting so many times. And now, he was speechless. But then, she'd often left him speechless.

Breathless, as well. His breath caught in his throat as he recalled their first kiss.

As they strolled, he turned away from her and stared at the ocean sparkling in the sun, keeping an eye on the energetic dog. "You didn't come back because... Was it because of a man?"

Her face changed, and her eyes hardened. She kept silent for a long while. "I guess you can put it that way."

It hurt more than it should have. Maybe it was best not to ask those questions. Not to know. She'd fallen in love with someone else. The most logical reason to break off their engagement, and yet for years, he'd kept telling himself it couldn't have been the reason.

To distract himself, he scooped up a stick and threw it in the air. Breeze jumped and caught it.

"Well!" Skylar gave out a squeaky laugh. "Someone knows how to play fetch. I guess she must've been someone's pet."

Dallas merely grunted. He knew how the animal felt. She'd been loved and abandoned like Skylar had loved and abandoned him.

So she'd met someone in the city. Most likely, someone polished and dashing who knew much more about art than Dallas, a simple cowboy growing up on the ranch, ever could. That man must've been very important to Skylar. He swallowed hard.

Breeze brought back the stick, and he rubbed the dog's back and praised her, then threw the stick again, further this time.

He asked the question again, the one she'd avoided answering. "Skylar, why did you stay away so long?"

"I can't tell you. I'm sorry," she whispered.

Hmm. There was no ring on Skylar's finger, and if she'd married and divorced, the grapevine would've brought the news to the ranch. Even if Skylar had asked her grandmother to keep it a secret, everyone knew Mrs. Rafferty couldn't keep secrets. At least, not from his mom.

Skylar's mother and her sister were close friends with Dallas's mother, and the trio had practically raised their children together. When Skylar's mother had left her family for another man, Skylar's grandmother had, in her own way, taken her daughter-in-law's place in their friendship circle.

Snippets of Skylar's dating a few years ago had put daggers in his heart. But nothing had circulated about her being in a serious relationship. Ever. Had she managed to conceal it even from her grandmother? But why?

Everyone was in everyone's business here. Maybe things worked differently in a city. Still, it didn't feel right.

"Did he... did he let you down?" Was he poking in her wound? In his? In both? His brothers had told him to let it go. He'd thought he'd done just that.

Until she showed up.

Her lips thinned, and her eyes narrowed. Then Breeze brought the stick, and Skylar bent and stroked her luxurious fur. He took a breath of salty air, waiting. The pause stretched.

Finally, she said a single word, releasing it like an exhalation after a long time of holding it in. "Yes."

He asked the question he didn't want to ask as if he just needed to put all the salt in the ocean into the wound. "Did you... did you love him?"

"It's not..." She turned tormented eyes to his, blinking furiously. Yet a tear escaped her. She just nodded.

Pain and compassion warred in his heart. Did she love that man still?

Then Breeze took off in the direction of *that* cottage. It had a sad history, and locals avoided it. It had changed owners often until the legend started reaching even prospective out-of-town buyers.

"Breeze, no! Come back!" Skylar screamed.

Dallas took off running after the dog. Once another owner died a mysterious death, the heirs wanted nothing to do with the small house and couldn't sell it. They'd rented it out through a local agency, but guests had trashed the house repeatedly until, after a few tries, the heirs let it be. Rumor had it someone had rented it again, but the renter had asked that their identity be kept confidential.

The town had scoffed. Nothing stayed a secret here for long. But of course, the locals never liked hanging out close to the out-of-the-way cottage, anyway, and the few who'd dared didn't stick around in the twilight or darkness. So nobody had seen anyone driving up or walking to the cottage, and the town was shocked they still had no clue which of the tourists in town was the mysterious renter.

There was no car near it now, either.

Dallas caught up to the golden retriever and clipped her back on the leash. "It's best not to go there, Breeze."

Breeze gave out a whine and stayed standing, her head cocked on alert. It took three tugs on the leash to get her to trudge back to the ocean. Even then, she growled in the cottage's direction.

Panting, Skylar leaned over and tried to calm the dog as she rubbed Breeze's back. "Look, I don't like it, either." Then she looked up at Dallas. "Thank you for catching her."

"You're welcome."

As expected, the place was deserted. Yet a weird feeling made the hairs stand up on the back of his head. As if... as if he were being watched. Not like people watching each other's backs, like many would here. In a completely different way. But nothing seemed out of place. So why was he getting this strange feeling? After all, this was a peaceful town.

Still, he moved closer to Skylar protectively. The whiff of her peach shampoo still wreaked havoc on his senses.

"We'd better head home. I need to unpack, and I'm already way behind on Grandma's wedding preparations." Without looking at him, Skylar tugged at the leash.

"Okay." His heart skittered strangely, especially for someone who totally, definitely, absolutely didn't want to see Skylar any longer.

Breeze dug her paws into the sand, and after about ten tugs, it took Dallas's help to get her moving. Maybe Skylar was affecting him this way, but as they left the shore, it was as if someone's gaze sent a shiver through him.

"WHY DON'T YOU JUST tell him?" Grandma's words made Skylar look up from her porcelain teacup that evening.

Drinking tea on the terrace and watching the sunset or sunrise used to be their tradition. Every time, it was spectacular. Skylar had just had to paint it. Her heart shifted. She missed those days. Then it registered. Grandma had asked her a question. "Tell who what?"

"Tell Dallas about—you know?" Grandma's eyesight behind thick glasses might not be the same, but she still saw everything. Even things Skylar didn't want others to see.

"You know why." Skylar clattered her smooth dainty cup onto its saucer, nearly sloshing the liquid over. Though she'd asked herself the same question many times. She repeated the words she'd told herself. "Besides, it's no use anymore. It's too late."

"I saw the way Dallas looked at you today."

Hope stirred her heart.

No. "What you saw was annoyance. I made my choice all those years ago. I have to accept the consequences."

A spectacular play of peach, gold, and crimson reflected off the choppy waves. She'd painted it many times before, but her skills would never be enough to show its beauty. The gorgeous hues used to distract her. But not any longer.

How long had it been since she'd put anything on canvas? Nearly fifteen years. Ever since one painting had nearly brought her downfall and put her grandmother's life at risk. Would being back here put her grandmother's life at risk again?

Skylar winced. But how could she say no when Grandma asked for help with the wedding?

"Why do you keep punishing yourself? For something that wasn't even your fault." Grandma's pale eyes, amplified by glasses, were kind, as always. Somehow, it only hurt more.

"I'm being realistic." Skylar closed her eyes.

Then she took a deep breath of salty air, reopened her eyes, and pasted on a smile before lifting the cup emanating the fragrance of mint tea. Her hand didn't shake this time. Good.

She sipped the soothing liquid. The open-air lattice canopy, thick with climbing wisteria vines, shaded them while the whimsical patio stones she'd painted in vivid oceanic blues, teals, and purples cooled her bare feet.

She needed to distract her grandmother from the tragic past, and she knew the perfect topic. "Why don't we talk about your upcoming wedding? You must be so excited. And I can't wait to meet your fiancé."

"Yes, except Earl took off for an unexpected trip. In some mysterious place where cell phone coverage is close to nonexistent." Grandma grimaced as she helped herself to a cherry turnover. Usually, cherry turnovers or speaking about her fiancé brought a smile to her lips. But not today. "He should be here, helping me with all the difficult decisions about the cake, decorations, and invitations."

Skylar blinked. Well, she'd distracted her grandmother all right.

Grandma's whirlwind courtship and short engagement with a tourist Skylar knew little about and never met had worried her, but a thousand more times now. Why would a happy husband-to-be take off instead of helping plan the wedding?

And where exactly was cell coverage nonexistent these days? At the bottom of an ocean?

Chapter Three

With thoughts buzzing in her head, Skylar slipped behind the steering wheel of her car to visit her aunt.

Grandma went to visit her friend—Dallas's mother—and it was best Skylar didn't accompany her *there*. Considering how much grief she'd caused his family by breaking Dallas's heart, she wasn't sure they wouldn't meet her with rotten eggs.

She'd done her best to think about planning the upcoming wedding, but her thoughts kept returning to him. The way hurt flashed in his ocean-blue eyes before those eyes became distant again. The way everything in her wanted to erase these last fifteen years and curl up in his arms. The way she longed to see his smile while knowing she'd caused his frown.

Even upset with her—*upset* was the understatement of the century—he'd still jumped in to help her and somehow even enlisted the help of his mechanically inclined brother to repair her sedan. Dallas had also brought her car from the vet's office to her grandmother's cottage.

Her heart contracted. That was the kind of man he was. That was the kind of man she'd lost.

And here she was, staring at the windshield without having started the car. It had been a while since she'd been so distracted. She prided herself on being organized, being focused. Routine helped her do more in her job... and remember less.

She turned the key in the ignition, and the engine turned over easily this time.

As soon as she drove from her grandmother's cottage driveway, her hands-free phone rang. She smiled at it announcing her aunt was calling and answered. "Hello, Auntie. I'm on my way."

"Hello, Little Miss." Aunt's voice sounded a tad uncomfortable. "I can't wait to see you, but something came up at the restaurant and requires my presence."

Skylar's heart dropped somewhere to the gas pedal, and she deflated like an airbag long after an accident. Was this Auntie's polite way to say she *didn't* want to see Skylar?

After all, it was a long time since Skylar had visited her. And while she'd called her aunt, it wasn't the equivalent of being present. She'd alienated a lot of people she loved, and she only had herself to blame. Acid coated her stomach.

"I understand, Auntie." Skylar made her voice chirrupy. Maybe too much. "Some other time. We can reschedule. Unless... unless you don't have an opening in your schedule?"

"Are you kidding me? When would I have no time for you?" Auntie coughed as if realizing she'd said just that. "Meet me in an hour at the restaurant, all right? I should be done by then. I'm glad you're here. I'm not going to pass up the chance to see you."

Skylar perked up and pressed on the gas pedal, guiding the car toward Main Street. She could breathe easier now. "Great. I can pick up some desserts in the interim. Get chew toys for my new dog."

Aunt laughed. "She's going to be spoiled rotten."

"As she should be." Skylar stopped at one of the few traffic lights in town, then swallowed hard. Some difficult words had to be said. "I'm sorry for being away so much."

"Don't mention it. I understand. Children grow up. Leave the nest." A note of sadness coated Auntie's words.

Skylar had a feeling her auntie didn't mean just Skylar. The light changed to green, and she drove forward. "See you soon."

"Sounds great." Auntie disconnected.

As Skylar made it to Main Street, her heart shifted to give space to a familiar guest—guilt. She woke up accompanied by guilt and brushed her teeth with it by her side. She shared her morning coffee with guilt.

Even if her aunt couldn't hear her now or maybe *because* she couldn't hear, Skylar whispered, "I'm sorry, Auntie, for what I did. Or rather, for what I didn't do."

Inaction was as much a choice as action.

Growing up, she'd sensed some guilt on her aunt's part, too, as if Auntie had somehow blamed herself for her sister falling in love with someone other than her husband. Or maybe Skylar was a painful reminder of the tragic past. Could they ever mend those bridges?

In those days, Skylar had felt closer to Mrs. Lawrence, Dallas's mother, who'd become sort of a substitute mother and didn't have Auntie's qualms. Skylar grimaced as she made a left turn. She might've burned her bridge with Mrs. Lawrence beyond repair. Mrs. Lawrence adored her sons, and Skylar had done a lot of damage to Dallas.

She pursed her lips and did what she'd learned to do over the years—redirected her attention to something else. Something to stay in the present and semi productive.

This time, it was local businesses. She took her foot off the gas pedal as she guided her car along the main district.

In her previous visits, she'd always rushed to do as much as possible for Grandma, from scrubbing floors to catching up on laundry and trying to spend all their time together, so she didn't have time for anything else.

She passed the stationery-souvenir store where Dallas's brother worked sometimes. Once upon a time, it had carried her paintings and watercolors.

Okay, fine, she'd avoided stores here because she'd been scared to run into Dallas. Even if he spent nearly all his time on the ranch.

Her gut tightened again. But what other choice could she have made fifteen years ago?

Yeah, keep telling yourself that.

She sighed as she drove past a clothing store. Mannequins in the shop window displayed bright-colored shirts and teal or salad-green shorts and raspberry-hued sundresses and yellow straw hats. The T-shirts didn't have her prints with local scenery anymore, and they shouldn't have. Regret uncoiled in her stomach, nonetheless. She'd been so thrilled when the local businesses had started to carry her designs, and Dallas had celebrated it with her with peach ice cream and lemonade in their little cove, so hidden away it had somehow stayed undiscovered by tourists.

Once upon a time, she'd made matching T-shirts for the two of them. To tease him, she'd put her prints on blushing pink T-shirts, but he wore his proudly. If anyone questioned the color, he'd say, "It's not pink. It's salmon."

Regret was another familiar guest. In some ways, she welcomed it. The moment she stopped feeling regret about the choice she'd had to make would be the moment she stopped respecting herself.

She parked near the only pet store in town and ran inside to get a couple of chew toys. As she paid the young cashier, her gaze flicked to a row of cars parked on the opposite street.

One of them attracted her attention, and she studied it as she walked outside, met with warm and humid air and a cloudless sky.

Hmm. A black SUV with tinted windows. The latter wouldn't be a surprise but a wise decision here in summer if one wanted to wear shorts but avoid getting blisters from leather seats. But mud oddly covered the license plate, which was unusual as it hadn't rained here for a while.

She drew a deep breath and slid inside her sedan, then turned on the engine. The SUV was probably out of state. They had people from all over the country here. Yet the dirt didn't seem to be spread evenly over the vehicle.

Maybe she was just paranoid. The SUV didn't take off when she did, and she released the air she'd held in her lungs. She paid attention to the rearview mirror, but the SUV didn't follow. She considered making several right turns, then scolded herself.

At a crawling pace, she drove by the store titled Pirate's Treasures. They still sold fashion jewelry made from seashells and more upscale pieces like pearl necklaces and bracelets. The sun shone brightly, showcasing those treasures in the shop window together with a mini treasure chest. That same sunlight played off the glass and metal ridges.

Then there was the barbershop that couldn't be named anything other than Black Beards and More. It still had her drawing of a pirate on the shop window. Not many things changed in her hometown.

Something about the familiarity of it all soothed her soul. Her world had gone upside down several times, and she'd craved stability. Then she'd created it for herself the only way she could.

The next stop was the pastry store, and she parked, grateful to find a vacant space. Soon, it would be at a premium. And in Charleston, parking space was nearly *always* at a premium.

As she walked to the store, she bumped into a young couple exiting the door. They seemed to have eyes only for each other.

"Sorry!" said the redheaded girl with freckles all over her face, shoulders, and arms. Even as she spoke, she didn't pause from looking at the young man whose long blond, sun-streaked and salt-dried hair and tanned skin made him resemble the stereotypical surfer.

They both wore white shorts and tangerine-colored flip-flops, but their T-shirts were different from each other. Hers bore a university logo while his—a skeleton.

"No problem." Skylar smiled as she went inside.

There had been a time when Dallas and Skylar only had eyes for each other, as well.... Wonderful times. She shook her head to shake off the nostalgia and focused on something more practical.

Like checking her pockets and purse. While the couple appeared lovey-dovey, one never knew when a bump could be intentional in a tourist town.

Satisfied everything was where it should be, she approached the enticing row of pastries that smelled just as enticing. She did her best to switch her thoughts to where they should be going as she studied the desserts, then took photos of the cakes. Most likely, this would be where they'd get the wedding cake. Even without much choice in a small town, Grandma didn't want to order anywhere else. And while she used to make fantastic cakes, it wouldn't be right for the bride to bake for her wedding day.

Once Skylar bought eclairs and croissants that made her mouth water, she checked the shop window, this time deliberately. She flinched at the sight of the SUV on the opposite street, parking near a pharmacy.

Was she imagining things?

She stepped outside, bracing for another change from the coolness of air-conditioning to the warmth of a beautiful day. Then she shielded her eyes from the sun and considered her options.

An ice-cream parlor was within walking distance. Not a great idea to eat ice cream before lunch—or more likely, before pastry. But she felt like buying time.

Would the SUV leave if she lingered?

Once she was inside the well-air-conditioned place, her eyes widened. They kept her watercolors. The place was renovated with a new menu display and more modern metal chairs with white leather cushions, and the walls were now of pistachio ice cream instead of vanilla. But they kept the fun watercolors she'd done for them with cute animals eating ice-cream cones. Her favorite was a penguin in a red knit hat and scarf.

Just like in other stores, the young uniformed girl at the counter was unfamiliar under her visor that matched cherry-flavored ice cream. Everyone knew each other in their small town, but Skylar didn't. Not anymore.

It tugged at her heart.

"What flavor would you like?" the girl asked, her voice as perky as her ponytail.

"Butter pecan," Skylar said without thinking. "Two scoops."

"Coming right up."

Huh. Butter pecan wasn't Skylar's favorite. Why had she ordered it? She didn't change her order even when she realized it was *Dallas's* favorite. They used to come here often. And Skylar would often tap his cheek with her ice cream, teasing him—

Enough.

She was like a girl who cried over everything, complaining it reminded her of her boyfriend who'd broken up with her. Even when someone breathed, that girl sobbed that he breathed, too.

Chin up, Skylar settled at one of the few tables facing the street and gave the ice cream its due. She welcomed the sweet, cold, creamy taste. When the SUV was gone, so was she.

It must be a coincidence. Totally.

She glanced at the time on the dashboard as she drove off. She still had some time until meeting with her aunt.

Why not take a drive outside of town, first along the ocean embankment and then along the fields? She could use it to clear her head, and the view was spectacular.

Her fingers tightened around the steering wheel as she glanced in the rearview mirror, watching for a tail. So far, so good. There was no reason for someone to follow her. Unless...

She shook her head in response to her thoughts. The fifteen-year-old threat, though still hanging over her head, had never materialized, and she had a legitimate reason to be in her hometown. She was the maid of honor in her grandmother's wedding. She couldn't do her duties over the phone.

That could be understood, right?

Yet a shiver of suspicion traveled down her spine.

She also drove out of town to make it easier to spot a tail. After the threat, she'd taken a defense course and a shooting course at the range and bought a small gun, though she'd hoped she'd never have to use either of the skills. She'd never thought to take a course on how to spot a tail.

The ocean sparkled under the bright sun, the peaceful beauty a contrast to her troubling thoughts. She slowed to let the breathtaking landscape soothe her raw nerves.

So many times in their childhood and teens, she and Dallas had walked along the beach on sand the color of her morning cappuccino. She could almost feel the warm grains under her toes as her skin tingled pleasantly from having her hand in his, even from mere memory. The memories lulled her senses for some time.

When she glanced in the rearview mirror the next time, every cell in her body went on high alert. The SUV was approaching fast.

Adrenaline surging in her veins, she floored the gas pedal. Her sedan's motor roared unhappily. How could she let herself get so distracted?

Calm down.

It could still be a coincidence. She drew several deep breaths of air filled with the sweet scent of the peach air freshener. She felt anything but sweet right now.

Okay, okay.

The SUV was approaching fast, growing in her rearview mirror. That could just mean someone was in a hurry, right?

Another deep breath. Rational thinking.

What were her options? It was a two-way road, and a head-on collision didn't sound appealing. Besides, she'd never want to hurt people in an oncoming vehicle. It didn't look like she could outrun an SUV.

If something happened to her, it would be disastrous for her grandmother, though surely Auntie and Mrs. Lawrence would step in as they had before. And Dallas... Would he grieve her?

Stop the negativity!

There seemed to be only one option left. She took her foot off the gas pedal. She knew this road well. The incline near the road was rather steep, but it led to the fields. It would become a forest soon. Then she'd be on the bridge over a ravine. The time to act was now.

Breathing fast, she tapped on the brakes. The car was probably silently asking her to make up her mind. Her heartbeat thundered in her head as she called 911 on her hands-free phone.

"What's your emergency?" the female voice asked.

"There's a vehicle following me—I believe with the intent to hit me." She'd look ridiculous if she were wrong, but better safe than sorry.

She slipped to the shoulder to let the SUV pass. But that clearly wasn't the driver's intention. She rattled off her location based on the landmarks, then the make and model of the SUV before the dispatcher had a chance to ask anything.

The first hit shook her but didn't surprise her. The steering wheel nearly jumped out of her hands, but she managed to hold on. "The SUV hit me."

"We're sending a team. Can you see the license plate?"

"It's covered in mud." It was a split-second decision, but she didn't wait for the next hit.

Her stomach clenched as she directed her car down the incline, terrified to roll over. The SUV didn't follow her immediately. The driver must be having the same concern. At least, this was still a field, and she wouldn't be wrapping her sedan around a tree.

The next moment, she went airborne. Everything inside her went cold.

I'm sorry, Dallas. I'm so sorry for all the pain I caused you.

Would that be it for her?

Chapter Four

This was so not a good idea.

Dallas nearly turned around and went back to the ranch three times. Spending time with Skylar brought back too much pain and longing for things that couldn't be.

He twisted his fingers around the steering wheel. When Mom relayed the news that someone had tried to run her off the road, it put him on edge and reawakened his protective instincts. He couldn't fall in love with her again, but he didn't want anything to happen to her, either.

Yes, thankfully she was safe. Someone had seen her car go into the field and called the police. But still. He resisted the urge to grind his teeth as he slowed around a curve.

He took a deep breath of air filled with the scents of wood and the stale french fries he'd grabbed on the go yesterday.

Was it an accident? Or did someone deliberately try to hurt her? Did a person in her past wish her harm and follow her to Port Sunshine?

Granted, they had some crime in tourist season, but it was mostly pickpockets or disorderly conduct from visitors who downed too much of the local wine.

Nothing more serious. Except for the things that happened at *that* cottage...

He frowned. That was many years ago. Never solved, it had become sort of a legend. Just like the legend about the pirate's treasure buried somewhere on the shore, but that one was from centuries ago.

At least, her car had only suffered minor damage that he'd heard was already repaired. The small-town grapevine made sure even if Skylar wasn't telling him things he wished she would, he'd find out, anyway.

Dallas pulled up to the canary-yellow cottage with her artsy seashell mural and turned off the engine.

What was he even going to tell her? Bringing the cherry pie was a flimsy excuse. Offer of protection? But from what? Besides, she hadn't asked for a bodyguard. And even looking at her still hurt him. Breeze barked somewhere inside, more in greeting than in warning. Skylar already had a dog to protect her. The thought of Breeze brought a smile.

Well, he should just leave.

Then the front door opened, and Skylar walked out to the porch. Too late now.

He jumped out of his truck and lifted the pie. "Mom sent this for you and your grandmother."

"Oh." Skylar squinted at the sun. "That was sweet of her. Thank her for us, please."

He ran up the steps to her and gave her the pie. Their fingers touched, and awareness jolted through him.

Her eyes widened, and she edged back, changing awareness into disappointment. She stared past him at the ocean. "I'd invite you for tea, but Grandma and I are leaving soon."

Did she seek an excuse not to invite him in? His disappointment deepened. "Okay. I was just dropping off the pie, anyway."

"How kind of you." She walked inside and waved him in. "Come on in."

He stepped inside the house sweet with the nostalgic scent of tea and safety. Breeze jumped at him and licked his face as he bent to pet her.

"Breeze, stop!" Skylar seemed to try to sound stern and failed. Then she called out, "Grandma, Mrs. Lawrence sent us a pie."

Inside, the house was the kingdom of teapots where a touch of the nautical reigned. The teapots conquered everything—the steady antique cupboard, the round table, the granite countertop. A set of them was even painted on the red dining room wall young Skylar had splattered with white polka dots. She'd painted those teapots too when she'd been a child, and the spout was a tad crooked.

Mrs. Rafferty collected teapots, and her husband and later their son—Skylar's father—used to bring them to her from their sea travels. Her late husband had been a sailor, and their son followed in his footsteps. Until Skylar's father didn't come home from a late-night boat trip two months after her mother had left town with a tourist she'd met at the beach.

The wind had brought his boat ashore the next day, but he'd been nowhere to be seen.

Speculation abounded about what had happened to him and why he'd gone out on the ocean late at night and in bad weather. Some said he'd fallen overboard by accident. Others said that he'd been drunk, but that was unlike him. One rumor spread that he'd drowned on purpose after losing the love of his life. A few even said he didn't want to return to the place that caused him so much grief.

That wasn't all.

On the night her father disappeared, Skylar had escaped the house, probably to look for him. Her grandmother, out of her wits, called the police when she stopped by the next morning, then Dallas's mother, and they'd gathered a search party. They'd finally found Skylar near *that* cottage when they'd checked everything a second time. She'd been hiding under the porch where she'd sneaked in by taking out a broken wooden plank, and they probably hadn't noticed her the first time.

In the following three weeks, she hadn't talked and only cried. When she'd started talking again, she'd said she couldn't remember anything. Years later, she'd never recalled what had happened that night.

Or so she'd said.

Dallas suppressed a shudder about the trauma she'd gone through. She couldn't even get closure, because how can you get closure to something you can't remember?

The place breathed the sea this family so loved. In wrinkled maps of the bay. In miniature ship replicas. In fishing nets hanging from the ceiling. In a lighthouse figurine with a chipped-off shoreline. And in something that always drew his attention—Skylar's watercolors of the ocean. Once, they'd changed often, a row of fresh works replacing the ones before them.

His heart contracted as he searched for new works. No, there wasn't a single new one since she'd left.

Would there ever be?

He didn't understand much about art. But her sunshine-filled works used to bring her joy. What—or who—was bringing her joy now?

Skylar's grandmother wobbled into the living room, and his stomach tightened. Her shoulders were more stooped today, and her movements were slower than usual. He and Skylar exchanged concerned glances. They used to understand each other so easily before.

Did she miss that understanding? Did she miss him at all? A rush of heat bubbled under his skin. How could she discard everything they had?

"Hey, stranger." Mrs. Rafferty smiled, but it didn't hold the usual warmth. What was happening? She didn't look like an excited bride. She picked up her purse. "We're going to choose the wedding cake and invitations. Would you like to join us?"

There was his opening. Not that he knew anything about wedding preparations. All his brothers were single. And the only time he'd thought he'd be shopping for a wedding cake would be with Skylar. His heart shifted.

"Why would Dallas want to join us in wedding preparations?" Skylar rolled her eyes.

"Actually, I'd love to." He offered Mrs. Rafferty his elbow to lean on.

Skylar's jaw slackened. "Seriously?"

"Yep." He couldn't pretend this wouldn't hurt. But he could make the best of it.

"You must really love cake." Mrs. Rafferty placed her hand in the crook of his arm.

He helped her walk outside and down the stairs while Skylar trailed them with a bewildered look in her eyes. Yes, he glanced back several times.

Breeze trudged along, but Skylar wiggled her finger at her. "Stay."

When Breeze whined, obviously scared she might get abandoned again, Skylar's expression softened. "I'm sorry. We can't take you inside the pastry shop, and it's going to be too hot for you to wait in the car. I'll be back before you know it."

Dallas winced. That was what she'd told him.

I'll be back before you know it.

"Before you know it" turned out to be fifteen years. And he'd felt every moment with every fiber of his being, especially the first two years.

The dog tilted her head and eyed Skylar skeptically but stayed in place.

He followed her sedan in his truck, and a short drive later, they were at Candy's Pastries. The place welcomed them with the aroma of freshly baked goodies, and his stomach perked up. But the instant he entered the pastry shop, he cringed. Of course, he knew Patty covered for her sister sometimes, but did it have to be today?

In a desperate attempt to forget Skylar after their breakup, he'd dated Patty. But soon he'd realized his feelings toward her would never be anything close to his feelings for Skylar. It wouldn't be fair to her to continue their relationship. He'd broken it off as kindly as he could. Probably with the finesse of a horse let loose near Mrs. Rafferty's teapot collection.

According to his brothers, Patty harbored hopes she and Dallas might still get together one day. Argh.

Patty had her long sandy-hued hair in a French braid, and her face lit up when she spotted him. "Hello, Dallas and Mrs. Rafferty! How may I help you?" But her smile flattened when Skylar stepped into the store behind them. "Hi, Skylar. I heard you're back in town. Did you and Dallas reconcile?"

Why did everyone assume that? He cringed but did his best to smile. It must look like Breeze did when she growled. "No. I'm just here to help Mrs. Rafferty shop for her wedding cake."

"Oh." Patty blinked, but at least she didn't ask why. He was about as much of a cake expert as the cattle his family raised, and yet here he was.

"I could use a male opinion on cakes, and my fiancé had to go on an emergency trip." Mrs. Rafferty patted his hand. "Wasn't it nice of Dallas to volunteer?"

Patty's eyes narrowed a fraction. "Very." She recovered fast enough and foisted off a smile. "We don't have any wedding cakes on display, sorry. But we do have a catalog with photos depicting what my sister can make. And we have some samples of the cakes that can be used as a base for frosting and other decorations to be added."

Mrs. Rafferty nodded. "Sounds like a great idea."

"This way, then." Patty hugged a glossy catalog with laminated pages to her chest and led them to a tiny café area with two round, white wrought iron tables.

He pulled out a chair for Mrs. Rafferty. Skylar didn't wait for him to do the same for her but took a seat.

The bell announced more customers coming in, all tourists from what Dallas could tell, and Patty slipped back behind the counter after touching Mrs. Rafferty's shoulder. "Let me know what you decide."

His fingers fisted as he sat. He drew a deep breath of air scented with pastries, vanilla, and cinnamon. Skylar planned to shop here for their wedding cake. He'd offered to drive to Charleston for a fancy cake order, but she'd wanted a small wedding and nothing too pretentious. She'd already known then what kind of cake she'd wanted. But now her gaze was distracted, and she appeared... lost?

At fifteen, he'd found his place in life and the person he'd wanted to share it with. He'd thought she'd done the same. Instead, she must still be searching for both.

Apparently, far away from him. The thought was so bitter even the yummy samples Patty brought didn't sweeten it.

Skylar reached for one sample with artistic fingers that looked beautiful whether she'd been holding a paintbrush at the beach or a grooming brush in their barn. But he loved them the most when she'd worn his engagement ring. And best of all, those delicate fingers had been so soft when they'd touched his face. Warmth pooled in the pit of his stomach.

No thinking like that!

"What do you think, Grandma? Peach or chocolate? Or both together?" Skylar must be oblivious to his struggle.

"Of all your silly suggestions. They do *not* go together. I tell you, Little Miss, sometimes you remind me too much of your mother." Mrs. Rafferty wagged a finger at Skylar, using the childhood nickname Skylar had earned for the way she'd tried to imitate her mother even as a toddler. Her face set in grim lines, Mrs. Rafferty helped herself to a chocolate sample.

Indeed, in the past, Skylar had managed to mix many things that usually didn't go together, be it clothes, colors, or food, and somehow, she made them work. He didn't think a silent, steady guy like him would fit with a mercurial chatterbox like her, but she'd made it work.

Turned out his first instinct had been right. They didn't fit together, or she wouldn't have broken the engagement. They'd grown up building castles in the sand, and in her stories and early drawings, she was a princess and he was her knight in shining armor. He smiled at her wild imagination. But it turned out, he'd been the one who built sandcastles in his mind, and she'd stomped on them.

A mischievous thought teased him, and he acted on it before he could change his mind. He forked up a sample of the white sheet cake with peach filling and brought it to her mouth. "Would you like to try this one?"

Her eyes widened.

Mrs. Rafferty sent her granddaughter an innocent glance. "I'd love your opinion."

Once again, this was so not a good idea. But his gaze lingered on Skylar, and he didn't back off. "Peach flavor used to be your favorite." Whenever he bought her ice cream, she always picked peach. He remembered the creamy, cold taste of it on her lips.

The room temperature seemed to kick up.

"It still is," she whispered before she accepted the bite.

A memory surfaced. They'd walked on the beach, the sunset painting the sky in a peach hue. She'd run barefoot, splashing the water around, and laughing. Back then, she'd said he wouldn't have to feed her cake delicately at their wedding because *she* was going to smash it in his face. He believed she would.

Now he fed her a substitute for a future wedding cake delicately, but it wasn't their wedding. The empty fork clattered as he put it back on the porcelain plate.

Mrs. Rafferty looked from her granddaughter to him and back. "What did you decide, Little Miss?"

A few heartbeats passed before Skylar spoke. "It was great, but I'll let you choose. It's your wedding, not mine. And I still like the same things, but sometimes, it can be the wrong choice in different circumstances."

The wrong choice in different circumstances? He tried to wrap his mind around her words and failed. He didn't get hints. He liked things open and clear. Not diluted. Not alluded to.

Silence hung between them, thick and heavy, underscored by the customer's lively chatter at the counter.

Did she have the same memories he had, or did she push them away to start a new life without him?

"I made my decision." Mrs. Rafferty broke the silence. "No offense, Skylar, but it's going to be a white cake with pineapple filling." She got up, and this time, Skylar rushed to her grandmother and offered her elbow, leaving him just tagging along. Mrs. Rafferty placed her order at the counter.

"Sounds great. I'll let my sister know. Thank you very much." Patty talked to Mrs. Rafferty but stared at Dallas.

Skylar's gaze flicked between him and Patty, and then her eyebrows edged up. A sad, understanding smile curved her lips. She wasn't even jealous. But then, why would she be?

Besides, he was here on a mission—sort of. And it wasn't to pay attention to Skylar's lips or eyes. It was to ensure her safety.

Stepping away from the counter with Skylar, Mrs. Rafferty patted his arm with her free hand. "Let's go to the stationery store now."

He nodded. "I'll ask my uncle to give you a good deal."

A small town was a small world indeed, and his uncle owned that store. As his cousins left for other states, Dallas and his brothers sometimes helped at the store. He'd done the heavy lifting of unloading new merchandise and moving things around while his more sociable brothers covered the counter from time to time.

He walked to the front glass door of the pastry store, checked the outdoor surroundings, then opened the door for Skylar and her grandmother when nothing seemed suspicious. But then, would he even know what was suspicious?

Unfamiliar people? Though the season didn't start yet and they didn't have crowds, tourists had already trickled in. His senses on high alert, he walked close to Mrs. Rafferty and Skylar across the parking lot to Skylar's silver-gray sedan. Then he followed them in his truck on the way to the stationery store. Skylar wasn't going to be run off the road on his watch.

He wasn't the best candidate for a bodyguard, but he was the one who showed up. That should mean something, right?

Soon, he pulled up to the artsy stationery store that doubled as a gallery and souvenir shop, grateful to find a parking spot. No, he didn't resent tourists. After all, they helped their small town survive and thrive. He just preferred large open spaces occupied by cows and horses over small confined ones with crowds.

His gut tightened. He didn't like confined places since... Well, best not to remember.

The store's floor-to-ceiling window display boasted framed watercolors done by local artists, the artwork placed on a bed of seashells and smooth pebbles. Skylar's gaze stopped on the watercolors done by other people, then moved along, carefully blank. Unable to read her mind now, he opened the teak front door for her and her grandmother.

Once, this place had displayed her work. But those watercolors had sold out over a decade ago. Yet her presence somehow lingered even here, maybe because of some of the greeting cards.

Skylar's eyes widened. "They still carry my designs."

"Welcome back, Skylar. Good afternoon, Mrs. Rafferty. Hi, bro." One of Dallas's younger brothers stepped out from around the counter. Kai's dark hair—the darkest in the family—was mostly hidden beneath a black bandanna, and a gold earring glistened in his ear. The hoop earring, bandanna, striped T-shirt, and mischievous look weren't just a pirate disguise to attract tourists. Kai was one of Dallas's rebellious brothers, or at least used to be when he'd gotten them all in trouble in their teens. Behind the counter, however, he was politeness itself. Mostly.

Kai also had the most mysterious story of them all. One morning, early, Mom had found a one-year-old boy abandoned at the beach. He could say a few words, but couldn't answer where his mommy was or where his home was. After settling some legal matters and lots of arguments with her husband, Mom adopted the little boy. She guessed the boy must have Asian heritage, but they'd never learned more of his story. Mom treated Kai like one of her sons. Dad didn't—meaning Kai was the only boy in the family Dad hadn't beaten up.

"My aunt says those designs are popular with customers." Kai grinned, layering on his charm. The only thing missing was a parrot on his shoulder, but that was because Quiet was at home today. Two days ago, the bird had learned a few swear words from a store visitor and then swore at a customer. Their mother wouldn't stand for swearing, and neither he nor their brothers ever swore. Now all of them had tried to teach Quiet to unlearn those words, but so far unsuccessfully.

"You're very talented, my dear." Loving pride gushed in Mrs. Rafferty's voice, but did sadness underplay it?

"I'm sure my uncle would love to sell your work again," Kai said.

"Thank you. Please give him my thanks, but..." Based on the way Skylar's neck moved, she swallowed hard. "I–I don't think that's going to happen."

"That's a pity." Kai voiced Dallas's thoughts. Probably all of their thoughts.

Her fingers touched a postcard, and his heart skipped a beat. He knew the place where the breathtaking sunrise photo was taken. It was one of their favorite places at the bay. And it still hurt. Did her eyes glisten?

Her gaze swept over key chains, refrigerator magnets, mugs, towels, T-shirts, and other ocean-themed souvenirs. It slid along the walls with other artists' watercolors and oil paintings until it stopped at a new one Dallas hadn't seen before depicting a cliff, pelted in the rain. The dark sky zigzagged with a lightning bolt, and the steep drop overlooked the churning ocean.

Her entire demeanor changed. She shuddered and took a sharp breath. And the look in her eyes... It was pure horror as if she were the one in the painting, standing on the cliff's edge, being buffeted by the wind, and scared to make the next step.

He stepped toward her, aching to comfort her despite everything. "Are you all right?"

But Mrs. Rafferty was closer. She squeezed Skylar's delicate fingers and shook her head nearly imperceptibly.

Skylar drew a deep breath and turned away. When she turned back, her expression was unreadable again. "I'm fine."

She kept secrets from him. Way more than he'd realized. Disappointment shouldn't have ripped through him, but it did before he let compassion overtake it.

"If you'd like to leave—"

"I'm perfectly fine." Her lips straightened in a smile as she answered her grandmother, but it wobbled. "Let's find you the perfect wedding invitations."

"Sure, Little Miss." The woman's pale eyes narrowed on Skylar. Then she refocused and pointed at the cards she wanted to see.

What was going on?

An alarm sounded in his head. Why did the painting affect her so badly? Yes, it was a dangerous place many locals avoided even on good days, much more during a storm at night. But she was familiar with it. They'd been there before in his more daring days. Though, of course, they didn't step close to the edge.

Why would it cause such a strong reaction now? Was it because her father had disappeared on a stormy night? Dallas had never understood why the man had ventured out to the ocean in such weather. It was common sense to stay ashore, but as a sailor, he especially should've known better.

Mrs. Rafferty didn't deliberate for long. She chose a wedding invitation with a romantic couple on the beach, the girl dressed in an unembellished white sleeveless dress, her long hair and veil floating in the breeze. She walked on the sand barefoot, holding hands with a similarly barefoot guy in a tuxedo. The man turned to gaze at his bride, so Dallas couldn't see his face, but the girl's face showed so much joy.

It was one of Skylar's designs and what he'd imagined their wedding would look like. They both had. His rib cage contracted.

Skylar opened her mouth as if to protest. Then her lips thinned, and she didn't say anything. But the sadness in her eyes spoke for her, glossing them like seafoam coating ocean waters.

"Great choice. Uncle says it's our most popular design for wedding invitations and anniversary cards." Kai looked from Dallas to Skylar and back as he input the order. At least, he didn't ask if they'd reconciled.

Dallas was often grateful for air-conditioning, but he was even more grateful for sunshine and its tender rays on his skin—almost like her fingers—when he opened the stationery store's door for her and her grandmother, then stepped outside after them. The sky was clear and the brightest shade of blue without a single cloud. All the foggy clouds were inside his head now, and he couldn't untangle his feelings toward her. It wasn't love any longer, couldn't be, but there was regret, longing, resentment, disappointment, and so many others he wasn't sure how to name. And yes, deep inside, there was still a bit of affection. After all, she'd been the center of his world for most of his life, his sun and his moon, and all the stars in the sky they used to count while lying on the sand.

Pay attention!

He scanned his surroundings.

The place seemed peaceful and quiet with only cries of seagulls in the distance and an occasional whir of a motor interrupting it. Her narrowed gaze moved around as if she didn't trust the peacefulness.

In their childhood, she'd often been the one to cheer him up, especially when his father became abusive again. Thanks to her, he didn't wince anymore at the memories of shouts and shattered dishes.

Whatever their past was, the desire to cheer her up and return the favor stirred in him. He opened the front passenger door for Mrs. Rafferty after Skylar had clicked on the fob. "If you've worked up some appetite while shopping, I'd be glad to take you lovely ladies out for lunch. And you could use it to discuss what menu you'd like at the wedding."

Mrs. Rafferty paused before climbing inside. "You two youngsters go ahead, but please, drop me off at home first."

Skylar frowned, giving him a stab of disappointment. Did she dislike the idea of having lunch with him that much? "Are you feeling unwell, Grandma?"

Ah. Of course, Skylar worried about her grandmother, hence the frown. The world didn't revolve around him.

"I'm good, missy. Don't get so fussy." Mrs. Rafferty slipped inside the car as Skylar helped her. "I just want to get some rest. I hope you don't mind. But please go ahead. How about Bay and Basin? Bring me back a few samples, too. That would be helpful. Your aunt already agreed to cater the wedding."

Mrs. Rafferty had been to all the local restaurants many times, especially the one belonging to a family member, so she knew the menus by heart. Though Skylar's mother had cut all connections with them after abandoning her husband and her child, Mrs. Rafferty didn't hold a grudge against her daughter-in-law's family. But a part of him was glad she'd encouraged Skylar to go with him. And not only because another part of him missed the times spent with her.

She turned to him, her eyes pensive. "Is Bay and Basin still pet friendly?"

He breathed out. "Yes, the patio side. And we can look at the ocean or walk to it later." He nearly added "Like old times," but he managed to stop himself.

She walked around the sedan to the driver's side. "Do you mind if we pick up Breeze and take her with us?"

He opened the door for her. "Sure. Go ahead."

He liked the newly adopted stray, and he also appreciated how the dog could alert them if something went wrong. Hopefully.

The inner alarm sounded again. Was it safe for Skylar to have lunch out in the open? But he was walking on shifting sands as it was, so he didn't bring it up. Rather, he resolved to be more alert to his surroundings.

And to be honest, he didn't like to be inside closed-in spaces, even when those spaces weren't that small. His scream rang in his ears, the little fists hitting the heavy door with no results... *Trapped.*

He shook off the feeling of desperation. It all had been decades ago. He wasn't that terrified child anymore. No need to remember.

His glance kept flicking to the rearview mirror for any tail. If it were up to him, he'd make a few extra turns, but he had to follow Skylar's car.

The canary-yellow cottage with green trims, like dandelions in the grass. Everything around it seemed quiet, and only familiar vehicles passed the street so far.

He pulled up after her nondescript gray sedan, regret hanging in the air like car fumes and poisoning his lungs. For Skylar's sixteenth birthday, her grandmother had gifted her a used lime-green car. The contraption screeched when turning corners and had a plastic sheet taped in place where the passenger side window should be. His brothers had spent hours making it drivable, and even then, it would only start after about fifteen minutes of sweet talk to the car.

Exhilarated, Skylar had danced around her first car, then had painted it with bright fairy-tale flowers and covered it with fun decals. There wasn't a single decal on this one. It was brand new and chosen to blend in.

More than Skylar had changed. Everything around her had changed, as if her bright fire had burned out to ashes. His heart ached for her and her losses—the losses he didn't even know about—more than it ached for his own loss.

After scanning the peaceful neighborhood, he rushed out of his rusty-trusty truck to carry the pastry boxes they'd brought back from Candy's Pastries.

"Thank you, dear." Mrs. Rafferty leaned on her granddaughter as they shuffled up the porch.

Again, he and Skylar exchanged concerned glances.

"A ramp?" she mouthed at him over her grandmother's head.

He nodded.

"Are you feeling okay, Grandma?"

Mrs. Rafferty conquered another step. "Yes. Just tired."

He'd install a ramp, just to be on the safe side, as soon as he figured out how to approach the issue with Mrs. Rafferty. She could use a cane or a walker, as well, but she'd refused so far.

Breeze met them with an enthusiastic bark that became even more enthusiastic once the dog realized they were going to take her with them. Breeze started licking Skylar's hands, then her face when Skylar knelt to pet her.

"Aren't you awesome?" A now-rare smile lifted Skylar's lips. "We're not going to leave you behind again."

Like she'd left him behind?

The time to mope about that had passed many years ago if there had ever been such a time to start with. He'd had to let her go and live his life. Only his heart had difficulty comprehending it.

She paused from petting the dog and looked up at him. "How about just taking your truck? No need to take two vehicles as we're going to the same place."

"Sure." He nodded. He liked the idea of her being in his truck again. A bit too much.

Whoa. She'd left him. Remember? Without a clear reason. Without an explanation.

Once they were on the road, Breeze barked again, and this wasn't a friendly bark any longer. Dallas tensed as his gaze jerked to the rearview mirror again. A sleek white car with tinted windows had stayed two cars behind them at several traffic lights already. Now it pulled up close.

Too close for his or Breeze's liking.

Chapter Five

Skylar wasn't as tuned into Dallas as she used to be, but she could still tell when something was wrong. She flinched at the memory of the hurt in his eyes when she'd broken off their engagement.

As they walked along the restaurant patio overlooking the beach, Breeze licked her hand again perhaps to provide much-needed support and encouragement.

"Is this spot okay?" His gaze roamed over the place as if he needed to take in every splinter on the wooden deck and every grain of sand on the shore.

"Sure." She nodded. With it too early for the lunch hour, only one other couple occupied the patio—not that Skylar thought she and Dallas were a couple.

He pulled out a wooden chair for her, and she sat while Breeze stretched on the deck near Skylar's feet.

The place smelled of fried fish and lime, and she waited to exhale, desperate to hold it in because, just like Dallas's cologne or Grandma's peppermint tea, it smelled like home.

All these years later, they still displayed her marine watercolors. The tables sported the pelicans and fish she'd painted on them, even though scratches and grooves now carved across them and the sun had faded the teal and gray colors she'd chosen.

The waitress sauntered over, a lanky teen with blonde hair in a ponytail. She must work here on weekends and summer breaks.

Just like Skylar used to. Partly to help her aunt during busy times, partly to aid her grandmother with their living expenses, and partly to raise funds for art supplies. Now all the art supplies had stayed untouched for almost fifteen years. The paints were surely dry at this point. Nostalgia turned to regret, but then those two often danced together.

After the girl took their drinks order and walked away, Skylar scooted forward. "What's going on?"

He met her gaze. "What do you mean?"

Breeze tilted her head as if feeling the tension in the air, but she didn't move otherwise.

"You seem to be... to be on edge." Argh. Skylar shouldn't have asked. She drew a deep breath of air where the ocean's saltiness mixed with the scents of fried shrimp and fresh-baked biscuits.

He could still be upset about their breakup, and she couldn't blame him. He wouldn't forgive her. She hadn't forgiven herself.

For more things than one. She stared past him at cerulean waters so serene it was difficult to believe they could rise dangerously in a storm. Rise so high and come so fast they could swallow a person and carry them far, far away.

She suppressed a shudder. When she'd been growing up, the ocean used to calm her and bring at least some peace after both her parents had disappeared one after the other.

But not any longer.

What could she have done differently once she'd remembered some things? She wasn't sure, but there must've been something.

She opened one of the laminated menus she used to know by heart. Her drawings of Aunt's dishes stared at her. Everything in this hometown mocked her former passion, and it was difficult to bear. It was easier to deal with numbers in spreadsheets. But Dallas was watching her, so she hid behind a menu again, angry at the heat in her stomach. Some passion wasn't exactly former.

A few unfamiliar dishes had joined the menu but not many, and she took comfort in the familiarity.

Their third date was here. Weirdly, sometimes she couldn't remember the things she did last week. But she could remember their every date, every kiss, every word, every glance....

She slid her fingers over the smooth menu as if she could touch the lost hopes and desires that had been crushed like debris in a shipwreck. Her fingers shifted toward his, finding a familiar path, but she stopped herself. Touching him now was forbidden.

Then she peeped up again at the man who embodied her past and had once embodied her future.

His eyebrows lifted, his expression puzzled. He must've said something, and she'd missed it.

"What did you say?" Just looking at him pained her, but then what did she expect?

"Do you think it was an accident that someone tried to run you over? Or is there danger in your life?"

Did he worry about her? And why did the thought bring her a pleasant wave? There couldn't be anything between them any longer. *She'd* made sure of it.

"I hope it was an accident," she said. "Though I don't know why someone would do that to a stranger."

Was this connected to...? She winced. No, it couldn't be. So many years had passed. Or could it?

But one thing she was sure about. "Nothing's dangerous about my present life. It's as boring as it could be."

He studied her. "Boring is one word I'd never think you'd use to describe your life."

She chuckled without mirth. That girl who'd danced barefoot on the beach and painted everything in sight with bright colors seemed like a different person, not her at all.

The young waitress with pink flowers on her nails and hope in her eyes showed up with their drinks. "Ready to order?"

A new generation to take over hoping and striving—and a bit of waiting. Maybe this girl wouldn't encounter all the disappointment and disillusionment Skylar had.

Skylar handed over her menu. "Yes. Fisherman's Catch. It still comes with coleslaw and french fries, right?"

"Sure thing." The waitress's heavily penciled-on eyebrows rose a tad. "And for you, Mr. Lawrence?"

The waitress knew him. Of course. People in small towns knew each other, and Skylar must've met this girl as a toddler. But she couldn't place her now, which made sense as she no longer belonged here.

"I'll take the same thing. Thank you." He handed his menu back as well without a glance at its contents. He didn't need to. This was his town, his place, his shore while she was still swept far away in an ocean of regrets.

"Got it. Thanks." The waitress in the same kind of flamingo-hued uniform Skylar used to wear walked away, her high blonde ponytail with streaks of cherry highlights bouncing at every step.

In high school, Skylar had worn blue highlights. Blue like her beloved ocean. Or Dallas's eyes.

Don't think about his eyes. Those eyes haunted her dreams forever. Yet they were much better than what else had haunted her dreams.

She took a long sip of her lemonade, cherishing the cold, tangy liquid. Dallas had helped her with lemonade stands for tourists. Another memory. Another loss.

Enough.

She drank some more. "My life is truly as mundane as it could be. I don't go to parties. I keep to myself in the office and avoid any conflicts. I often telework, like this month. I don't know most of my neighbors' names. Never had an issue with them. I didn't even have a pet. Well, until now." She petted Breeze.

"What about..." A muscle twitched in his jaw. His fingers wrapped around his glass, but he didn't lift it. "About an ex-boyfriend?"

She cringed and listened to seagulls crying out as if they could give her good advice. Dallas and Skylar used to tell each other everything since they were children.

Now she didn't want him to know just how pathetic her personal life was. She'd wanted something more vibrant once. But life in the shadows required one to be a recluse. "I used to date, but it never moved into boyfriend-girlfriend territory. You're the only ex-boyfriend I have."

He'd finally sipped his soda at that moment, and it didn't go well. He coughed and placed the glass back so fast the bubbly liquid sloshed over. He didn't expect that answer, did he?

"Are you all right?" She mopped up the soda on the table with a napkin and got up to pat him on the back.

He raised his hand to stop her. "I'm good."

"Okay." Probably wasn't a great idea to touch him, anyway.

The waitress brought their food and left. He said grace. Skylar didn't. Another loss. Another regret.

Then they ate in silence. They'd never eaten in silence before. She'd always found something to chat about. To ask about. He'd never talked much, but it hadn't bothered her.

She itched to ask him about someone in his life. But it wasn't her right to know.

He munched on the fried shrimp. "What about your job? Anything suspicious there?"

"Seriously? I'm an accountant." She resisted the urge to roll her eyes. Instead, she just dipped a french fry in ketchup. The bright dark-red color screamed at her, and she shifted back. She evened her breathing. It was just ketchup. Not something... she associated that color with ever since the memories had come back. But not all of them had. She'd still had a lot of blurs. Too many.

Or maybe not enough.

Usually, he'd been the one to finish his food first—she'd been too busy doing all the talking. Now she'd been making a dent in it much faster than he did. The same french fries tasted different here, even without ketchup. Crunchy and salty outside, soft inside. Better somehow.

"Well, could you have come across some unsavory information in the accounting books?" He studied her over the rim of his glass.

What did he see? It was wrong of her to wish he'd look at her with the same affection, just once.

Then his gaze roamed over the place again, like it did most of the time at lunch. Was it because he was vigilant after her accident? Or did it pain him to even look at her? That thought gave her a bitter taste, and she chased it down with sweet and tangy lemonade.

When she glanced around as well, her gaze lingered on a woman in a white short-sleeved dress with red polka dots and a crimson belt who must've come in recently. Several diamonds sparkled in the sunshine on fingers that also bore an elaborate manicure. A wide-brimmed straw hat shaded her, and ice-blonde hair spilled over her shoulders. Fancy oversized sunglasses covered most of her face, leaving visible only overdone lips highlighted by lipstick as bright as those polka dots. Straw hats and sunglasses were a staple here because of the bright sun, and yet something about this visitor put Skylar on guard. An uneasiness clenched her stomach.

First, the woman's hair didn't match her eyebrows, which were at least a shade darker. Second, her body was sort of turned in their direction, even though her attention seemed to be taken with a small salad and her phone. Her posture was tense, and she wasn't scrolling or typing anything. She wasn't eavesdropping, was she?

Of course not. Why would she? Skylar nearly snorted.

"I work for a *very* reputable company. Nothing suspicious there." She squeezed a lime over the fish fillet and gave it its due. She didn't know who the cook was here now, but the fillet was nice and tender, and the herbs were flavorful. Did her aunt still do some of the cooking?

"Why?"

She blinked at him. "Um, why would I work for a reputable company?"

He forked some of his coleslaw. "No, why did you become an accountant? You always wanted to be an artist."

Though her appetite started to evaporate, she helped herself to the coleslaw, too, mostly to stall. "But I was good at math, remember?"

"I do, but that doesn't answer my question."

He was right. Her fork clattered to the plate, causing Breeze to get up and growl, but then she settled at Skylar's feet again.

What could Skylar tell him? That one day she remembered something horrifying? That she had to stop being a dreamer? That she'd needed to distance herself from their beach town and what she used to be here? Or that one of her paintings could've cost Grandma her life?

"Getting a degree in accounting gave me a reliable, steady job." Completely true, but the lesser of several reasons. "There's a reason the expression 'starving artist' exists."

"But you loved it." His voice went quiet.

She loved *him*, too. But she'd walked away, hadn't she? A sharp knife turned in her belly. Maybe the same one with which he'd thought she'd stabbed him in the back.

Slowly, she drained her lemonade. Partly because she was thirsty. Partly because she needed to buy time again to answer without giving too much away. She put the glass on the table, empty like her heart.

Then she stared at the gentle cerulean waters as if the ocean was telling her the right words and she could decipher them in its whisper.

"Sometimes, we have to leave what we love the most," she finally said. Based on his frown, it wasn't the answer he wanted to hear. But it was the only answer she could give.

Heat prickled her eyes, and she dropped beside Breeze to hide her face in the luxurious, smooth fur in case the tears slid free. She clutched the dog as if Breeze were her lifesaver.

Could she still tell Dallas everything? Or whatever little she remembered? Would he understand her decision, then?

No, it was too dangerous. And too late anyway.

A LOW GROWL THREW SKYLAR out of her dreams. She dreamed of Dallas again, and her heart was beating faster than usual. Only it wasn't the Dallas of her teen dreams but the man he was now. The man she'd hurt and kept hurting.

She opened her eyes and blinked, disoriented and adjusting to the darkness. Where was she?

The whisper of the ocean... A faint scent of peppermint tea... It wasn't her apartment.

Her childhood home. Her grandmother's sea cottage. Offering many familiar and calming scents and sounds. But one that wasn't.

The low growl. Breeze, warning about something. Skylar's heart skipped a beat. Was someone outside?

Alarmed, she slipped out of bed where her preteen self had decorated the frame with seashells. Her bare feet drowned in the soft carpet, and she didn't bother to look for slippers. The moon must've emerged from behind the clouds because moonlight filtered through the closed curtains together with the lantern light.

The silhouette of the golden retriever froze near the window. Breeze cocked her head on high alert, and her posture sent a dart of worry through Skylar.

"What's wrong? Did you hear something? Or... somebody?" She whispered as if Breeze could understand her.

Maybe she could because Breeze turned her head and barked. Another warning. A shiver traveled down Skylar's spine, despite the room's warmth. She crouched toward the window. "What did you hear?"

Should she get her gun? It was small and fit in her hand well, and she hoped she'd never have to fire it. But after the threat fifteen years ago, it had become a necessity.

Shouldn't it all be in the past by now, though? She plastered herself near the window and lifted the curtain a fraction to look outside.

A shadow shifted near the fence and vanished fast. Skylar flinched. A cloud shrouded the moon, and without more moonlight, she couldn't see anything beyond a black hoodie in the dim lantern light. Besides, it happened too fast.

Breeze edged closer but didn't bark anymore. No more growling, either.

Afraid to breathe, Skylar stared at the white sand for several more minutes. Her beloved ocean appeared dark and menacing, threatening her with mysteries like the one she never should've seen. A shiver traveled down her spine, but she didn't move. Then Breeze stretched on the carpet as if nothing had happened.

The threat, if there was a threat, had passed.

Or did this place wake up her paranoia?

She needed to check on her grandmother. Skylar forced herself to move now and tiptoed out of her childhood room still covered in her drawings and watercolors, wincing at the cold tile, then to her grandmother's bedroom, the only other bedroom in the house.

She moved quietly in case Grandma was asleep as low snoring coming from the bedroom suggested. Skylar peeked into the room decorated with doilies and embroidered tablecloths on the dresser and nightstand. Yup, Grandma was asleep indeed.

Relieved, Skylar turned around and stumbled onto Breeze in the hall. She held in a gasp somehow, then steadied herself while holding onto the dog.

Did she scare herself for nothing? Or had she brought danger to her grandmother's place?

Getting cold, she rubbed her palms over her forearms, her silk pajamas smooth under her skin but no protection from cold or fear. The words of the threat she'd received after leaving her small town were imprinted in her brain forever.

Or could danger still wait for her here?

Chapter Six

Skylar told her grandmother about the night scare over breakfast on the terrace.

"Oh, my darling Little Miss." The woman who'd raised her hugged her gently.

"Do you think it was nothing?" Skylar voiced her wishful thinking. "Just some tourist who couldn't sleep roaming the beach?"

"I hope so." Grandma sipped yellow chamomile tea from a dainty porcelain cup seeming as fragile as its owner, wrinkles deepening around her pale eyes. Her hair, usually combed, was a bit disheveled after the night.

"We really should get you outside cameras." Skylar stirred the spoon around in her small cup, though the honey had most likely dissolved long ago. She preferred larger more practical mugs, but the tea ritual was important to her grandmother and routine even more so.

Hmm, she'd talked her grandmother into the indoor cameras but hadn't succeeded with outdoor ones. After a while, she'd given up insisting on those. She shouldn't have.

The metal spoon clanked against porcelain edges, and it grated on her raw nerves. She hadn't gotten much sleep last night. When she'd finally fallen into a restless slumber in the morning, she'd dreamed of the night of the storm. She'd woken up drenched in a cold sweat and wishing she'd dreamed of Dallas.

She raised her chin and gazed at the ocean, spectacular in its morning awakening of flamingo and canary hues and looking much friendlier now than at night. Somewhere in the trees, birds sang a hymn to the new day. She'd have to figure it all out somehow. She had to.

From a dreamer, she'd become practical and pragmatic, and she stood firmly on her two feet, even if those feet were back in shifting sands.

The wind rustling the wisteria also played with her grandmother's white hair, and she pushed it back. With the movement, three seashell bracelets Skylar had made many years ago clattered on Grandma's wrist. A strand of her hair nearly snagged on a seashell but then slipped back and spilled over her shoulders.

Skylar didn't have a problem with the wind pushing her hair in her face or catching on bracelets. She wore her long hair in a tight bun these days, and unlike in her childhood and teens, not a single bracelet jangled on her arms. The only jewelry she still wore were golden earrings—Grandma's gift, and the necklace, Dallas's gift.

Grandma reached for a cherry turnover. "On a brighter topic, I need you to take a blueberry pie to the Lawrence ranch."

Skylar cringed. Of course, her grandmother tried to change the topic, but why the pie delivery? "What is this, some kind of neighborhood pie exchange?"

Going to the ranch could mean running into Dallas. And while he'd trailed them yesterday and had even taken Skylar out for lunch, seeing her clearly pained him.

What a difference from the times when his face lit up at the mere sight of her. She swallowed hard, then took a sip of her sweet tea before it could grow as cold as her heart.

"You say that as if a pie exchange is something bad." Grandma put the pastry on her plate and pinned her with a stare. "Here, we help each other. And send good things and good wishes to each other."

Skylar lowered her gaze. Great, now she'd upset her grandmother. And after all, maybe she wouldn't run into Dallas. "Okay. But do we have a blueberry pie to send?"

"Not yet. You're going to make it."

Skylar nearly dropped the dainty cup. "You said you send *good* things and *good* wishes to each other. If I make a pie, it won't turn out a good thing. And believe me, they wouldn't be sending good wishes back."

Her grandmother chuckled and bit into her pastry. Delicate flakes sifted to her plate after her dainty bite. "I'll make it then, and you'll help. I used to bake many pies in my days."

"And they were great ones. You were the best baker in town, or maybe in the entire state. As far as I'm concerned, you still are." Skylar smiled.

But her heart constricted at how her grandmother had seemed smaller now, more vulnerable, instead of the pillar of Skylar's life she'd always been. If her parents had been like wooden boats set adrift in the sea and vanishing, her grandmother had been a steady ship anchoring Skylar to reality and survival. Well, Dallas had been, as well, but she'd jumped that ship fifteen years ago.

To distract herself, she picked the gooiest chocolate chip cookie from her plate. "I'll do my best not to ruin the pie while helping you. As we work, we can also discuss how you want to decorate the venue."

"You can discuss it with Amelia."

Skylar's hand with the cookie froze in the air. She didn't like where this was going. "Why would I discuss it with Mrs. Lawrence?"

Grandma blinked at her, all innocence. "Because the reception is going to be at their barn."

This was just getting better and better.

An hour later, heated up more than the oven she'd taken the blueberry pie out of, Skylar was driving to the ranch. She was supposed to avoid Dallas. And now she was going to his ranch. How did she get herself into this situation?

Her gaze roamed over emerald-green fields, and cheery baby-pink and turquoise flowers waved back in the breeze. She'd fallen in love with this ranch long before she loved Dallas. Her mother had two friends—her sister and Dallas's mom—and they'd babysat for each other and spent whatever time they could together. Their children had become friends by default. Well, after some squabbling, of course.

Thinking about her mother sent a sharp pain inside Skylar. So much betrayal. Her throat clogged up, but she pushed the tumultuous thoughts away and turned to happier scenery and happier thoughts.

Those times of petting baby critters, grooming ponies, and running in the sun-dappled, flowery meadows were another part of childhood she missed. Okay, the Lawrence boys didn't exactly welcome the girls at first, but they'd tolerated them. With time, the brothers had even shown Skylar and her cousins the way around farm animals—at least the ones who were relatively safe.

It felt like an eternity ago. She lived in a different world now, and she'd better remember it.

She powered down the window to breathe fresh air tinted with a wildflower aroma. Still, her stomach tightened. Would the Lawrence family hate seeing her? After all, she'd broken the heart of their son and brother.

She straightened her shoulders. If Grandma thought it would be too horrible, she wouldn't have sent her. They did offer their barn for the wedding reception, even knowing Skylar was going to be the maid of honor, right?

Yet she wouldn't blame them for a hostile reaction right now.

Soon she climbed the porch to the sprawling Cape-Cod-style ranch house sheltered by live oaks with wispy Spanish moss, while balancing the heavenly-smelling blueberry pie. Her aunt's recipe that Grandma had improved further. Her cousins, except Skylar's best friend Marina, had inherited the cooking and baking gene. Saylor, the cousin with the name so like hers they'd joked about it often, was a great cook. But the cooking gene had skipped Skylar entirely. The only pies she'd been decent at were mud pies, and she was five then.

She knocked on the front door, then tried the handle, and it gave in, sending her a nostalgic jolt. They'd never locked doors here before, and they still didn't. She couldn't imagine leaving a front door unlocked in the city. Especially after...

Stop it.

Inside, the homey aromas of steak, baked potatoes, and steamed broccoli met her, and her mouth watered. Dallas's mom had always made tons of hearty food, which Skylar had appreciated. Despite Aunt's and Grandma's efforts, Skylar's mom had never mastered good cooking. From what little Skylar could remember, Mom seemed like an ethereal creature nearly floating in the air rather than walking on the earth. Skylar had learned to entertain herself early on with drawings because Mom could pass by her like her little girl wasn't even there. Often, Mom had forgotten cooking altogether. Dad had either thrown something together fast after returning home from work, or relied on his mother or sister-in-law. Sometimes, Mrs. Lawrence would just drop off casseroles without being asked.

It had been a miracle Mom had managed to hold down a job with the local florist, but then she was as fleeting as the flowers she fondled and as flighty as the butterflies that landed on them. She'd been a genius at putting bouquets together. Domesticity, not so much. It was Skylar's father who'd taken Skylar to the ice cream parlor or brushed her hair or made sure she had clean clothes, and

Auntie, Grandma, or Mrs. Lawrence had often stepped in, Auntie shaking her head and Grandma looking resigned.

The three girlfriends of that time couldn't have been more different. Auntie and Mrs. Lawrence were down-to-earth and present in the moment, often with throaty laughs. Mom was melancholic, her eyes sad and looking somewhere far beyond her daughter or her husband and nearly always in her own fantasies. Auntie and Mrs. Lawrence were like a pot roast in a Crock-Pot, sturdy and reliable. Mom was more of a soufflé on a thin porcelain plate, something gentle, fragile, and easily breakable.

There had been some great days with Mom, too. When she'd woken up in a cheery mood, dressed Skylar up in a pretty dress, and taken her walking on the beach. Or when they'd painted together or created bouquets in the florist shop. Dad's face lit up on those days.

Or was it the story Skylar had told herself over the years? Her memories, existing and returning, mixed with her imagination, like different hues in her mom's watercolors, and at this point, she wasn't sure which memories were the real ones.

"Over here!" Mrs. Lawrence called out from the dining room, returning Skylar to the present.

Skylar's low-heeled, sensible black pumps clicked against the hardwood floor as she entered the dining room. Her stomach clenched, and guilt and apprehension nearly ripped her apart. After her mother had left, her aunt and Mrs. Lawrence had helped Grandma raise the traumatized and terrified girl. And how had Skylar repaid the kindness?

Right. By shattering Mrs. Lawrence's son's heart.

For years, she'd dreaded this. But it was time to face the consequences. And if the blueberry pie got thrown in her face, so be it. She should've asked Grandma to make lemon meringue, though. Much easier to wash off.

In the dining room, four pairs of eyes fixed on her. One pair was frosty. Darius barely waved before stomping out. Well, she knew where she stood with him.

"Hi, Skylar." Kai lifted his tall sweet tea glass in a salute, his dark hair spread on his shoulders instead of being hidden by a bandanna. He was semi friendly territory.

She smiled her gratitude, though the smile wobbled. "Hi, Kai. Hi, Mrs. Lawrence. Hi Dallas." She avoided looking at him once she saw how his eyes narrowed.

Austin should be at the vet clinic, and the rest of the brothers must've left for the fields already.

"Hello, Skylar," Dallas muttered. But he didn't leave like his brother, and that was something. Though maybe it would've been better if he left the room. Just having him in the same space electrified it.

"I brought a blueberry pie." She placed the covered plate on the table, ready to duck and run. While her mother was a shy and reclusive artist, her mother's friend had a much spunkier spirit, especially after her abusive husband died. Skylar had seen her rope horses and her teenage sons with the same skill.

"Welcome back!" Mrs. Lawrence slapped the table, pushed up from her seat, and captured Skylar in a tight hug. "It's about time!"

Was... was this for real?

"Thank you so much." Skylar could breathe again as if a mountain—no, an entire mountain range—dropped off her shoulders. Could this be happening? The sweet homecoming she didn't dare hope for. As her spirits soared, she returned the hug, leaning into Mrs. Lawrence and breathing in her familiar comfort. Tears burned her eyes, but she kept them at bay. "I'm sorry. For everything."

"Your grandmother told me what you had to do," Mrs. Lawrence whispered in Skylar's ear.

Skylar went cold.

No, no, no. Just what had her grandmother revealed? But she couldn't ask here. Maybe it wasn't a good idea to ask at all. Did Mrs. Lawrence tell the others?

As if reading Skylar's mind, Mrs. Lawrence kept her close. She even smelled like home, of yummy foods and warmth. "Don't worry. I didn't tell anyone. Even Dallas."

That must've been difficult. Skylar didn't think she could do the same if she were in Mrs. Lawrence's place. Relief whooshed out of Skylar's lungs in a sigh. "That means a lot to me. Everything."

"We were just finishing lunch. The others already left. Care to join us?" Mrs. Lawrence gestured to the table.

It felt painfully familiar. Skylar had stayed a lot of times for meals there. There was always a place for one more person at their place—especially without Mr. Lawrence. But there was no return to old times, and her insides ached for that. She didn't deserve to be at their table any longer.

"Thanks, but it's okay," she said.

"Oh, and thank you for the pie," Mrs. Lawrence said, but with much less enthusiasm.

Kai's smile became a frown. Skylar didn't know what Dallas's reaction was because she still refused to look his way.

She resisted the urge to roll her eyes. Just because the boys had gotten indigestion from her dishes a few times didn't mean she hadn't learned to cook. Even if she, well, hadn't. "Oh, come on. My cooking isn't that bad. Anyway, my *grandmother* made this pie."

"Oh, good." Mrs. Lawrence exhaled in a whoosh. Grandma's baking was legendary.

"I did help make it, so there's that." Wait? Did Dallas just chuckle? She couldn't say for sure because, once again, she didn't look in his direction.

Mrs. Lawrence took her rightful place at the table. "Please thank your grandmother on our behalf." Her brows pinched together before she raised her chin. She styled her chocolate-brown, wavy hair shorter now, and her wrinkles were a bit more pronounced. But she was the same woman who'd welcomed Skylar into her house with no questions asked. She still wore the seashell earrings Skylar had made for her, and it warmed Skylar's heart.

"I'd love to visit her sometime soon," Mrs. Lawrence said. "Would that be okay with you?"

"Of course!" Skylar nodded once and then another time for good measure. "You don't have to ask."

When Grandma had lost her only son and her daughter-in-law, the latter's friends, including Mrs. Lawrence, had formed an unspoken agreement to visit her and help with chores if needed, but most of all, simply to be there in her grief. Skylar had never forgotten that. Guilt stabbed her again.

Mrs. Lawrence gestured at the vacated chair again. "Please join us."

Skylar swallowed hard. Talk about awkward.

Thanks again, Grandma.

"Um, I was just leaving. And your lunch is over."

"But you brought the dessert." Kai winked. "Come on. We won't bite—well, other than the pie—and you promised it won't bite back."

He didn't flirt with her. It was just his nature, though he'd been rumored to have left a lot of broken hearts.

How could Mrs. Lawrence and Kai forgive her so easily? Some of Dallas's brothers hadn't forgiven her, and neither had he, not fully. Spending time with him yesterday had caused her to toss and turn for hours, thinking about him, remembering all the things they'd shared. And even when she'd fallen asleep, he'd invaded her dreams. Until Breeze's growl had awakened her.

Having lunch with Dallas yesterday was a bad idea. It would be a mistake to have dessert with his family today. Spending *any* time with him was a mistake.

But when he got up and pulled out a sturdy oak chair for her without saying a word, her legs carried her to the chair. Her heartbeat increased just from breathing his intoxicating cologne with woodsy notes of cedar and juniper. She'd given him the first bottle after she'd sold one of her paintings. He'd never changed his cologne. Yes, he'd matured, his broad shoulders filled out, and his arms were more muscular now. But he hadn't changed much, while she had.

She sat.

"Thank you. I appreciate it. Thank you." She cringed. How many times was she going to say that? She was worse than Kai's parrot.

"We're glad to have you back." Mrs. Lawrence cut the pie. She paused, then shrugged. "Well, some of us are."

Did that include Dallas? Skylar cringed again, too desperate for the answer for her liking.

She attempted a smile and tried to infuse some of her former humor into her words. "Are you sure you don't need me to try the first piece of the pie? To make sure it's edible because, you know, I did help make it?"

Kai chuckled as he helped himself to a slice. "Nah. They have me for that."

She stole a glance at Dallas this time. Not even a hint of a smile, and her heart fell a little. She missed the times when she could make him laugh so easily. She missed the sound of his laugh itself. The way her heart fluttered when he looked at her with so much affection. The tingles across her skin when he whispered tender things in her ear.

The certainty she'd once taken for granted that he'd always be there for her. That he'd catch her every time she fell. He was the steady, reliable, all-encompassing influence then. These days, she could rely only on herself. There was no one to catch her, and every time she'd fallen, she'd gotten lots of bruises.

She missed *him*, everything about him. But even more, she missed herself, the way she used to be when she was with him. Carefree, hopeful, inspired, loved. And happy.

"What would you like to drink?" He sounded gruff. Since he'd had time to think, he must've decided seeing her wasn't a good idea.

Her heart fell even more—and of course, he didn't catch it or her. She glanced at the lemonade carafe on the table. "Lemonade sounds great."

He got up and returned with a glass, then poured her the drink.

"Thank you. I appreciate it." At least, she didn't say thank you a second time. So, that was progress, right?

"You're welcome." But he didn't sound like she was welcome. Not in his house and not in his life, and the thought hurt. He placed a slice of the blueberry pie on a plate and shifted it toward her.

What else could she say besides "Thank you, I appreciate it" again? Who'd believe there were days when she'd talked nonstop?

The pie, sweet, gooey, and yummy, failed to lift her spirits. And the place that once had couldn't this time, either.

If her grandmother's place was all about the ocean, here it was all about the land and the livestock they raised on it. Cows decorated a ceramic container with the sweetener on the table and looked at her from the paintings on the wall. Except the painting she'd done for Mrs. Lawrence of cows lounging in a meadow was no longer there. Skylar didn't expect it to be. Still, she suppressed the feeling of loss.

"This was scrumptious." Kai pushed his empty plate away. "You and your grandmother did a great job. Unlike the time Dallas had to use a fire extinguisher in your kitchen."

Dallas cracked half a smile this time.

Okay, Skylar was going to roll with it. "Or the time I used salt instead of sugar. In my defense, I was half asleep when I was pouring it into the container. Apparently, I used the wrong container."

"And you liked to improvise with recipes." Dallas's voice was less gruff. Good.

She drank her lemonade, welcoming the cold, tangy liquid, though not as much as the change in his voice. "Who knew some substitutes wouldn't work so well?"

"Even when your culinary creations weren't great, watching you dance and sing in the kitchen while making them was worth it." Dallas's eyes widened, and then he frowned as if he'd said too much.

When was the last time she'd danced? When was the last time she'd sung? She couldn't remember. Probably about the last time she'd painted.

Once everyone finished their treat, she helped clean the table. She was careful to avoid touching his hands. Her emotions were running amok as it was.

"Okay, I got to go." Kai left for the fields, waving at her before he sauntered away. In a navy-and-white striped T-shirt instead of a Wrangler's shirt and tall black boots, he didn't look like a typical cowboy. Why had he forgiven her, after all?

She shouldn't ask herself those questions but be grateful.

Once the last plate was loaded into the dishwasher, it was time for her to get out. Grandma and Mrs. Lawrence could discuss wedding decorations over the phone or when Mrs. Lawrence came for a visit.

"Thank you so much for having me." Especially under the circumstances. But Skylar didn't add that.

Mrs. Lawrence's phone rang, and minutes later, she disconnected. "Garnet ran away. Dallas, you need to go find her!" Then she turned to Skylar. "Would you help him look for our missing horse?"

"Excuse me?" Dallas and Skylar said in unison.

"Would you mind doing it?" Mrs. Lawrence blinked innocently.

Skylar cleared her throat. "I don't mind, but—"

"Great!" Mrs. Lawrence beamed. "I'm going upstairs, then. Please keep me posted."

Skylar stared at Dallas once they were alone. "What just happened?"

He shrugged as he put on his Stetson. "Looks like you *volunteered* to search for a horse."

Huh? Did she look like a good candidate for said job?

"Well, are you coming or staying?" He called over his shoulder as he walked into the hall.

In a way, she did promise Mrs. Lawrence, didn't she? Skylar hurried after him.

She walked outside, squinted against the sun, and found the four-wheeler waiting for her. "Um, we're going on this?"

"Would you prefer to do it on foot? You do remember this is how we move around the ranch, right?"

"Right." And she did remember. But she also remembered she couldn't get behind him there without touching him. And while in motion, she'd have to hold onto him. Of course, it had never been a problem before, rather the opposite.

Oh boy.

She managed to climb behind him with minimal touching, then placed her hands on her knees, avoiding the muscular man right in front of her. Because how could one physically hold onto something without touching anything? She jerked back as they took off but stayed on the seat. Her heart was beating erratically as he darted onto the gravel road.

After some time, he yelled back over the growl of the motor. "Are you there, or did you fall off?"

"Well, if I fell off, how would I answer you, then?" she yelled back.

"That's my answer! Finally, some of your spunk is back!"

Seriously? Did he think she became a pushover? Or as bland as her clothes? She scoffed. "You should watch where you're going! Or we'll end up in a ditch!"

That would help neither the runaway horse nor them. She kind of hoped he looked around, as well, because her primary concentration was on not falling off. Which wasn't much help to Garnet.

Why would a horse run away? Was she looking for a greener pasture like Skylar's childhood girlfriends who'd left their hometown? Did Garnet wander off from the dear and familiar by accident?

Or had something spooked her so badly it had sent her running for a long time? A shiver went down Skylar's back as she recalled the night of the storm. A danger, unclear but no less scary, or maybe even scarier because of that.

Okay, she shouldn't be projecting her fears on a horse. She was far from the best candidate for a search party, and it was a surprise she was asked. Dallas had grown up in the reality of hard labor and outdoor work. She'd grown up in the fantasy of colors and hues that later had become her escape when her parents disappeared.

And Dallas. Like watercolors and oil paints, he'd become her escape. Except unlike her paints and the imaginary worlds they'd unlocked, he'd been real, solid, her rock to hold onto in the storm. But not any longer.

"Argh." She grunted as they jumped over a bump, and she latched onto him before she could think of it. "Oh. Oops." She let him go. Touching him created a whirlwind of emotions she didn't dare examine.

"I'd rather you hold onto me than fall off," he yelled over his shoulder.

Right. Because the only reason for her to touch him now would be to avoid falling off a vehicle. "Um, thanks!"

He went uphill. She had zero desire to roll down the same hill, so she snatched fistfuls of his T-shirt. Thankfully without snagging skin in the process. A compromise. But she still leaned into him too much, and it made her heart thump.

The air smelled of fresh flowers and fresh promises mixed with the intoxicating scent of his cologne because of his proximity.

"What does Garnet look like?" she yelled. Great. Just the way to have a conversation.

"An American quarter horse. Bay coloring."

Usually, Skylar associated the word *bay* with the ocean, not with horses.

"She's calm and gentle. I don't know why she'd run away," he yelled back again.

Then she spotted something near the creek. "Could that be her?"

"Yes! Great job!" He turned to the left.

Her chest swelled like when she'd won an art competition in sixth grade. When she'd gone to the stage to receive the award, she'd waved at her grandmother first. Then her gaze switched to the Lawrence family. They'd all cheered the loudest in the crowd, and Dallas's cheering was the strongest of them all.

He went downhill now, just like their relationship, and she got plastered against him against her will. Well, not exactly against her will, and she took a moment to shift back. Her nostrils stayed filled with his scent, and even the scent of grass didn't push it away. Her pulse went erratic again.

He stopped and turned off the motor a fair distance from Garnet. Then he swung to the ground and offered her his hand. "Are you okay?"

She hadn't been okay for fifteen years, but she'd made the best of it. So she nodded. They walked toward Garnet who stood peacefully grazing. Would they be able to sneak up on her?

Skylar needed to keep quiet, but she might not have another chance to make things at least somewhat better. "Everything you've done for me... It meant a lot to me. And I never meant to hurt you." She'd give the last drop of blood in her veins for him, but what did it matter if she put poison in his?

"Then why?" His question cut through her.

"I can't tell you. I'm sorry." She ducked her head. So much for making things better between them.

"Stay here, okay?" He walked to Garnet while Skylar didn't move.

Garnet let him get close, and he stroked her gently. The mare seemed to welcome it.

Skylar wasn't surprised. He was a great guy, kind to people and animals. Even when she'd had doubts, he'd supported her in her art and her dreams, unlike her dad, maybe because it reminded him too much of Mom. Grandma had tried to be supportive, and she had been. But sometimes, Skylar had caught doubt in her eyes. Grandma also probably associated art with Skylar's mother who'd hurt their family so much. When Skylar had won an art scholarship, Dallas seemed happier than even she'd been.

He gestured for her to get closer, and she stepped carefully forward. The last thing she needed was for Garnet to start running at the sight of a stranger. The mare's tail swished, but otherwise, she didn't show any signs of distress.

Skylar whispered, "Beautiful Garnet. Wonderful Garnet."

Dallas was feeding Garnet a treat, and he handed one to Skylar when she got close enough. "Would you like to give her a treat? But be careful, sometimes horses can bite."

And based on the size of those teeth, those bites would hurt a lot. But she lifted her palm to him. "Sure. I'd love to."

His lips slid up a tad. "Here we go." He handed her a round raspberry-colored thingy. When did he have a chance to get treats? Or did he always carry them?

"Here." She lifted the treat close to Garnet's mouth. "Yummy!" Hopefully, Garnet would consider it yummier than Skylar's fingers.

Garnet nipped the treat from Skylar's palm, her lips surprisingly soft on Skylar's skin. No teeth chomping on her fingers. "Good girl. Good girl. We'll take you home, okay?" She stroked the mare's gorgeous smooth coat, then her luxurious mane. She used to decorate the Lawrences' horses' manes for the town parade. Then she'd watched with admiration while Dallas rode in the parade. All that seemed in another century now.

"You're great with her." Dallas's voice softened. And he'd always been great with her, Skylar.

She'd declared an art major in college but changed it to accounting once she'd started to remember more of that stormy night, and her art scholarship had gone to waste. She'd wanted to paint many masterpieces but hadn't painted even one.

No, it wasn't true. Her one masterpiece—on the canvas she'd sliced and ruined later—was her love for Dallas.

Chapter Seven

Working in the field was peaceful for Dallas. Usually.

But Skylar's arrival turned his world upside down.

"Hello! Earth to Dallas." Kai tapped Dallas's shoulder as they finished putting up hay the next day, the scent calming and refreshing. *Usually.*

Dallas frowned. "Why are you saying that?"

"Because I asked you three times if you want to check the bridge over the creek, and you didn't answer." Kai winked. "Thinking about Skylar, aren't you?"

Dallas shook his head so vehemently that he rocked his brown cowboy hat askew. "What? Of course not. Why would I? There's nothing between us now. There can't be. At all. Ever."

"A simple *no* would've sufficed. And that's the way you'd normally answer a yes-or-no question." Kai nodded at the vehicles. "Do you want to take four-wheelers?"

The memory of Skylar's arms around his torso sent a wave of apprehension through him. "No!" How about that answer to a yes-or-no question?

The creek sparkled in the afternoon sun. The wooden bridge he and his brothers had constructed years ago disappeared around the bend far enough from here not to be seen. "Let's take horses."

He saddled Garnet and sank into memories of Skylar with the mare while Kai got an Appaloosa.

The horses started slowly, but neither he nor his brother nudged them into a gallop. The view from horseback was much better than from the ground. A breeze stirred, swirling the tall grass across the lush green hills and sending pink, blue, and white clusters of flowers dancing. Languid herds lolled below an endless azure sky, and a familiar sense of awe shivered over him.

God's gorgeous creation.

Once upon a time, Dallas had thought the same about Skylar. Oh, and she'd captured the beauty of nature perfectly on canvas. "God-given talent," his mother used to say. His heart skipped a beat.

Why did his thoughts keep returning to Skylar now? He cringed, and Garnet looked back when he had pulled the reins too much. He patted her to prompt her to keep moving.

Forgive me, Lord. I know we're supposed to be more forgiving. But even thinking about Skylar hurts too much.

His mother was a much better Christian than he was. She'd seemed to forgive Skylar fast enough. Darius was angry with her for that, and Dallas did harbor some resentment but tried to do better.

Lord, what am I supposed to do now? Why do I keep meeting Skylar?

"What are you going to do about it?" Kai asked.

Dallas sent his brother a sidelong glance. Did he miss a question again? "Do about what?"

"About Skylar's return." Kai's expression grew uncharacteristically serious. Something must be on his mind.

But Dallas wasn't one to pry. *Unlike some people.*

He stared at the line where the sky met land. This was his place, where God meant for him to be. And once upon a time, he'd thought God had meant for him and Skylar to be. "There's nothing to do. And she didn't return, not really. She just came to help her grandmother with the wedding. After it, she'll drive off to her life in Charleston. Besides, did you forget she broke up with me?" And it still made his heart ache. "Years ago."

"I didn't forget. I just thought... Do you want a second chance? You've been hanging around her a lot since she got here."

"By accident! Well, and because someone tried to run her off the road." His stomach clenched. He must've stiffened in his seat because Garnet halted as if he'd sent her a stop cue.

"It's okay, Garnet. It's okay." He leaned forward, patted her again, and relaxed into a go motion, urging her forward. Then when she did, he straightened. "Whatever happened between us, I still don't want someone to harm her."

"So you volunteered to be her bodyguard." Those teasing notes in Kai's voice sure were irritating.

"I didn't! And she might not need a bodyguard. Can we talk about something else?"

"Sure. Just a sec. Let me check on 128." Kai veered off the path to check on a cow that had looked off yesterday, then galloped back.

Do I want a second chance with Skylar? Dallas's heartbeat increased in rhythm with the gallop. It wouldn't matter even if he wanted it. Skylar had shown she didn't love him any longer. They were done. Over. More than over, if there was such a thing.

Now he could see the small bridge.

Kai caught up. "Rumor is Marina and her sisters are coming back to town soon for a couple of weeks to help around the restaurant."

So *that* was what was on Kai's mind.

Kai and Marina had grown up together due to their mothers' friendship. They'd been best friends since they'd known how to walk. By their teens, Dallas had thought Kai and Marina would become more than friends, and the glances his brother sometimes sent Marina's way hinted as much. But it had never happened.

Then, in high school, flirty and laid-back Kai had dated a lot and changed girlfriends often. Geeky and studious Marina hadn't dated at all until meeting a dashing lawyer while waiting on tables at her mother's restaurant. The guy had returned the following summer for his vacation. Marina had just graduated high school then, ready to leave for college in Charleston. When he'd left, they'd left together, and she'd had a ring on her finger.

Marina had visited home sometimes, but not for long. Why would she stay here for weeks?

Right.

"Oh yeah." Dallas whistled. "Mom said Marina's mother decided to go on a singles cruise. One of the tourists and restaurant patrons found love and got married that way and highly recommended it."

"A singles cruise? What's happening? Suddenly, everyone wants to get married? First, Skylar's grandmother. Now, Marina's mother." Kai gestured wildly with his hands and nearly dropped the reins. "Is there a marriage bug going around?"

"No marriage bug. Because none of us caught it. Neither did Skylar." Dallas swallowed the bitter taste in his mouth. He was fine living as a bachelor. And so, it seemed, were his brothers. So what if Skylar made his blood run faster?

"Right." Kai raked his fingers through his dark hair. A few strands escaped his low ponytail, giving him a roguish look. Well, more roguish than usual. No wonder he played a pirate in the pirate ship performances for tourists. "Doesn't look like Marina will be catching that bug, either. A year ago, I heard she got divorced."

Dallas didn't comment because they'd reached their destination.

At the bridge, he dismounted and started checking the planks. One did seem loose, so he put a few nails in to keep it in place. Another one was missing a nail, so he nailed it down. And one more had a nail loose. He remedied that. They should've worked on this a long time ago.

Meanwhile, Kai checked the support posts underneath. "All good."

Dallas got up and wiped his hands on his jeans. "Let's go back. Or do you want to check on the herd nearby?"

"Let's check it first." Kai mounted his horse again. "I had to find out from Marina's mom that she's coming back. We just lost touch."

Dallas pulled himself into the saddle. Then he studied his brother as they rode side by side along the pasture. Was this about Kai missing his best friend? Or was this about more? Much more?

"Your friendship with Marina surprised many people." Dallas tensed because Garnet's ears twitched, and her tail swished as if she heard something suspicious. But then everything went back to normal, and his shoulders relaxed.

"Why's that?" Kai sounded defensive.

Huh. Did Dallas hit a sore spot? "You're complete opposites. You're outgoing, talkative, often loud, sociable—"

"Are you sure you're not describing my parrot?" Kai chuckled. He rose in his stirrups, gazing at the herd in the distance.

Undeterred, Dallas continued, "With a short attention span often jumping from one thing to another." Or one girl to another, except where Marina was concerned. But Dallas kept *that* comment to himself.

Kai laughed. "Now you're *really* describing my parrot."

"Can you be serious for a moment? But right, then it would be Marina. Serious, quiet, studious, focused, and goal-oriented."

The smile slipped off Kai's face. "With a father like hers, she had to be. He favored his son over his daughters so much that it made me cringe. Then when the son didn't measure up, he made Marina follow his own dreams. I said things to him, but it only made it worse for the family. Marina asked me not to interfere." He stopped, his jaw set tight.

Anger surged inside Dallas like hot lava when he thought about their own family. His uncle was a much better father figure than their father, and Dallas had envied his cousins sometimes.

As Dallas and Darius had been the oldest, they'd tried to stand up to their father, but they'd only gotten thrown around and punished. Kai had joined in sometimes, though Dad had never hit his adopted son. Then something horrible had happened....

No, don't think about that.

"Marina and her sisters always had to prove themselves and, even then, received little of their father's affection." Dallas frowned.

"Well, in the end, their mother got fed up and divorced him." Kai's eyes narrowed.

"Right." Dallas nodded. "After he publicly humiliated her and her youngest daughter for what had seemed the thousandth time. But the damage was already done."

"Marina always wanted to get out of the house and from under his control."

Something about the way his brother said her name clued Dallas in. "Do you like her?"

Kai didn't answer, and that was an answer in itself. Or maybe it was because they made it to the herd. They steered the horses around it to make it to 128.

Dallas studied the cow. "She looks okay to me now." If not, they'd have to call Austin.

"I think so, too, but glad to have you confirm it." Kai nodded. Then they worked together to make sure everyone else looked healthy and fine. It was nice to have the inoculations done for the season. Finally, they headed to the ranch house. Dallas wasn't about to let it go. "Do you like Marina?"

Kai groaned. "Aren't you the talkative one today?"

"I'm taking lessons from your parrot." Dallas shrugged.

"Okay, okay." Kai laughed. "I do like her, but it doesn't matter."

"It matters a lot." Dallas's thoughts switched to Skylar. "Why have you never told her?"

This time, Kai edged his horse to go into a gallop, but Dallas caught up to his brother fast. Kai wasn't running away from this conversation. Stubbornness ran in the family.

"Come on," Kai finally said. "Marina knew she was going to leave this small town and worked hard for her goals. She had big dreams, also spurred on by her father diminishing her. I couldn't stand in the way of her dreams."

Dallas tried to wrap his mind around that. In school, everyone thought the charming Kai was great at getting dates and the silent Dallas—well, not so great. Yet Dallas had done everything to pursue a relationship with the girl he'd liked while Kai had done nothing at all. In the end, Dallas ended up with a broken heart and Kai with an aching one.

What could they do now? They should steer clear of romance to avoid more heartache.

Dallas eyed the sky as if he could find answers written there. "You could've left with her."

Kai hesitated as if he wanted to say something, then shook his head, making a golden earring dance in his ear. "I belong here."

Dallas had thought the same about himself. But then, maybe it had been easier to support Skylar in her dreams because she'd promised to return after getting her art degree in Charleston. There wasn't much work for a lawyer in their small town.

"In high school, you told me you thought about leaving."

Kai frowned. "Yeah, to follow Marina. I had no clue what I was going to do in a city, but I'd figure it out once I got there. Okay, fine, I was going to tell her everything. When I met her that evening, she couldn't stop talking about the new guy she met at the restaurant. She was smitten. A lawyer, he also fit her better than I ever did. He could help her in ways I couldn't."

Dallas gazed at the ranch house in the distance, the entire story reshaping in his head. "I'm sure she didn't marry him just because of that."

"Oh, she was in love." Kai's voice turned bitter. "Very much so."

How could Dallas miss all this right under his nose? He urged Garnet to slow down. He needed to have the rest of this conversation. He sent up a prayer for Kai and Marina. "It's over between them now. And everyone deserves a fresh start. Don't you think?"

Lord, please guide my brother to his happiness.

Kai raised an eyebrow. "Including you and Skylar?"

"I said 'a fresh start.' Not rehashing one-sided relationships." Dallas changed his mind and urged Garnet into a gallop as if to outrun the longing inside him. Everything between him and Skylar was over. It had to be, right?

Then a frightening sound far away made Garnet neigh and buck. Her nostrils flared. Dallas tensed, then patted the horse reassuringly. "It's okay. It's okay." But he wasn't sure it was okay. "Did you hear that?" he asked his brother.

Kai stopped, too, keeping a tight rein. His eyes narrowed. "Yes, a weird blast."

"Was it a gunshot?"

Kai rolled his eyes, but his mouth remained taut. "And they say I'm the one with the wild imagination in the family."

"It came from the direction of the beach. The place of... of *that* cottage." Dallas swallowed hard, everything in him protesting against going there. Even his blood seemed to curdle at the thought. "Let's check it out. It's the right thing to do."

Kai groaned. "You're kidding, right?"

Surely, he thought about what had happened at that place, too. Well, lots of things had happened there, but one of them concerned their family directly.

"No. Someone might need help. We don't have to go inside *that* cottage." The coppery scent of blood appeared in his nostrils at the memory, and forgotten fear rippled over his skin again. Weird because Dallas hadn't been at that place the night his father died there. He'd learned about it from his brothers. Yet the mention of the place sent a shiver over his back.

But if the recent sound was a gunshot, after all, and someone got hurt, he needed to help them. Before he could change his mind, he took off in a gallop without waiting for his brother.

Based on the sound behind him, Kai didn't wait to follow, though Dallas wouldn't blame his brother if he'd stayed. Dallas leaned closer to Garnet and listened intently. Hopefully, it was just his imagination indeed. Such a blast could be other things. But his gut tightened nonetheless.

They stopped at the border of their property and eyed the distant sandy beach. It spread out before him, peaceful and surprisingly deserted. Waves lulled against the shore and reflected the sky, clear and bright. Deceptively peaceful?

Dallas's gaze strayed in the direction he didn't want to go. At all. "Do you think it came from *that* cottage?"

"Hmm." Kai shrugged. "I don't think so. I don't know. It could've come from the road further down and been a tire blowout. Or it could've been a twig."

A twig? Seriously?

"Or not? We should make sure." Not that Dallas wanted to. Reluctantly, he steered Garnet toward the cottage.

Kai grunted. "Do you always have to be the good guy?"

"That's the way Mom raised us."

With no vehicle near the run-down place or lights inside, it was difficult to believe it could be inhabited. Dallas dismounted, ground his teeth, and forced his legs to walk toward the porch, even if it seemed like huge weights encased his feet. Blood pounded in his temples, just like the night he'd found out about his father. Should he be ashamed that his first feeling was relief? Guilt had replaced it soon enough. But the second feeling had been fear and worry that one of the people he loved so much had done it.

His father wasn't the type of person to take his own life, but then what did Dallas know?

Neither Kai nor Dallas had been here that night. They only knew from their brother about what had happened. They didn't have the horrifying images seared in their brain. But one of their brothers did. Dallas could still hear the whisper that sent a shiver down his spine.

He can't hurt us anymore. Right?

It was a long time ago. Dallas had to man up and get this done. He squared his shoulders as he ran up the porch. He knocked on the door but received no answer.

Kai didn't dismount and waved from the horse's back. "Do you want to break and enter? I can try to pick the lock."

And here Dallas thought his brother's rebellious years were behind him. "It's private property. You wouldn't!" But he wasn't so sure about the latter.

Either way, he mounted Garnet again, eager to get out of here as fast as possible. "Never mind. Let's go."

Without discussing it, they both went into a gallop.

Why had his father gone to that cottage that night? Why had he done what later had been ruled a suicide?

All these years later, Dallas still had no answers. And he wasn't sure he wanted to.

Chapter Eight

"Are you going to the ranch again today?"

On the terrace enjoying the breathtaking view, Skylar looked up at her grandmother from her breakfast plate the next day, her mouth agape. Her fork clattered to the blue metal bistro table, bounced, and would have hit the bright patio stones if she hadn't caught it. "Why... why would I do that?" She wasn't looking for excuses to see Dallas. Absolutely not!

Breeze, stretched on the sun-warmed patio stones, lifted her head as if also confused.

"To discuss the wedding reception at their barn. Why else?" Grandma blinked, her expression harmless.

Right. Skylar's brain must be as scrambled as these eggs. "But... but... but, Grandma, how about I drop *you* off there? And *you* discuss the reception and decorations for *your* wedding?" Wasn't *that* logical? And Skylar was all about logic these days.

She must've raised her voice because Breeze leaped to her feet, gave out a bark, and pressed in close. "It's okay, sweetie." Skylar reached to calm the dog and rub her smooth, gorgeous fur.

Breeze sat near her chair, vigilant.

"Nah." Grandma waved her off. "I trust *your* judgment."

The issue was Skylar didn't trust herself anywhere near Dallas. Her heart fluttered. She didn't even need to be *near* him to feel all these palpitations. She didn't trust herself with him—period.

Concentrate on the things at hand.

She went over her mental list of wedding preparations. Yesterday, she'd taken Grandma to the local florist where Mom once used to work to choose the bridal bouquet and one for the maid of honor. The flowery aromas seemed as unattainable and fleeting as her memories. Grandma had chosen the bouquet with pink hibiscus, reminding Skylar of the days she'd called her friendship with her cousins "The Hibiscus Sisterhood." "Okay, I'm glad you're happy with your bridal bouquet order. And I'm happy with mine. But we still need to decide on the table centerpieces and wall decorations. Chair decorations, too."

Breeze gave up her watch and trudged after some insect on a jade-painted stone. Skylar tensed, then relaxed at the sight of a ladybug. Not a spider.

Grandma smiled like a Cheshire cat. "Hence, your visit to the ranch."

Well, two could play this game. Skylar pressed her feet against the smooth stones beneath her, grounding herself as she leaned across the indigo-blue metal table. "You mean *our* visit to the ranch? I want everything to be to *your* liking."

After a pause, Grandma nodded. "Okay. Good point. While we want to get married only once, the reality is we never know. But I'm sure there's going to be only one wedding in the time left for me. I don't need it to be perfect. But yeah, it needs to be to my liking."

Skylar's heart contracted as she gulped a sip of her morning tea. Would there ever be a fairy-tale wedding in her life? Well, she'd stopped believing in fairy tales a long time ago. And a beautiful wedding and a happy marriage weren't an entitlement or a right but a privilege.

Then she realized something was off in Grandma's expression. Most of her scrambled eggs remained uneaten, and even her cup of tea was full. Grandma *never* left her teacup untouched.

"What's wrong?" Skylar asked. Oh no. Grandma didn't suggest picking up her fiancé to go with them. "Earl is still on a trip, right?"

Grandma's gnarled fingers tightened around her cup. "He was supposed to be back by now. But he's not. And he's not answering his phone. I guess the business trip is taking longer than expected. And if he's in a no-coverage zone, I understand he doesn't get my calls. But wouldn't he get some way to let me know?"

Skylar's heart dropped onto the patio stones, and she pushed the plate away. "Do you have any other ways to contact him?" Sometimes places without cell coverage had internet reception or at least landlines. "A work phone number or social media, maybe?"

Her grandmother shook her head.

Okay, okay. No need to worry yet. Skylar touched the necklace over the smooth fabric of her blouse that happened to match the table. Despite the hurt of the breakup, Dallas's necklace had brought her comfort throughout the years. "You said he works with antique cars. What is his business's name? We can look it up on the internet."

"I don't know the name." Grandma scrunched up her nose and blinked damp eyes behind her glasses.

Not good.

Breeze barked as if to confirm it.

"How about his family? You said you met his son, right?" Skylar spread out her hands. She should've interfered a long time ago. What if someone was trying to take advantage of Grandma? Her grandmother wasn't rich by any means, and the tiny cottage was willed to Skylar already. But one never knew.

"Well, we sort of met via videoconference. I have his son's phone number." Grandma grimaced. "But that guy, um, isn't exactly fond of me."

Skylar got up and placed a kiss on her grandmother's cheek. "How can anyone not be fond of you?"

Grandma just spread her hands. "In other circumstances, I'd say some people have no taste. But we're talking about the son of the man I love. I want us to get along. I mean, Grant wasn't rude or anything. I just got that vibe. But I'd better call him, anyway." She sighed and gestured at her plate and cup. "I'm sorry. I have no appetite today."

"It's okay, Grandma. I understand. I'll take care of the cleanup." Skylar whistled for Breeze to follow her, then carried utensils, cups, and plates inside through the green-framed French doors. She washed and dried the dishes as the fragrance of peach-scented dishwashing liquid spread through the small room. Then she gave Breeze fresh water and filled the kibble bowl by the time Grandma came into the kitchen.

Skylar's fingers pinched around the spoon she was drying as she took in her grandmother's worried expression and the glasses sitting a bit crooked now. Grandma fidgeted with her seashell bracelet, which usually wasn't a good sign, either.

Whatever it was, they'd have to figure it out together. Skylar dropped the spoon in the drawer and pulled out a chair at the breakfast nook for her grandmother. "What did he say?"

The scent of wildflowers from the table reached her nostrils to tease her with memories of running beside Dallas in the fields. Oh how carefree they'd been then! How naïve. How very much in love. Her heart shifted, but she needed to concentrate.

Grandma lowered herself onto the chair. "His son says he can't reach his father, either. Grant called Earl's work but couldn't get much. He has no clue where the business trip must've been. He's flying here. That's not all. He said his sister was already supposed to be here." Grandma grabbed a paper napkin and started tearing it into tiny pieces.

Breeze finished her breakfast, then trudged to the nearby living room, and stretched out on the colorful sea-toned rug spread across the floor as if the bay had been brought inside.

Putting two and two together, Skylar frowned. "But his daughter didn't contact you."

"No. I got a feeling neither of his children like me much, though his daughter's never met me."

"I'm sorry." Skylar reached for her grandmother's wrinkled hands. "I'm sure they'll love you when they get to know you."

Then Grandma lifted her chin and placed the rest of the poor napkin aside. "I understand they didn't expect a stepmom at this age. Not that I'm trying to become their mother. The family dynamics might be weird, too. I didn't mean to impose on them."

"You didn't impose on them." Skylar squeezed her grandmother's hands before letting them go. Then she took a deep breath, and it filled her lungs with the scent of wildflowers again and her mind with memories of Dallas. She cleared her mind with an effort.

It was best not to mention another delicate nuance. Inheritance.

Skylar resisted the urge to tear apart the rest of the napkin. From what she understood, Grandma's fiancé was well-off. If he got married without a will and something happened to him, everything would go to the wife. His children might've been upset for reasons other than the new family dynamics.

The image of the woman in sunglasses and a straw hat at Auntie's restaurant floated in Skylar's memory. Could it be...?

Her mind whirled for what other options they had. "How about we stop by Earl's place if you like? You said he stayed at the hotel at first and then rented a cottage, right? We can go by the cottage."

A deep sigh left Grandma's lungs. "I don't have keys to his place. I... I've never even been there. He invited me a couple of times, but I always found an excuse not to go."

Skylar's eyes widened. Something didn't add up. "Why?"

Grandma looked away and snagged another napkin, folded it, and unfolded it again. "He rented *that* cottage. You know."

Uh-oh. Skylar shuddered. Not because she worried about the things that had happened inside the house, though the trauma Dallas and his family had gone through had weighed on her. But because she carried snippets of memories of crawling inside the porch, hiding, and shivering from cold and fear. "*Th–that* cottage? How come the town grapevine doesn't know about it?"

"He said he'd asked the owner to keep it under wraps. The owner, glad to finally rent it out, agreed." Grandma paused as if seeking a plausible explanation. "See, my fiancé is a very private person. Besides, he only rented it a few days ago."

A very private person? Hmm.

Guilt clenched Skylar's stomach. She was letting her grandmother marry a stranger. She should've been here a long time ago. "Wouldn't someone have seen him when he went in or out of the house?"

Grandma shrugged those bony shoulders wrapped in a tawny-hued shawl she'd crocheted herself. "Earl said he left early and returned late, mostly after dark. Besides, you know the locals avoid the place."

Which could be why he'd rented it. Skylar took the half napkin and tore off a piece. Their coastal town offered plenty of great accommodations. Why would he choose a run-down place with a bad reputation?

Was it because it was secluded? Was Grandma's fiancé hiding from someone?

Skylar needed to talk to someone about this, and she'd always turned to Dallas. Her heart contracted. She couldn't turn to him any longer. Probably not ever. And she only had herself to blame. Things were getting more and more complicated. And here she'd thought her biggest issues would be avoiding him or not getting the right centerpieces for Grandma's wedding.

Skylar leaned toward her grandmother. "What would you like to do first? Do you want to go to the police station and file a missing person report?"

Grandma hesitated, then nodded. "Yes. I think we should."

Skylar stifled a frown as she helped her grandmother get up. She should've gone to the police after she'd started college.

But what did she have to report? Fuzzy memories that resurfaced too late? A phone call in the middle of the night when a distorted voice told her something would happen to her grandmother if Skylar went to the police? If she as much as returned to visit her hometown?

It didn't matter that she still didn't remember much. It was her fault. It was all her fault.

After they visited the police station, Grandma insisted on going to the ranch. "We should continue the preparations. The wedding *will* happen."

Didn't they need a groom for that? Thankfully, Skylar didn't blurt *that* out.

Soon, she was pulling up to the spacious white Cape-Cod-style ranch house, its familiar trio of dormers rising from the roof, and stone chimneys flanking its sides. The moment she saw Dallas walking down the porch, her heart started beating faster. Why did she still have this reaction to him? She'd let him go years ago. Or so she'd thought.

She turned off the engine, and Breeze gave out a joyful bark as if to greet Dallas. He waved but didn't move closer.

"Wait a sec, Grandma, please. I need to let Breeze out before she tears up everything in the car." Skylar hurried to open the door for the energetic dog.

Breeze shot up the steps to Dallas as if the man was someone dear. Skylar knew the feeling. Her entire being longed to run to him, fly into his arms.

Earth to Skylar.

"Please lean on me," she suggested as she opened the passenger door for her grandmother and helped her to climb out. She had a sting of guilt for stealing a glance at Dallas.

"Well, hello, Breeze." Dallas chuckled and petted the dog who was jumping at him and preventing him from moving forward. "I'm glad to see you, too."

The smile slid off his handsome face as his gaze moved to Skylar. He obviously wasn't glad to see *her*. Her stomach dipped, but she couldn't blame him. The goofy dog was joy itself and had never harmed him the way Skylar had.

"Hello, Mrs. Rafferty. Hello, Skylar." Dallas made it down the steps even with such an obstacle as an excited golden retriever. "Did you come to see my mother?"

"Where are you off to? Are you avoiding us, stranger?" Despite her words, Grandma's voice was soft and kind.

"No! Not at all. I was just leaving." He frowned. "I wanted to check *that* cottage. Well, not really wanted to. I thought I should, well, look around."

Skylar pulled her shoulders back. She wasn't a scared, shivering child any longer. She didn't need to flinch just at the words. But his words surprised her. His experience with *that* cottage was much more traumatic than hers had been. His entire family had a good reason to avoid the place. "May I ask why?"

"Kai and I heard a suspicious sound from the area yesterday. Like a gunshot."

Skylar's eyes widened while her grandmother paled and staggered. "A... a gunshot?"

Skylar wrapped her arm around her grandmother tighter, steadying her. It was only fair that now Skylar could be the rock for her grandmother. Especially considering she hadn't been a good granddaughter for years, making guilt eat her up inside like acid. "It might've just been a tire blowout."

"Kai said the same thing. But there's word in town about a new renter there." He shoved his hands into his jeans pockets and avoided looking at her. "I, well, I wanted to make sure everything was okay."

That was Dallas for you. Always doing the right thing. All the Lawrence brothers were born protectors. But how far would the protective streak go?

Dallas shifted from one foot to the other. "I mean, what kind of person would rent that place?"

Grandma's lips pursed. "My fiancé."

"Oh."

In other times, Skylar would've enjoyed seeing Dallas's jaw agape.

"It's okay." Grandma patted his hand, then turned to Skylar. "Would you mind terribly if we went there, as well? Considering this fine man can accompany us? I know it brings back bad memories, but—"

Something inside Skylar trembled, but she nodded. "It's fine." Neither one of them wanted to go to *that* cottage, but apparently, they had to.

Well, except for the golden retriever, who was overly excited. Breeze barked and ran in circles, chasing her tail.

Dallas's eyes narrowed before he walked Grandma back to their vehicle. "You want to meet your fiancé there?"

"See, Earl was supposed to return from his business trip by now. But he hasn't shown up and isn't answering his phone. Maybe he returned, and something's wrong with his phone?"

Skylar doubted the latter, but it was kinder not to point it out.

Grandma sighed as Skylar helped her back in the car. "I could've saved myself the difficulty of getting in and out if I just stayed in the car."

Skylar's rib cage contracted as she slipped into the driver's seat, and this time it wasn't from the things that couldn't be between her and Dallas. Grandma was such a permanent fixture in her life and the most necessary one. Skylar refused to think she could lose her. It would tear her apart worse than she'd torn apart that napkin.

All the years she'd spent away from Port Sunshine and the only family she had left weighed heavily on her shoulders. She'd told herself she had no choice. But maybe she was just placating her conscience. She'd studied art. She knew how differently artists could paint the same thing.

It was all about how you look at it.

But no matter what way she looked at it, her feelings for Dallas were returning. She waited for him to get in his rusty truck, her gaze taking in his muscular form while her entire being begged to be in his arms again. Then she started the engine.

"You miss him, don't you?" Grandma clicked her seat belt closed.

Why deny the obvious? Especially to the person who knew her the best? "Yes." Skylar pulled onto the gravel road, checking that he followed her.

"Then why don't you—?"

"Grandma, please!" Skylar's throat clogged up. Too many things, too many realizations were happening at once. "I'm here for you, not to rekindle a love that can't be."

"One thing doesn't have to exclude the other," Grandma muttered. "One day, you'll realize how precious time is and how fast it flies."

Skylar had already realized it. She just didn't know how to change anything. Her throat clogged up further. But it wasn't her grandmother's fault. "I love you, Grandma."

"I love you, too, Little Miss." Her grandmother's voice softened, and she sounded like she wanted to say more but chose not to.

Minutes later, they were all walking to *that* cottage, the dog included. The closer they got to it, the more Breeze tugged on the leash. And her bark turned anything but friendly.

Dallas and Skylar exchanged glances.

"Do you think she senses something?" He voiced her thoughts.

"Or maybe she's spotted a seagull she wants to chase." She infused light notes into her words since she didn't want to worry her grandmother, but her heart was heavy.

Her grandmother's face looked ashen as it was, and Skylar suggested turning back several times. But Grandma put on her resolute expression and hurried forward, albeit in small steps.

Up close, the place still appeared menacing. Even if Skylar no longer saw it through the eyes of a terrified child, shivering from pouring rain and wincing from every rumble of thunder, who couldn't outrun what she'd seen no matter how hard she'd tried.

The house squatted as if embarrassed by its sad history, especially against the spectacular backdrop of a gorgeous ocean, like a speck of dirt on a postcard. The roof missed a few shingles, and the windows were dark like gaps in teeth punched out in a fight.

A web on one of the windows with a fly in it made Skylar wince, and she jumped back.

"It's okay," Dallas whispered in her ear, his breath hot on her skin. He shielded her. "There's no spider I can see."

But she couldn't hide behind his broad back. So even as her heart was beating fast for several reasons, she moved forward, carefully staying away from the web, though.

What flourished here were the weeds eagerly hugging the house, and the breeze brought a faint scent of stale french fries someone must've thrown there that might be moldy by now.

She eyed the porch warily. She remembered the porch from underneath as she'd huddled on the cold ground in the dark but dry place, howling an unhappy duet with the wind. Knowing she could never, ever go outside again.

But this wasn't about her.

Concerned, she glanced at Dallas. No matter how painful what had caused her to run here had been, for her, the porch was a refuge from that horror.

While what had happened inside the cottage for Dallas was something no teenager—no, no human being—should ever have to see.

"Are you okay with being here?" She shifted toward him.

"I don't think either one of us is okay with being here. But what needs to be done needs to be done." A muscle jerked in his jaw. But it was the only sign of his distress, and she forced herself to stay in one place instead of reaching out to him.

There was a surprise, too. The once-rickety porch was propped with new boards, and it and the front door sported fresh white paint, probably done for the renter. Yet contrasting with peeling mud-hued paint on the rest of the house, it seemed like a Band-Aid slapped on a gunshot wound.

Dallas frowned. Skylar could guess what he was thinking. The same thought she'd had before. Why would an affluent businessman stay in such a place?

Grandma's eyes widened. "I didn't expect... this." Her hands shook, and she clasped them together. "Earl said the cottage was renovated."

Breeze barked wildly as she bolted up the steps. One of them seemed to have a plank loose because her paw nearly went through, and she whined.

"No! Stop!" Skylar screamed as all kinds of alarms sounded in her head.

Dallas ran after the dog, carefully avoiding the loose plank. Skylar jerked forward, then glanced at her grandmother. "Sorry, the porch doesn't look safe enough for you."

"You go ahead." Grandma eyed the steps warily, then waved Skylar off. "I'll just wait here."

"Breeze!" Worried, Skylar climbed the steps fast, but the dog was already at the front door.

Breeze scratched at it and whined again. If anyone was inside, Skylar doubted they wouldn't hear this ruckus, but she still knocked.

"Why don't you stand aside?" Dallas moved her away from the door. His touch sent a wave of apprehension through her.

As her brain stuttered, she struggled to find her tongue. "Why? Do you expect bullets to start flying?"

He didn't answer, just frowned. She missed their former camaraderie, how easy it once was. She nearly leaned into him, then remembered to step back. No answer inside the house, either, just as she'd expected. She told Breeze to keep silent and listened. Dallas seemed to do the same.

After a few long minutes, she shook her head. "I don't think anyone is inside. Or... or hiding there."

His brows furrowed. He didn't look convinced, but he nodded. "I'll walk around the house. Maybe I'll see something in the windows. Would you like to wait in the car?"

She avoided the urge to roll her eyes. He needed to start seeing her as the independent, accomplished woman she now was, not a young girl he'd needed to protect. "Now, why would I want to wait in the car?"

"Maybe because it's safer, Little Miss?" Grandma pointed out the obvious.

Skylar jammed her hands on her hips as she marched from the front door toward the steps. "I'm not a scaredy-cat!" Then she spotted something dark moving on the freshly whitewashed porch step. An insect? Relatively small, but moving in her direction...

She squinted. Did it have six or eight legs?

"Spider!" she screamed at the top of her lungs when she realized what that insect was. In just moments, it could run up her leg! Her heart leaped into her throat, and she leaped into Dallas's arms.

With his eyes wide, he caught her in his strong arms. Held her. Her heart jumped into her throat for a different reason.

What... what just happened? Her ear was so close to his broad chest that she could hear his heartbeat. Like many times before. And when she'd tell him that, he'd reply, "It beats for you."

Always.

Somewhere in the back of her mind, it registered as Breeze slapped her paw against the wooden plank where the spider was.

Skylar wound her arms around his neck before she could think of it, then looked up into his ocean-blue eyes and got lost there. Or maybe *not lost*. Maybe, once again, she found her way back to where she was supposed to be all along.

"Are you all right?" Grandma's concerned voice threw Skylar out of her mental fog.

"Yes, Grandma." Her voice came out raspy, so she tried again for more normal tones. "Yes."

"I believe you're safe now." Dallas's eyes crinkled around the corners, and his lips tugged up. "Breeze got your spider."

Despite her fear of spiders, compassion for it tugged at her heart. The insect wasn't at fault for her irrational fear. And a part of her—a scarily significant part—even felt grateful for the excuse to be in his arms again.

Unlike the other children at school, he'd never made fun of her for her fear of spiders. And after a school bully had put a live spider behind her collar, making her nearly lose her mind, Dallas punched the bully. Never mind that Dallas had been smaller than the bully at the time. Well, everyone knew how the Lawrence brothers had stood up for each other.

Enough of the trip down memory lane. Enough of leaning against him. No matter how good it felt.

"You, um, you can put me down now," she whispered somewhat reluctantly.

"Okay." He did just that. Did she imagine it was also somewhat reluctantly?

"Thank you." She missed his arms around her.

Stop this.

She should be aware of her surroundings and help her grandmother, not go googly-eyed over her first love. "Good job, Breeze." She patted Breeze who preened.

With legs wobbling, Skylar picked up the leash and walked down the porch, careful not to step on the loose plank with Breeze in tow. Grandma joined them in their walk around the house, her expression more worried by the minute, her cobalt-blue silk scarf trailing her. Her lower lip trembled.

Skylar nearly ground her teeth as her favorite woman in the world leaned on her. All these new developments couldn't be good for Grandma.

Then Skylar tried to peep into the windows with zero success. "Argh. Thick curtains. We can't see anything." She glanced around. "Anything suspicious around the house?"

"Not that I can see." His gaze swept over the weeds, and his brow furrowed. "Except for maybe the excessive amount of trash thrown into the weeds."

She'd always cringed when people left their trash on the beach. She, Dallas, and their group of friends used to walk along the beach late in the evening and gather plastic bottles, paper cups, soda cans, foam packages, hamburger wrappers, and other things she'd rather not name into trash bags. Considering locals had avoided this place, it must be tourists.

Then Breeze jerked forward again, barking.

"Oh no. I hope it's not another spider." Skylar's gut tightened. Though to be honest, her heart somersaulted when she thought about being in his arms again.

He stepped forward, spread the tall weeds apart, then frowned. "I don't think it's a spider."

Air whooshed out of her lungs. "Good."

"I don't think it's something good, either." His voice was grave. "There appears to be dry blood on the leaves."

Her grandmother gasped.

"It could be some animal," Dallas said for Grandma's sake.

But Skylar went cold. "We'd better call the police."

Chapter Nine

The uneasy feeling inside Dallas wouldn't go away after they visited the police station and talked to the only local detective, a man who was nearly as much a fixture in Port Sunshine as Skylar's grandmother was. Every year he was going to retire, and every year he postponed it. He'd been the officer on call the night Dallas's father died.

Dallas had hoped he'd never have to set foot in the place again.

But *that* cottage seemed to live up to its sad history once again. He frowned all the way back to the ranch. Or could the missing renter, the gunshot, and what seemed to be dry blood on the leaves be a coincidence?

Even shaken up, Skylar's grandmother had insisted on going back to the ranch, saying talking to his mom would be a good distraction.

Once they got there and left their vehicles, Mrs. Rafferty declared, "I'm a bit tired. I'll stay with Amelia and chat inside. Why don't you two youngsters take a walk to the barn and see what needs to be done for the reception?"

Worry clouded Skylar's expression as she opened the door to let Breeze out. "Grandma, are you okay? Would you like me to take you home?"

Breeze leaped out of the car, clearly excited about the many new smells.

"Not so fast, darling." Skylar secured her leash before the dog could get too excited about a distant moving scent of an animal. Some cows could charge an untrained dog, even one as friendly as Breeze.

"I'm fine." Mrs. Rafferty waved her granddaughter off, though her hand shook. "Well, fine under the circumstances. I just want to talk to my friend. She's going to be one of the bridesmaids, and we need to decide on the dresses." Then she sized Dallas up. "How do you feel about being one of the groomsmen?"

Dallas flinched. That would mean spending even more time with Skylar, who was the maid of honor.

"Grandma, shouldn't that be up to your fiancé to decide?" Skylar seemed as reluctant about the idea as he was, and for some reason, it irritated him.

"Well, he's not here, is he?" Mrs. Rafferty waved around. "He said he didn't have many friends. And I have a feeling his son's not keen on our wedding."

Dallas's mother loved Mrs. Rafferty, and he loved her, too. So he cleared his throat. "It would be an honor."

"Thank you." She patted his hand with cold fingers. "We'll see when we can get you an appointment for a tuxedo fitting."

Riiight. He'd never had to wear a tuxedo and never intended to squeeze into one, but remember, his mother loved Mrs. Rafferty. After a long series of tragic events, she especially deserved to be happy. And really, his wants couldn't count when the wonderful woman had been so shaken up lately.

"Do you mind holding the leash, please?" Skylar stepped to him, giving him a whiff of her peach shampoo.

It sent his thoughts to all the times he used to run his fingers through her silky long hair, and his treacherous heart started beating fast. "No. Yes. I mean, no."

"Which one is it?" Her lips twitched up.

"I mean no, I don't mind." He lifted his palm.

"Thanks." She passed him the leather leash.

Their hands touched, sending something akin to an electric current, but a pleasant one, through him. Why did he still react to her touch? His mind said no, but his heart didn't want to follow.

Her eyes widened, and she let out a low gasp, giving him a jolt of satisfaction. So the touch affected her, as well.

"I... we... I..." Blinking rapidly, she seemed to come to her senses, squatted near the golden retriever, and hugged Breeze. Or did she hug the dog because she needed to compose herself? "Don't try to run, okay, Breeze? Be good. I'll be right back."

Then Skylar straightened and helped her grandmother inside the house.

Dallas and Breeze looked after Skylar, then at each other. Breeze whined and tugged the leash to run after Skylar to the porch.

He stayed firm. "Yeah, I miss her already, too. The difference between us is you'll get her back soon and I won't."

Seeming satisfied with his answer, Breeze started chasing her tail again. Then she plopped down on the grass and tilted her head as if she couldn't understand something.

"I know I should've come up with an excuse not to go with her to the barn." He voiced his thoughts. "But what was I supposed to say? That I was too busy and refused to accompany her?"

Kai walked from the stables. "Talking to the dog, I see."

Right. "Well, you talk to your parrot."

"But my parrot talks to me. The dog doesn't."

Breeze sneezed derisively and barked, perhaps saying that just because humans didn't understand her language, it didn't mean she didn't talk.

Dallas slapped his brother on the shoulder. "Any more words like that, and I'll make sure you're fitted into a tuxedo for a groomsman, too."

Kai laughed. "Oh, you got roped into that?"

Formal events and formal attire were so not Dallas's forte. He raised his chin. "Hey, Marina might be part of the bridal party."

Kai stopped laughing. "Um, I've got to... to do something." He marched to the porch.

"Keep running away!" Dallas yelled after him.

Breeze tugged on the leash again, this time in the direction of the sprawling oak that once housed a treehouse. Now, only Spanish moss hung in the branches where Dallas and his brothers used to play. Many days, the girls had joined them.

Breeze sniffed the oak's trunk.

"It's difficult to understand humans, right?" Dallas said, maybe to the dog or maybe to himself.

Skylar ran down the steps. "Thank you for taking care of Breeze."

While Breeze barked again, maybe to say Skylar was mistaken about who had taken care of whom, Skylar took over the leash. This time, she was careful not to touch him. It was the right thing to do but still sent a bit of sadness through him.

They walked to the tall red barn with white trim with Breeze exploring things and especially tree trunks on the way. She scared a few birds into the sky who didn't understand her friendliness. One of them was a Carolina wren with its cinnamon-hued body and orangish belly, its beak long and curved. It could sing beautifully, when not scared away by a dog, of course. A ladybug stayed longer on the grass before it took off. Nobody and nothing stayed forever, and he'd best remember it.

"Do you think Grandma is all right?" Concern tightened Skylar's voice. "That she just wanted to talk to your mom? Or was she playing matchmaker?"

He opened the massive door of their quintessential red barn for her with a characteristic gambrel roof, double pitched for more storage. Just like the barn, the door was bright red with white trim, only here it also had a zigzag pattern.

She slipped inside, then glanced back. "Remember, you told me that red color started from the time rust was used as a sealant and against moss and fungi? When paint became available, farmers painted the barn red to honor the tradition."

"Of course, I do." His heart constricted painfully. He'd forever remember everything he'd told her. And everything he hadn't.

Inside, it smelled of wood and hay. A few artificial flowers still dangled on the wall, skillful imitation of local oakleaf hydrangea and yellow jessamine, gathering dust after the previous event. "I hope so." Oh no. That sounded as if he... He coughed profusely. Heat crept up his neck. "I mean, I hope she's all right. Not that she was playing matchmaker."

Skylar let Breeze off the leash, and the happy dog dashed to explore every corner.

"Right. I know." Her voice echoed in the tall empty building, bouncing off the walls and coming back to him, staying inside. She seemed to want to say something else but then shook her head as if in answer to her thoughts. She pulled out her phone and swiped the screen to bring up the camera. "All this about her fiancé's disappearance worries me. The man himself worries me."

He didn't like what was going on, either, but despite everything, he didn't want to see her stressed. "We'll figure out something." He winked, doing his best to sound cheerful. "We just need to get the groom back and make sure he deserves Mrs. Rafferty."

She snorted like in childhood as she captured photos of the walls, floor, and even the ceiling. "Such a little detail." She lowered the phone. Then she walked from wall to wall, counting steps as if taking measurements, and punched something into her phone.

Until she stopped near him. "Thank you for doing this for us."

"Anytime." He stepped closer, all the memories clouding his judgment. When she was near, when she looked at him like that, he could forget she'd left him, forget she'd broken her promises to him.

The tight bun on the back of her head was secured with pins, and his fingers twitched to shake her luscious golden-bronze hair free, to run through its silkiness again, and to bring her close. Close enough for their lips to touch. His pulse skyrocketed.

He ached to free the caged bird she'd become, but it could be his misconception. She must've wanted a different life away from him, or she wouldn't have led it. A white scarf was wrapped around her neck, the end thrown over one shoulder, but it was his ship that had hung the white flag of surrender to her a long time ago.

"Would you like a barn dance? You know, to test it out for the reception?" He spoke before he could think about it.

Argh. He shouldn't have let it slip. The barn had been tested out for dances plenty, and it wasn't a good idea to succumb to the desire to hold her in his arms again.

Visibly trembling like the baby bird he and Austin had once found under a tree, Skylar didn't say anything. Then she stepped closer and put one hand in his while placing the other one on his shoulder. Was it her gift to him before she disappeared again?

There was no music besides birds chirruping outside, but just like she once used to march to the beat of her own drum, she moved in tune with the silent melody now. It wasn't a country dance, but it was a dance of their own. He cherished these moments of having her close because he realized how rare they were going to be, how irreplaceable. He whirled her around, then looked into her hazel eyes where regret and tenderness lingered and yet they sparkled.

His feelings were coming back in full force and growing further as the two of them moved along the empty floor with only Breeze as a spectator. With each passing second, his chest ached with longing while he held her close, her small hand delicate in his large callused one.

Could they still change anything? If only she would talk to him like she used to.

"Skylar, what if…" His voice trailed off because he wasn't sure what he was going to say, just that he shouldn't be saying it.

Her gaze lingered on his face. In her beautiful hazel eyes glowed the same gentleness he'd seen and treasured. She leaned into him. Their foreheads touched, and for the few moments they stayed that way, all the regrets ebbed away.

Then she stepped back. "I'm sorry."

The regrets sluiced back in. He didn't need her to be sorry! Disappointment surged in his veins, but he only had himself to blame. So many times, she'd shown him they had no future together. Yet he'd gotten distracted by those doe-like eyes and the person once so dear to him.

"It's all in the past. I know." He stepped back, putting even more distance between them.

"I didn't mean that." Her gaze became tormented. "I, well... We should go back. Grandma might be waiting for me. Thank you for bringing me here. I–I have a few ideas for decorations now."

As if feeling the change of atmosphere in the room, Breeze stopped running, sat down, then whined, and covered her head with a paw. Skylar put her back on the leash. "It's time to go."

Yes, it was. And it was high time for him to let go, as well.

They covered the same distance three times faster in a brisk walk back from the barn. Then they helped her grandmother walk down the porch steps and get inside her car.

"I'll follow your car to the sea cottage," he grumbled. He was doing this for Mrs. Rafferty's safety. Absolutely.

"How sweet of you." Mrs. Rafferty smiled at him, though her smile was still wobbly.

Skylar looked away. "You don't have to."

"Humor me," he insisted with more force than necessary.

Skylar hesitated, nodded, then slipped into the driver's seat, and revved the engine. "Thanks for everything you've done." She fell silent briefly, then added, "And for what you haven't done, too."

Minutes later, she seemed eager to get away from the ranch or most likely from him because she drove fast, zipped between cars, and flew forward on the yellow light.

His fingers tightened around his truck's steering wheel, the peeled-off edges grating against his callused palms. He'd see them safely home and then avoid seeing her again. He'd skip the tuxedo fitting. He didn't care if the tuxedo hung on him or choked him during the wedding. Enough was enough.

They made it to Mrs. Rafferty's sea cottage in record time, and he was about to turn around when a flashy apple-red sports car parked at the curb made him linger. It was out of place here.

Did some affluent tourist get lost? Or could Mrs. Rafferty's fiancé have come back?

Or...

Dallas parked at the opposite curb to make sure Mrs. Rafferty and Skylar made it safely home. Skylar had already pulled into the driveway and was helping her grandmother out of the vehicle.

A man in his late forties, dressed in a black suit and tie and leather shoes, leaped out of the sports car, his face blotchy and features taut. "What did you do with my dad?" the man bellowed.

Adrenaline surging, Dallas shot out of his truck.

SKYLAR'S BLOOD WENT cold, and her first reaction was to recoil.

What on earth?

The man's features twisted into a menacing scowl, and his loud voice assaulted her eardrums. With his shoulders bunched and his hands fisted, he widened his stance, and fury emanated from him in waves. "What did you do with my dad?"

What did he expect? Her to produce his father out of her pocket?

Breeze barked in the car, demanding to be let out to defend them, but Skylar hesitated. The guy'd be the type to sue if Breeze bit him. Skylar raised her chin. She'd had years of practice reining in her emotions and learned to exude confidence. The latter helped her land new clients.

"Good afternoon, sir." She stepped in front of her grandmother, shielding her. Skylar kept her voice even and her posture assertive but non threatening. "You're Mr. Lane's son, I presume?"

"That's him," Grandma said behind Skylar's back.

"Don't you dare talk to them like that!" Dallas was already rushing to her, and it gave her a pleasant jolt.

No matter how many times she kept ruining things between them, even smashing to dust the small crumbs of friendship, here he was—offering her his help again. Joy warred with guilt, though. She'd kept feeding guilt again and again while starving joy.

Okay, it wasn't about her right now.

She eased her purse containing her gun closer and drew a deep breath of fresh air now tainted with an unwelcome addition of the guy's expensive cologne and fury. She'd dealt with difficult clients and managed to maintain her cool. And the last thing she needed was to get Dallas into a fistfight again. This could escalate.

Breeze kept barking in the car, prompting Skylar to say, "It's okay, Breeze. Quiet, please."

"I'm Skylar Rafferty, Dolores Rafferty's granddaughter." She offered her hand to the guy, keeping her grandmother tucked behind her, which wouldn't last for long. Whatever spunk she used to have, she'd gotten from her grandmother. "I can't say it's a pleasure to meet you, but it appears we have a common problem. So why don't we join forces?"

The man startled and appeared to apply the brakes like Breeze when she rounded a corner too fast. "Excuse me?"

Dallas shielded her, his hands fisted. "You're trespassing!"

She didn't need to be shielded, at least not from this visitor, but it gave her a surge of gratitude nonetheless.

The man shifted back. "I have the right to be here. My dad was fine until he met that—"

She cocked her head, her hands sliding to her hips. "That wonderful, amazing Dolores Rafferty, you mean?"

Dallas growled. Breeze echoed that growl in the car and scratched at the window, her claws scraping against the glass.

"And that wonderful, amazing Dolores Rafferty invites you all for some tea. I still have some pastries, too," Grandma said, as much of an awesome human being as always.

Dallas's eyes narrowed. "Or we just call the police if you don't leave."

The man gaped at him, then deflated. "I'm Grant Lane, and yes, I'm Earl Lane's son." He shook Skylar's hand and to her surprise held it longer than she'd expected. He needed to make a decision.

Meanwhile, she needed to calm the distraught dog. But first, she edged forward and opened the purse wider to help him see the weapon. Grant's eyes widened, and the look in them turned different. Calculated.

That's right.

Her lips curved into a semblance of a welcoming smile with something feral on the inside. He'd expected a fragile elderly woman, easy to intimidate, but encountered her armed granddaughter, a younger man more muscular than he was, and a dog baring teeth. Ha!

Plus, he'd soon discover Grandma wasn't easy to intimidate to start with. "So... what is it going to be, Mr. Lane?"

"Fine," Grant Lane finally said. "Please call me Grant. Let's get that tea."

"Not *that* tea, but *the* tea." Grandma led everyone inside.

Skylar rushed to the car and released Breeze, then hugged her and rubbed her fur. "So sorry."

Once Skylar headed inside the sea cottage with Breeze, Dallas followed, probably for nothing else than to protect them. No matter how Skylar was used to taking care of herself and relying only on herself now, knowing he'd always have her back sure felt good.

In the house, she wiped Breeze's paws, using the time to gather her thoughts and develop a strategy while Grandma set the table. Dallas helped her grandmother, but his gaze never wavered from the newcomer. Skylar gave Breeze fresh water and kibble, but the golden retriever drank some water fast and then didn't let herself get distracted. Skylar petted her dog gratefully. Dallas wasn't the only one who had Skylar's back now, but the difference was she could hope to keep Breeze.

The instant Skylar sat down, Breeze stretched on the floor nearby, baring her teeth from time to time for preventive maintenance. Steam rose from cups with tea, sending off whiffs of peppermint, the aroma mixed with the one of flaky fruit-filled pastries. Once a baker, always a baker.

Her nerves still on edge, Skylar looked around the table and then realized her faux pas. "Sorry. I forgot to introduce Dallas Lawrence. He is..."

What was she supposed to say? An ex-boyfriend? Ex-fiancé? Childhood friend? The man of her dreams? Or all of the above? Only she didn't want any of his titles to have "ex" in them.

"A friend of the family," Dallas supplied the definition she couldn't. "I already introduced myself while setting the table."

He was so much more than a family friend. And the feelings she felt now... There was nothing *ex* about them.

"I'm a movie executive," Grant's voice interrupted her thoughts.

Uh-oh. She stared at Dallas for too long. Heat rose to her cheeks. "And I'm an accountant." A highly successful one, who'd made partner in her firm, but why go into details?

Hmm. Had Grant said his profession with an air of importance, or did it only seem so?

Dallas shrugged. "And I'm a cowboy. Let's combine our knowledge about Mr. Lane's disappearance so far."

"I made several women movie stars." Okay, there was certainly an air of importance this time. Why wouldn't Grant drop that topic? Wasn't he in a hurry to find his father any longer?

She wrapped her fingers around the warm, smooth cup and sipped her tea with mint flavor, eyeing him like numbers to fit in their proper column. Her appraisal must lack the eagerness and admiration he expected. "How admirable of you."

He wasn't bluffing, though. While her grandmother had been getting ready that morning, Skylar researched Earl's son online. Another thing she should've done before, considering he was going to become her family.

He'd been successful and had helped others become a success. He had a habit of dating beautiful starlets, and one of them had become his wife for ten years. No children, and two years ago they'd divorced.

Grant loosened his fancy tie and draped his arm over the back of his chair. He was probably more accustomed to slick tall leather chairs than stalwart scratched oak ones displaying the decades they'd served with love. Diamonds on his cufflinks sparkled in the lamplight, tarnishing the inheritance motive. The man must be rich in his own right. Or was this appearance as fake as a movie prop? "Maybe we should wait for my sister to have this conversation. Though I called her, she didn't answer."

"Your family seems to have a knack for finding places with no cell phone coverage," Dallas said drily.

"Well, after the wedding, it's going to be *our* family." Grant's smile, directed at Skylar, seemed too sweet, like tea when she'd added too much sugar. Huh. Why such a drastic change in demeanor? "Let me send her a quick text."

While he typed something on his phone, Skylar, Dallas, Grandma, and Breeze exchanged glances. Then Grandma pushed the pastry plate toward Skylar, and Skylar took a bite of a sweet bear claw, more to placate her grandmother than out of hunger. Well, at least he wasn't throwing accusations any longer. But how much of what he was about to say could she believe?

"While we wait, have you ever thought about becoming an actress?" Grant's voice became suave as he leaned toward her. "You have the looks for it."

Skylar chuckled. "Nope. Never wanted to be an actress. Never wanted to be famous." She didn't even want to be a famous artist. She just wanted people to enjoy her work. To bring them joy instead of sadness. Apparently, she'd wanted too much.

Her throat clogged up at the fate of the last painting she'd done, and she put the pastry aside.

As a teen, she used to wear her heart on the sleeve of her bright dresses. But then she'd had to learn how to conceal her feelings. So maybe she knew how to act a bit, even if it had been self-taught.

Hmm. If Dallas was like a storm cloud before, that cloud now carried not just rain but thunder and lightning. He couldn't be jealous, could he? He moved his chair closer to her. "Let's get started. Grant can explain everything to his sister later, right?"

"Good point." Grandma nodded. "We have a new development you need to know about." She paused, clearly reluctant to voice it.

Dallas did it for her. "Today, we went to the cottage Mr. Lane rented. The place seemed empty, but there was dried blood on some plants outside."

Grant gasped. "Oh no!"

"Most likely, it's not your father's," Skylar said softly, her heart going out to the man. She'd become too much of a cynic in the city. This was a man missing his father, and she should extend him some grace. She'd known all too well how it felt to lose a father. "It might've been some injured animal. The police are investigating whether it's human blood."

And more rumors and speculations were circulating in town about *that* cottage. Skylar suppressed a grimace. More people started discussing other things that had happened there. Including Dallas's father's suicide. Some folks still doubted it was suicide. Sadly, Skylar was one of them, though, for Dallas's sake, she hadn't voiced those doubts.

Grandma shuddered.

Skylar got up and hugged her, then took her empty cup, and brought her more tea. According to her grandmother, more tea was always a good thing. "Mr. Lane—"

"Grant."

"Grant, if you give the police a blood sample, maybe they'd be able to tell if your blood is related to that found onsite."

"I'll do that." Grant nodded. "I'm glad I'm here."

"Me, too." Skylar reluctantly admitted, nibbling on the rest of the pastry. They could get answers faster with him here.

But Dallas's eyes darkened at her words.

"Good to hear it." Grant's expression turned predatory. "Thank you for being so gracious." His gaze washed over her, estimating, calculating.

Should she let him think he had the upper hand? Arrogant men were easier to trip. But she'd never cared enough to play games. As an accountant, she'd never sold her looks, only her skills.

Dallas interjected, "The police didn't find anything suspicious inside the cottage except that several surfaces were wiped down."

Hmm. To remove fingerprints?

Grant brought the cup to his lips. His facial lines seemed too smooth for his age. Was it because he lived not caring about anything or anybody, or from plastic surgery? Again, that wasn't a kind thought. Argh. "I still want to see inside the cottage."

So did Skylar. "We don't have keys, but I can give you the local caretaker's name and phone number. He could give you access as he did to the police, considering the circumstances."

"I'm sure he will." Grant's eyes narrowed.

Uh-oh. Did he expect to steamroll everyone here? He was in for a surprise then. Skylar hid a mocking smile by taking another sip of her tea.

"We should talk to Dad's maid here." Grant drummed his fingers on the weathered, scratched table, attracting her attention to another diamond, this one on his pinkie.

"He didn't have a maid at the cottage," Grandma said.

Grant frowned. "Strange. He *always* had a maid."

They lived in different worlds. Skylar had started working as soon as she reached the legal age to do so, mostly as a waitress at her aunt's restaurant but sometimes also as a maid at the local hotel during the tourist season. Plus, she'd picked up whatever painting jobs she could find. Most of her income had gone to living expenses, especially after Grandma had to retire from the bakery. The rest Skylar had set aside for her college fund before she'd won an art scholarship, allowing herself only a little for art supplies, hoping she could see those as business investments.

Her mother had never gotten an art degree, marrying young and becoming a mom ten months afterward. Had part of Skylar wanted to live her mother's dream then, just like Marina had to live her father's? Or was this Skylar's way to keep her mother in her life for a while longer?

She had tried to escape those questions before, but it was difficult to escape them now. Both could be reasons, but art also used to make her happy and inspired just like Dallas had. Another loss, another regret. The tea turned sour in her stomach.

Grandma took a few more sips, her hand shaking again. "Okay, here's what I know. Earl said that most things at work he could handle remotely but sometimes things came up and he needed to be present. During all his time here in town, he never had to leave. Until a week ago. He looked distraught before leaving. Worried."

"Did he say what the issue was or how long he'd be gone?" Grant asked, the picture of a concerned son again.

Had he taken some acting lessons? Or was she suspicious for nothing? She should give him the benefit of the doubt.

"No." Grandma rubbed her forearms as if she were cold.

Skylar got up and brought her a tawny-hued crocheted shawl and a soft matching crocheted blanket, both thin and faded by now. She put the shawl over her grandmother's bony shoulders and spread the blanket over her legs.

Grandma sighed, misery in her eyes. "I should've asked, but I didn't."

"You didn't know this was going to happen." Skylar took her grandmother's hands in hers. She should be more compassionate to Grant. If something happened to her grandmother... Skylar's gut twisted again, more painfully this time. She couldn't even imagine it.

"I hope your father is okay." She turned to Grant, softening her gaze. "Could anyone wish him harm at his job?"

"He retired five years ago. I think he took on this consulting gig out of boredom. Or maybe to feel useful. Or both. He never mentioned having arguments with anyone at the company."

"Any friends at his job? Someone we can ask?" Skylar pressed on.

Grant spread his arms. "Sorry. I don't know." A text beeped on his phone. He read it. "Hart just arrived."

Skylar leaped to her feet and hurried to open the door for her. But the moment she flung the door open, she halted, staring at the woman walking up the porch steps.

There was something vaguely familiar in the posture, wasn't there?

Maybe if the woman's hair was covered with a straw hat and her face was hidden behind large sunglasses and she was wearing red lipstick... And if her hair was ice blond instead of ash brown like now... Different shoes, different clothes, different jewelry, but... Could this woman, now in joggers, tank top, and running shoes, be the one who sat two tables away from them at Auntie's restaurant?

Skylar's gaze moved down the road. And could this sleek white car with tinted windows be the one that trailed her a day ago?

"Hello. I'm Skylar. You must be Hart Lane. Please come on in." Skylar plastered a smile on her face with about as much authenticity as the one she got in return. She waved at another part of the family her grandmother intended to marry into, then stepped aside to let the woman pass.

"Hello, Skylar. A great pleasure to meet you." A distinct floral perfume with a note of pear glided into the house.

Skylar stilled. She remembered the scent from Auntie's restaurant. People who wore disguises needed to remember to change their scents. Or maybe it hadn't been a disguise and just a different style that day. Besides, the surf and turf restaurant was a public place and a popular one. It could be a coincidence Hart had happened to have lunch there then. Because why would Earl's daughter need to follow Skylar and Dallas and eavesdrop on their conversation? Did Hart seriously suspect them of harming her father?

How would this all affect her kind and sometimes too-trusting grandma? Concern constricted Skylar's rib cage, but she kept her smile intact as she returned to the round table.

Was all this her admittedly vivid imagination? Or were there more players in the game than she'd realized? And what kind of game were they playing, exactly?

Chapter Ten

Skylar's heart fluttered as she opened her grandmother's front door the next day and waved Dallas in. "Hey there. Come on in."

What was happening to her? She wasn't a lovestruck teenager any longer with naïve dreams. She was a rational adult with no more illusions.

Yet every time she saw him again, every time she *thought* about him—and she'd thought about him constantly since returning to her hometown—her heart did this weird dance in her chest.

He stepped inside. "I, um, I brought something for you." He adjusted the easel's strap on his shoulder.

"Oh. Right. Thank you." If she hadn't stared into his baby blues so long, she'd have noticed the easel and the large box in his hands right away. Curiosity won over. "What's in the box? I mean, I appreciate it, but you shouldn't have."

She thought she could guess, and it gave her mixed feelings. Just as the fact that he still wanted anything to do with her gave her mixed feelings—surprise, regret, hope, gratitude, and many others she didn't dare name.

Hope could be a dangerous thing, though. For so long, she'd hoped her parents would return. Look where that had led her.

"Is it okay if I place the rest on the coffee table?" He slid the easel on the floor.

"Sure." She edged a couple of Grandma's colorful crocheting magazines aside.

"I hope you like these. Kai said they had an extra supply of frames at the store." Dallas took out frames, canvases, paintbrushes, paints, and a palette.

Tears prickled behind her eyes. "I–I don't know what to say. I can't even promise I'll use any of this. I don't paint anymore."

"There are things for watercolors here, too."

A lump grew in her throat as she stroked one exquisite picture frame, the surface smooth and familiar beneath her fingertips even after all these years. She didn't dare even touch a paintbrush. What would it feel like to hold one, to wield it? Her heartbeat kicked up speed, and she stifled the emotion with a deep breath, pressing it down, burying it and that part of her soul. "You know what I mean."

With his gaze so understanding, it nearly ripped her apart. "I don't want you to promise anything." At least, he didn't add *because you broke your main promise to me*. "I just wanted you to have this. Just in case."

"But... but it's too much."

He shook his head. "No. I only hope it's enough."

For a few moments, no words passed between them. Then she gestured for him to step through the French doors onto the terrace. With wisteria overhanging them, they overlooked the turquoise ocean as it caressed pale sand while seagulls greeted a new day—or maybe signaled where the fish were. She longed to look at him, but it would be too painful. She longed to find the right words, but did the right words even exist in this situation?

He'd always been her biggest supporter.

She dragged her bare toes across a patio stone, letting her big toe trace the asymmetrical outline of one painted in cobalt blue. "I used to watch my mother paint on the beach or the terrace. It felt magical to me. I know lots of children liked to draw. But to me, drawing was trying to be part of her world where she seemed to disappear. It was one of my connections to her. And then... it was the only connection."

Her throat clogged up, and breathing became difficult. As her eyes became misty, she turned away and blinked furiously, keeping the tears at bay. The independent, self-sufficient woman she'd become didn't cry.

"I'm sorry she hurt you so badly. A parent abandoning her child... I can't understand how she could do it." Emotion roughened his voice. His hand touched hers, his palm callused from manual labor, but he withdrew fast.

She missed his touch immediately. And she always missed *him*. The void he'd left in her life had never been filled. Could never get filled, no matter what she'd told herself. But unlike with her parents' disappearance, she'd dug the ravine between her and Dallas herself, and then filled it with alligators for good measure.

He didn't realize it, but his words about her mother nearly ripped her apart. She'd managed to keep it all within for years, but it was getting more and more difficult.

It wasn't his fault because he still had no idea what had really happened. She opened her mouth to tell him, then reminded herself she needed to keep her promise. Even years later, she couldn't take the risk. Would she ever be able to stop carrying this huge burden pressing on her heart?

Some things she could tell, though, and many he already knew. She stared at the endless beauty of the ocean. Both her parents loved the ocean, though for different reasons and in a different way. One of the cottony clouds looked like her mother's palette.

"In some ways, she'd sort of checked out long before she disappeared." She spoke slowly. "I became Daddy's girl by default. Now I think she got married way too young and wasn't ready to be a wife and a mother. I don't know what she wanted, but our family wasn't it. My father loved her a lot, and she just... accepted that love. It wasn't just running away with another guy for her, but running away from the life she didn't want. After she left, Dad mangled all her paintings and watercolors with a saw and threw them away with all her art supplies."

"I'm sorry that happened."

She shuddered. "He drove far away to toss them out. I would've dived into a dumpster to retrieve them." She swallowed around the lump in her throat. "He threw away everything of hers she didn't take with her. *Everything.*"

The word felt as sharp as a razor and hurt just as much. "He gave away furniture and anything useful, gutting our house to bare walls. Empty." Exactly the way she'd felt then—gutted, empty. She gripped the jade-green—like the shutters—railing, the surface rough under her hands, like the bark of a tree but more protruding. It could use a fresh coat of paint, something she needed to do before she left Port Sunshine.

She suppressed a grimace because she didn't want to leave. Her resolve to return to Charleston could use a fresh coat of paint, as well. She'd covered her memories with so many layers she'd thought she'd never peel it down to the original one. But now she did, stripping all the layers with acid. After all, her large supply of acid had been eating at her soul for so long.

He grunted. "I understand he was hurt deeply." He would know. She'd seemingly done the same thing to him. "But"—he kept talking—"it wasn't right of him to do that. Or to take down your drawings from the refrigerator and throw away your crayons and paper and forbid you to draw."

"Dad wanted to erase anything connected with Mom. But I was her spitting image, except for the hair, of course, and he couldn't erase me." She stumbled and turned to Dallas, her eyes dry as they should be. "I mean, he loved me. Took care of me unless he was at sea. Besides Grandma, he'd been the one to brush my hair or put shoes on my feet. I loved him back. But he became a different man after she left. Often the same thing is the source of our greatest love and greatest pain." In more senses than one.

Surely, Dallas knew what she meant. He'd been her greatest love and leaving him her greatest pain. Perhaps he'd felt the same about her. But that's not what they were discussing, was it?

"True." He leaned to her as if he wanted to hug her but seemed to stop himself. "And still unfair to you."

"Thanks for sticking with me then. For finding ways to see me despite my dad." Her father had cut all ties with her mother's sister, which meant Skylar couldn't see her cousins anymore. Which meant she couldn't go to the ranch where she might see them.

Dallas had gone out of his way to see her during those traumatic two months before *everything* changed.

She closed her eyes to compose herself, then opened them. He was so close she could nearly feel his breath on her skin, get a lungful of his intoxicating scent of cedar and juniper notes. Yet an ocean still spread between them. Might be for the better because the compassion in his blue eyes already cut her to the core. If he tried to touch her, she'd come undone.

Back to the pressing matters. She straightened her spine. "Do you know whether the police are making any progress in finding Earl?"

"No." A muscle twitched in his jaw. "I mean, I heard there was no progress yet. How is your grandmother holding up?"

A deep sigh left her lungs. "About as you can imagine. Confused and worried. She's with my aunt right now, and she took Breeze with her. Auntie is applying the therapy of cooking and consuming hearty food. I did some research online about Earl and his family and coworkers, but it wasn't enough." She hesitated. "Sorry I dragged you into this mess."

"You didn't." He pulled off his cowboy hat and forked his fingers through his flattened hair, the rich russet brown glowing in the sunlight. "My brother, Barrett, is a private investigator. I can ask him for help if you'd like."

"Yes, please," she said without thinking.

Then she second-guessed herself. Was it a good idea? She'd done things without thinking as a child, and she'd regretted it now.

But how else could she help her grandmother? Skylar was out of her league with investigating, and she'd advanced at her job partly because she knew what she was good at and where she had limitations.

"Thank you." She sent him a grateful glance and nearly stepped in for a hug. But like he'd done minutes ago, she stopped herself. She lifted her face and let the ocean breeze caress her skin since she couldn't let his fingers do the same.

He'd always seemed to know how to help her. Well, when she'd let him. No, she'd never been a helpless kitten. Neither had she been displaced from reality like her mother had seemed to be. But unfurling the sails and sailing off on the tumultuous seas of life had been much easier when Skylar had known he'd always be her safe haven to come to in the storm.

"I need to go through the things in the attic," she surprised herself by saying. "Grandma hasn't been there in ages, and she asked me to. I should do some things for her while I'm here."

He winced at her words *while I'm here*, and she chastised herself. No need to remind him. She'd be leaving soon enough. Her heart shifted painfully. No need to remind herself, either.

Okay, she wouldn't just be looking through boxes for her grandmother. She had a selfish reason. As well as a reason she hadn't made it to the attic yet.

"I can help you move boxes and such." Understanding shadowed his eyes. "And I'll remove cobwebs from the way and make sure no spiders linger nearby."

She should thank him and tell him she'd do it herself. She could lift boxes and carry herself and had done both plenty of times. But, well, the spiders... Her lips curved up a little. "You're my hero."

His neck pinked. "Oh please. I'm no hero."

"You are to me. Always will be," she whispered.

He already stood tall, but her words made him stand even taller.

She'd accepted his help not only because of the spiders or because she hoped she could find some things in the attic by some miracle. But also because she'd always enjoyed being around him. When she'd been a traumatized, confused, abandoned child, he'd coaxed her out of the hole she'd curled up in, and she'd leaned into him like a fragile flower to sunshine. Because he'd been that sunshine to her for so long.

And fine, she needed his calm presence in the storm her life had become again with Grandma's fiancé's disappearance. But there was so much more to it, and it was dangerous for her heart to analyze it.

"Thank you." The corners of his lips lifted slightly, curving his trimmed beard around them. Even his half smile did strange things to her heart, and her gaze lingered on his lips longer than it should have. Knowing how they tasted didn't help.

Oh how she craved his touch or his kiss—fine, both!—that could raise her on such a high wave of sweet abandon. She had a great imagination, but she didn't need it here.

His breathing seemed to go shallow, too. Close, so close, yet so far away. That moat she'd built still yawned between them, but she'd jump into the alligator-infested waters to reach him. Not a rational thought there, was it? She tore her gaze away and stepped inside the house before she could do something reckless and kiss him.

Inside, the lavender scent still hung in the air from the cleaning solution she'd scrubbed the tile floors with this morning. She'd done lots of laundry for Grandma, too, though the faint scent of clean sheets might be her imagination.

But no clean scent greeted her when she climbed the narrow wooden staircase, following Dallas instead of leading the way because, again, spiders. "Be careful, in case one of the wooden planks has broken." Maybe that was another reason he'd volunteered to go first. She watched where she stepped.

"You, too. So far so good." He made it to the attic, carrying paper towels and a cleaning spray, and waved away the cobweb. "Only one cobweb and no spiders in the vicinity. And no other, um, guests." He put the cleaning supplies on one of the boxes and pulled her up.

"Thanks." The brief contact sent a wave of awareness through her. They were alone here, and the feeling was sharp and delicious like spicy food and even more dangerous.

No.

Off-limits.

The narrow attic seemed much smaller than when she'd been a child. It smelled musty, and specks of dust danced in beams of sunlight. Boxes seemed to multiply since she'd last been here. Most of them she didn't remember, but she did remember a heavy antique trunk.

Heat crouched in the rafters, pouncing as they ascended. Dust tickled her nose, and she sneezed several times.

"Bless you. And bless you again." He smiled. "Would you like me to bring you a dust mask?"

"I should be okay." She sneezed a few more times, sending more specks dancing. Hopefully, it also sent any lingering spiders running. "At this point, you can just say bless you a thousand times."

"Bless you a thousand times."

"Thanks." She approached boxes covered by a thick layer of dust. "What do I expect to find here?" She shivered. Did she even want to know?

She wiped down the first box with paper towels, then opened it. Books. She separated the ones she'd read while growing up to donate to the library and wrote down the titles of her grandmother's books.

"I hope it's something good. I know your father threw away your mother's dresses, but maybe you'll find one he didn't notice."

"No." Skylar blanched as the image of a red raincoat open to reveal a matching red dress emblazoned her mind. She straightened fast, her insides shaking.

Dallas stepped closer. Concern etched the chiseled features that begged to go on a canvas again. "Did I say something wrong? You once mentioned you wished you had your mom's dresses. But now you look like you've seen a ghost."

Because she did see a ghost. In her mind. She suppressed a shudder as if she were still in that cold night. Then she pushed the memories away with a familiar effort. "No, you didn't say anything wrong. She... she had pretty dresses, and a lot of them she made herself. She said I could have them when I grew up."

Skylar had even tried them on, dreaming of the time they'd fit her. Her mother was as pretty as a spring flower. Slim, with full pink lips, expressive hazel eyes, and cherry-hued hair, her skin gentle like petals—Skylar remembered soft kisses on the cheek every morning. Even the scent of her perfume was something floral and gentle.

Skylar's burly father, with legs as thick as trunks, unshaven with skin rough like tree bark—from the times he'd had little Skylar to climb onto his lap, rather resembled an oak. Her parents were opposites in appearance and character, and there was a seven-year-age difference, as well. According to Grandma, her son had courted Skylar's mother for a long time before she'd agreed to become his wife. Of course, Grandma had never said so in his presence.

Had Skylar's mother seen a mighty oak to rely on in him, as well?

Skylar had never met either one of her grandfathers, but her mother had always referred to her dad with great affection. He'd arrived in their small town with two little girls in tow, girls he'd doted on, and had settled there. He'd never said what had happened to the girls' mother. They'd remained somewhat outsiders, keeping to themselves. He'd homeschooled both girls, and they all had rarely been seen in town. Mom's more sociable sister had still made a few friends, but Mom hadn't.

Skylar's father had started courting the young beautiful artist when she'd taken a job with the florist. He'd become her best customer and gifted her back all the flowers he'd bought. She'd been polite but had declined to go out with him. All that occurred almost a year before her father had been diagnosed with cancer. A year after her father died, to the surprise of the Port Sunshine locals, they'd gotten married. On the wedding photos in Auntie's photo album, Mom appeared distant, but Dad had a huge grin. In all those photos, he gazed at Mom while she peered somewhere far away. In the gentle lace of her wedding gown, she looked like a mist about to disappear soon.

The age gap and the timing disturbed Skylar. As if her mother had been in grief rather than in love. Unlike Dallas's father with his wife and children, Skylar's dad had never been violent with his family members, and he'd loved his wife and daughter with a passion. He'd always said they were his entire world. But even though her mother had a sister, it felt to Skylar now as if her mother had been desperate for emotional support and a friend then. What she'd received instead was a husband. And while spouses could be and should be friends, it wasn't the same.

"I don't want Mom's dresses any longer." Especially the one that now looked like a bloodstain in Skylar's mind. "I don't even wear dresses anymore." Her wardrobe mostly consisted of business suits for work and sweatshirts or T-shirts and sweatpants for home.

"You used to."

"Yeah." Her voice echoed in the attic and her hollow heart as she did her best to ignore nostalgia. "Exactly. I used to. Now let's see what we have here."

She opened the box labeled Wedding. It wasn't her parents' wedding. Her father had thrown out anything connected to it and had probably burned it. If it wasn't for the treasured photos and keepsakes her aunt had supplied, Skylar wouldn't have a single one.

Nothing.

She swallowed the growing lump in her throat.

This was a legacy nonetheless as she stroked the album cover's cracked leather surface. Her grandmother's wedding photos, the cover and pages yellowed from age. Beneath it, she unearthed champagne flutes decorated with faded pale-blue ribbons, centerpieces with artificial flowers, and...

Gently, respectfully, she lifted the dress, the fabric taking on a champagne hue but still holding on. Something shifted inside her. "Grandma's wedding gown." Grandma had given her permission to wear it for her wedding to Dallas, but the wedding had never happened.

Ooooh, she'd love to have her grandmother's dress, with lots of lace on the bodice and a tulle skirt. Skylar would look like a swan, and she wanted to.

Well, no point thinking about it because she'd never get married. There was only one man she'd wanted to marry in her entire life, and she'd messed it up too much.

She swallowed hard and folded the dress, the silky fabric refined and glossy under her fingertips. "This box is for keepers. Let's keep moving." The way *she* had to.

Her mother hadn't worn this dress. Did she betray Mom by stopping painting? Doing what she'd loved, carrying on, would've been one way to honor her. Skylar had failed even there.

Now her mother had disappeared like seafoam. One more thing Skylar had to blame herself for, and the knife of guilt turned again.

"Sure." He hesitated as if he wanted to say something else, but then brought another box. It had Skylar's name on it.

"Mom was very talented," she said defensively.

"You are, too." He studied her.

His admiration always put wind in her sails, but she didn't deserve it now. Curiosity piqued, she opened the box. "Let's see what we have here."

It held her own paintings, the few she hadn't offered for sale before leaving for college, or rather, the ones Grandma had talked her into keeping. Skylar touched the surface of the canvas with raised paint strokes where a young girl in a canary-yellow dress ran barefoot along the tide, her long golden-bronze hair flowing in the breeze. A seashell bracelet adorned her wrist. Her arm was raised high as she waved at someone beyond the painting, beyond reach.

Out of habit, she reached for the smooth fabric of her blouse that hid the necklace Dallas had given her. She'd never taken off his necklace. But he wasn't wearing the one she'd given him. Not that she could blame him.

"I remember the first easel you built for me," she said slowly.

He shrugged. "It was wobbly."

"I remember the frames you made."

He glanced away. "They were crooked."

"They were the best I'd ever seen. It... it meant a lot to me that you put so much effort into them."

"I wanted to. And they were nothing compared to your work."

"They were everything to me." *You were everything to me.* She stopped the words before they slipped from her tongue.

They went through several more boxes, and some she put aside and marked for donation. Three boxes he took to the living room to throw away if Grandma agreed.

She tugged on the antique trunk, but it didn't budge. "Huh. Must be locked."

"Maybe your grandmother has some valuable jewelry there."

"It's not Grandma's. It's my aunt's. Grandma said she just provided the storage for it." The request was weird to start with. "Okay, I imagine only my aunt has the key." Curiosity stirred in her, but she suppressed it. Other people's secrets weren't her business.

Then Dallas and Skylar reached one more box. Crumpled paper and crumpled yellowed newspapers padded mason jars with seashells and pebbles also wrapped in paper.

Skylar unwrapped and rewrapped every one of them after examining them. Then before she was about to rewrap the last one, she gasped.

What was used as wrapping paper was a watercolor, the image on the internal side. And it wasn't Skylar's watercolor, though she recognized herself immediately. She was about five years old and walking hand in hand with a woman on the beach. Skylar wore a pretty dress with a pink rose pattern and matching shoes. They both wore straw hats her mother had decorated with yellow jessamines collected from their garden. Grandma used to garden then. Must be one of those rare days when Mom had been fully present.

"Dad didn't see this one," Skylar whispered.

Dallas's hand covered hers. "It's a good thing he didn't, right?"

Skylar wasn't sure because it caused an avalanche of emotions. But then gratitude expanded her chest. She pointed at the girl. "That's me there."

His eyes narrowed. "It's so gut-wrenching that she never showed up again. That she made no contact with the entire family. Never called you. Never answer your grandmother's or her sister's calls."

"She couldn't," she said before she had a chance to stop herself.

His eyebrows rose. He didn't ask her to elaborate, and she didn't volunteer.

How would her life have turned out if she hadn't *ever* remembered what happened that stormy night? If she hadn't done that painting of a woman in a red raincoat before she'd realized she shouldn't have? Or if she'd chosen a different path after she'd received the threatening call?

She'd told herself she'd been protecting her grandmother and Dallas. Instead, she'd been protecting herself. She'd been a coward. She'd chosen the path of least resistance, and several people had paid for it. Dallas probably most of all, through no fault of his.

Her eyes widened as she tasted salt on her lips.

"Don't cry." He swiped her tear with his thumb. "Please don't cry."

"I didn't realize I was crying." Her smile was as wobbly as he'd claimed her first easel was.

"Your mother isn't worth your tears." His voice hardened.

"She is. She was. Everyone makes mistakes. She paid for hers." Skylar felt like she was sliding on a slippery road. One leading down to alligators of guilt.

"You forgave her?"

"One day, I'll tell you everything, I hope. But not today." She sank onto one of the sturdier boxes with nothing breakable inside because her legs went weak.

"You don't have to."

"These are selfish tears. I'm crying for myself. For my mistakes. For us. For the things that could've been." She searched his eyes. "Will you ever be able to forgive me?" Asking that question was also selfish, but she was on a roll.

"Don't you know it? I already have." He wiped her tears, the gesture so gentle the caress seemed to touch her heart.

"How can you do that so easily?" She'd been right before. His touch, even fleeting, even only meant to comfort, even amid emotional turmoil, caused her to come undone.

His eyes darkened. "It hasn't been easy. Far from it. But it's worth it. You're worth it."

"Am I?"

"Yes."

All her emotions heightened to an unbelievable degree. A dusty attic was far from a romantic place, and she didn't deserve his touch or forgiveness.

But all rational thought evaporated as his fingers lingered on her skin, finding a familiar path. All the years of being rational and analytical, of suppressing her memories and emotions seemed to evaporate like a morning mist.

Without thinking, without questioning, she rose to her feet. Then, on her tiptoes, she wove her arms around his neck, finding a familiar path, as well. Her pulse skyrocketed as he dipped his head, a question in his eyes. She should pull away. She absolutely should.

Instead, she met him halfway and brushed her lips against his. His kiss was like his touch, gentle at first, but she deepened it, and he responded.

It was just like she'd remembered and yet somehow a thousand times better. Maybe because now it wasn't one of many, but the only one after fifteen years of longing and waiting. Every cell in her body responded to him, ecstatic, starved, and delighted. A delicious wave swept her up.

Once again, she was young, carefree, and filled with hopes and dreams. Once again, she believed happiness was possible and love could last. She went liquid like the ocean and refused to think, to know, to remember.

She clung to him like a sailor to flotsam after a shipwreck. *She* was the shipwreck, though, but right now, it didn't matter because he'd always seen her only as beautiful and complete.

With each kiss, she drank him in, and yet she was more and more thirsty.

The growl of a motor approaching the street registered in the back of her mind, but she didn't want the kiss to stop. She didn't ever want it to stop.

Ever.

Chapter Eleven

How did he end up in this situation?

Dallas helplessly eyed the bright balloons, motley paper plates, gigantic banners, and a myriad of other items at a party supply store.

"What do you think of these paper bells?" Pairs of eyes belonging to Skylar and Mrs. Rafferty, respectively, searched him.

He mentally scrambled for the right word. "It's... it's nice."

Mrs. Rafferty scrunched her nose. "Just nice?" She turned to her granddaughter. "Let's keep looking."

Dallas cringed. Apparently, *nice* wasn't the right word here. "I meant fabulous! Great!"

But Skylar and her grandmother had already disappeared further into the wedding decoration aisles. He swallowed hard as he stared at the endless shelves and shifted from one foot to the other. It was going to be a long day.

Even with the groom absent and his location unknown, Skylar's grandmother continued their wedding preparations. Maybe, in her mind, that would bring Earl back somehow.

Lord, please help Mrs. Rafferty. Um, and if it's okay to ask, please guide me on what to say next time they ask me about bells, ribbons, flowers, and whatnot so we can get out of here in my lifetime.

With Mrs. Rafferty present on the drive to the city and now in the store, neither Dallas nor Skylar had mentioned the elephant in the room.

Their kiss.

His heartbeat went into overdrive just at the memory of the kiss Mrs. Rafferty's return home had interrupted. When she'd come inside and suggested they head into the city to shop for wedding things, he'd eagerly tagged along. Just like he now tagged along after Skylar to a new row of shelves. Did that wondrous kiss change the dynamics between them? Or did it matter to him way more than it mattered to her?

He frowned.

What if for her it had just been a way to find comfort in the familiar while in emotional distress? One would think it would be easier to navigate these things with age. But he'd been much more confident where he and Skylar had been standing when he'd been a teenager.

"What do you think about these ribbons?" Skylar pointed at white silk ones.

This time, he was prepared. "They are *fabulous*."

"Really?" Skylar tilted her head. "I thought those light-blue ones would be better."

He suppressed a groan, then remembered to plaster a smile he hoped didn't resemble a scowl. "You're right. Those are better."

Then his heart squeezed. He'd always imagined he'd be shopping for wedding decorations—even if the shopping part wouldn't be entirely voluntary—for his and Skylar's wedding, not someone else's.

But here they were. And here he was, wishing for things that couldn't be.

After two very slow-moving hours, he carried an astonishing number of shopping bags to Skylar's car and placed them in the back. He didn't even want to think about setting those decorations up, but he already knew he'd either volunteer or be voluntold by his mother.

He opened the car doors first for Mrs. Rafferty, then once she was safely inside, for Skylar.

Skylar placed her hand on his, giving him a jolt of awareness and reminding him of the wonderful moment those same hands wrapped around his neck and brought her closer to him. "Thank you. You didn't have to do any of this. I know shopping isn't your thing. It's amazing you still want to be around me in the first place. And yet here you are." Her eyes glistened.

"Here I am." He echoed, the emotion in her eyes touching something deep inside him. "I'll always be there, whenever and however you need me."

"I need you. Far more than you realize." Her gaze lingered on him, vulnerable and longing. "I'm not saying this because I need you to carry my bags. Or to carry my burdens. Though it helps. I"—based on the movement of her neck, she swallowed hard—"I just need you to exist and... and not let me push you away."

His throat went dry. "I'll do my best, but I also want you to have the freedom of choice."

"I know." Raw emotion gleamed in her eyes, more exposed than he'd ever seen, even in the times when she'd been open with him and the world. Then she slipped into the driver's seat.

He perked up as he closed the door, then rounded the car. To think about it, shopping for decorations wasn't bad at all. He'd sign up for another round if it meant being near her. He got the answer to his unspoken question. The dynamics between them *had* changed. But would it be enough?

Soon, he folded himself into the small sedan's passenger seat, wishing for the space of his truck. But it was too high for Mrs. Rafferty to climb into, so he didn't mind going in Skylar's car. It also gave him the whiff of her peach shampoo that made his head spin.

They buckled up, and she drove off. Without having to drive and keep his focus on the road, he enjoyed the luxury of looking at her lovely profile. The raw emotion was gone from her face, and her features rearranged into a measured expression. Yet he'd never get tired of looking at his favorite face in the world, taking in her soft cheeks, pert nose, and dainty chin.

As a teen, she'd dreamed of creating a masterpiece, not realizing *she* was God's masterpiece already. Though now she resembled one of those paintings where fresh layers of paint were meant to conceal something far more valuable beneath them.

Of course, he was far from the art world, so what did he know?

"What kind of food would you like for lunch?" Skylar's melodic voice interrupted his thoughts.

He shrugged. "I'm not picky. Tex-Mex ahead looks good."

The corners of her lips curved up. "I was asking Grandma, but that sounds good to me. Grandma?"

"Looks good to me, too, dear."

Skylar pulled into the parking lot.

Minutes later, they were all seated in a corner booth well away from the noisier section by the takeout counter. The bright music danced in the air scented with grilled meat and onions while they munched cheery-orange nachos and fire-red salsa.

As they waited for their orders, Skylar leaned forward and lowered her voice. "Did your brother find out anything interesting?"

She didn't need to say which brother. And he should've told her and Mrs. Rafferty already, but he selfishly didn't prolong the shopping spree by distracting them.

His throat suddenly dry, he sipped his lemonade, the liquid tangy and refreshingly cold. "I'll forward what Barrett sent me so far to you. But a few details stood out to me. Earl's daughter Hart fell for a guy who bled her dry and then disappeared. Hart's neighbor heard her and Earl arguing about money, and then Earl stormed out. Oh, and his son's latest project ended up being a flop. Grant's usual backers turned away from him. There's a new project he's been courting, but he'll have to sell some of his things or find funds elsewhere."

"Oh, I remember now." Mrs. Rafferty held up a finger. "Earl told me Grant wanted him to finance his new project, promising it was going to be a hit. But Earl refused. Movies weren't his kind of thing."

"I imagine it caused a rift between them." Skylar scooped up salsa with a chip.

Her grandmother grimaced. "I think so."

A waitress brought their orders, so they stopped talking until she walked away.

He breathed in the enticing aroma of grilled beef fajitas with onions and green peppers that came with ginger-hued rice and a salad artfully arranged on the plate in vibrant splashes of green, red, brown, and orange.

Mrs. Rafferty took a forkful of her cheesy enchiladas, which arrived accompanied by the same feast for the eye and tongue of rice and salad. "But they wouldn't do something to their father, right? I mean, they're family."

Family.

The memory of his father's slaps and yells made Dallas wince, and his fingers tightened around a fork as hard and cold as his father's heart. The delicious fajita turned to rubber in his mouth.

He flushed it down with more lemonade. "Um, I hope they wouldn't. There's another suspect, as well. One of Earl's friends, Terrence Hirst, claimed Earl stole his ideas. According to Earl's household staff, Terrence even showed up at Earl's doorstep, yelling threats. He wasn't allowed to enter and was escorted from the premises."

Skylar's eyes lit up, and she thudded her water glass back on the table. "It's worth looking into further." Then she turned to her grandmother. "Remember, you said someone showed up on your porch, looking for Earl, saying he was a friend?"

"Yeah, but when I described the guy, Earl said he didn't have a friend like that."

Dallas's eyes narrowed, and he placed the fork back on his plate. He had an idea, and the result could be more than furthering the investigation. Would it work? His heart skipped a beat. "If an artist drew a rendering of that man, do you think you could recognize him?"

Mrs. Rafferty sighed. "Our police station is too small. They don't have an artist on staff." Then understanding dawned in her pale eyes, and she blinked them rapidly behind her thick glasses. "Oh!" She fished in her purse, then plunked a pencil on the table between her and Skylar. "Do you think you could draw a portrait for me?"

Skylar's eyes widened, and her fork clattered to the plate as she eyed the innocent pencil as if it were going to start jabbing her. Her pupils dilated, her mouth slid open, and she didn't say a word.

The pause stretched. "If you can, I believe it would help a lot." He held his breath.

Why did this small step seem so significant? It was just a drawing. She'd done thousands of them since the time she'd known how to hold a crayon. But not anymore. Dallas and Mrs. Rafferty exchanged a glance while Skylar's gaze stayed on the pencil.

She didn't even blink. "It's important, right?"

"Yes, dear."

Thank you, Mrs. Rafferty!

Skylar's hand slipped toward the pencil, then stopped. Then moved again.

After what seemed like an eternity, she nodded. "It's been a while since I did any drawings, but I guess I can try."

"Now, we just need some paper," Skylar's grandmother said.

Skylar flipped her paper place mat with its cartoon cacti to the blank side. "Not ideal, but why not?"

Dallas and Mrs. Rafferty seemed to exhale at the same time. "Great."

Skylar twisted the pencil in her fingers. "I don't guarantee the results."

"No expectations, Little Miss." Her grandmother patted her hand. "But even when I had expectations for you, you always exceeded them."

Skylar's eyes glistened again. "Thanks, Grandma."

Dallas's throat felt as parched as if he'd worked in the sun the entire day. He drained his glass of ice-cold water. He just hoped Skylar wouldn't change her mind.

She placed the pencil on the table and gave due to her chicken fajitas. If before she'd just poked into her food, now her appetite seemed to return, and she was putting a dent in her food fast. "Would you mind describing again how the man looked?"

Mrs. Rafferty chewed on her enchiladas thoughtfully, then helped herself to guacamole. "Let me think. Tall, though not as tall as Dallas here. White hair slightly thinning and a white beard. I'd guess he was in his seventies. He was stooping a little."

Skylar pushed her nearly empty plate away and slid a paper place mat closer. "Any tattoos? Maybe scars?"

"Sorry, missy. Only a few liver spots on his hands. He didn't have a wedding band, either." Skylar's grandmother's cheeks pinked. "Not that I'd look at him that way. I'm dedicated to Earl, you know."

Present tense. Dallas and Skylar exchanged glances, and his heart contracted. Mrs. Rafferty still believed that Earl was okay and would be back someday, or at the very least, that they'd find him.

Dallas would hate to see her heart broken. He sent up a prayer. For his part, he'd do everything to find her fiancé, not only for Skylar but also for Mrs. Rafferty who'd always treated him as if he were her grandson.

"Of course, we know." Skylar cleared her throat while her hand with the pencil glided fast over the place mat. "His hair... was it short? Or did it reach his collar? What about his beard? Was it shortly trimmed? Longish?"

"Hold on." Her grandmother touched her forehead, then took a sip of her iced tea with a lemon wedge hanging on the side of the glass for dear life. "Shortly trimmed hair. Combed. Um, hair missing a little on the top. His beard and mustache were short, too. Well taken care of. Something about him seemed familiar, but I don't know what. Oh, also he had a birthmark on his right cheek."

"Good job. Shape of eyes? Were they close to each other?"

Skylar went over those questions, then the forehead, nose, and chin, and soon, those features, the clothes, and everything else appeared while her pencil flew over the paper, her movements unsure at first but more and more confident with each line until she scooted back. "Does this in any way resemble the person you've seen?"

Her grandmother gasped. "Yes! That's him!"

He leaned toward Skylar, his chest swelling. "You're still amazing, and you always will be."

She waved him off. "Oh please. It was no biggie." But her eyes sparkled again. Almost like they used to.

He sent up another heartfelt prayer, this time for Skylar. He didn't just want her to find herself again, to do what she loved because it might bring her back *to him*. That ship had sailed, and just the thought soured the fajitas in his stomach.

Rather, he simply wanted her to be happy. After all, wasn't that what love was about? For the person you love to be happy, whether with you or not?

Wait a minute. Had he fallen in love with her again? His eyes widened, and he hid his confusion by scooping up the rest of his guacamole with nachos.

No, he couldn't. It would mean so much heartache when she left.

Skylar drained her water glass and placed it on the table with a resolute gesture. "I'm ready unless someone wants dessert."

"I'm full. No dessert for me." Mrs. Rafferty tapped her gnarled fingers on the table.

He gestured to the waitress for the bill and found his voice again. "We should show the drawing to the police. And I can email it to Barrett to see if he can get this person identified. And if by any chance it can be Terrence." He fished out his phone from his jeans pocket and took photos, then sent them to his brother.

"Thanks, and yes." Skylar also snapped photos with her phone. "Absolutely, let's give a copy to the police. And maybe someone at the local hotels or the inns will recognize this person? At least, we'll know when he was here and if he had an alibi." Her expression changed, and fire lit her eyes again, igniting a new flare of longing through him.

After the visit to the police station, Skylar dropped off her grandmother at the sea cottage to rest.

Two hours and three visits to the hotels later, they had an answer to one of their questions, and it wasn't something he'd expected.

Mrs. Rafferty's mysterious guest hadn't left yet. He was still at a local motel.

Chapter Twelve

Today Skylar felt different. More alive than she'd felt in years. More optimistic than she'd felt in years. Before, she'd been trying to escape herself and her memories and the person who'd terrified her.

Today, blood rushed faster in her veins, and her heart whispered hope to her soul. She had two reasons for it.

She stole a glance at Dallas who walked by her side from the parking lot toward the motel. She'd talked him into visiting the guest. While growing up, he'd been the more sensible, and she the more reckless one. After she'd left her hometown, she'd gotten sensibility to spare, maybe because she'd had to go on without him.

Now excitement bubbled under her skin. Being able to draw again was one reason. But he was another one. After all the years of acting sensibly, no matter how much her mind told her to stay away from him, her heart didn't want to listen.

That must've been the reason her hand slipped into his as they walked to the motel, sending awareness jolting through her. Causing him to look at her with joyous surprise.

"Remember, how we used to walk hand in hand on the beach all the time?" she whispered, nostalgia cloaking her insides.

"Of course, I do." His voice softened. "I remember every moment I spent with you. I remember everything." He paused before adding, "Even when I didn't want to. But now, I want to."

Could she allow herself to cherish these precious minutes while he was still by her side? "I thought it was going to be that way forever."

"Me, too."

Regretfully, she took her hand out of his as they reached the door. She shouldn't be establishing the foundation of a new relationship if she couldn't commit to it. Her stomach clenched as she stepped inside the hall. She was just going to hurt him again.

This two-story motel with mustard walls and numbered doors wasn't one of Port Sunshine's most prestigious establishments, though it was by no means seedy.

Did the budget hotel mean Terrence wasn't doing so well? But that also meant they didn't have to go through the lobby and could have an element of surprise.

Once Dallas knocked on the fern-green door with intriguing symmetrical scratches close to the floor, Skylar wished they'd gone with his suggestion and found out more information about the guy. But she didn't want him to disappear before they visited him. A faint scent of vomit drifted to her, and she suppressed a grimace and her gag reflex, hoping it wasn't from *this* room.

When the door opened, the smile she plastered on took an effort to keep in place. But she could mentally pat herself on the back. She'd still got it. The man looked a lot like her portrait of him, except his white hair was now disheveled and tiny pieces of food were stuck in his unkempt beard. The slacks themselves likely didn't remember the last time they'd been ironed. The room stank a bit of rotting food and cigarette smoke, but not of vomit, thankfully. After all, she could only suppress her gag reflex so much.

Dallas moved forward, but the man's gaze stayed on her. "You're Dolores's granddaughter, aren't you?"

Startled, she nearly stumbled back. Huh. So not what she'd expected to hear. "Um, yes. I'm Skylar Rafferty, and this is my, um, my friend, Dallas Lawrence. But... how do you know my grandma?"

"I'm Terry Hirst." His gaze didn't waver from her.

Bingo! Skylar's smile became sincere. They were right, after all. Well, that explained his connection to Earl but not to her grandmother. And so far, Terrence was offering no clarification.

"My grandma's fiancé, Earl Lane, disappeared. Did you have something to do with it?" Right, just blurt it out. Not her wisest idea. She'd likely earned them a door in their faces. In her years alone, she'd learned to think before she'd spoken and to tread carefully. Where were those skills now? Being near Dallas, breathing in the intoxicating scent of his cologne must be affecting her brain too much.

Her mouth slackened when Terrence waved them in.

His shoulders slumped forward. "No, I don't have anything to do with Earl's disappearance. But I wish I had."

Hmm. Could they believe him? Dallas led her inside.

The man didn't invite them to sit, and she could understand why. Most available surfaces were taken with either clothes or empty takeout boxes and ashtrays. The stench of stale food and cigarettes was overpowering. Didn't the staff clean here?

Terrence didn't say anything, and the silence hung in the air as heavily as the stench. So Skylar looked at Dallas and gestured to him that she got it. She hoped.

Then she went with, "You and Earl used to be friends, right?"

His mouth formed a thin, resentful line. "Yes, and he used it against me. First, with taking my ideas and funds from our company and launching a new one. I tried to keep my company afloat but had to give up eventually."

First? Skylar raised an eyebrow. There was another betrayal, then?

"Do you have any proof?" Dallas planted his feet wide apart.

Too bad, she couldn't lean on him, but she hadn't had that luxury for fifteen years. Probably wouldn't ever have it again. She pulled her shoulders back. She did fine for herself. Only...

Well, never mind. Anyway, she could totally stand for a few minutes.

"No." Terrence swiped an empty takeout box onto the carpet and sank onto a chair. "It was my word against his."

Whom did she choose to believe? For now, she'd keep an open mind.

"You said, first. What was the next thing?" Might as well address the issue they could address.

The man's face hardened. "He took Dolores from me."

"Grandma?" Skylar's knees went weak, and it would've been better if she were sitting down.

Dallas hugged her, steadying her.

Terrence shrugged. "To you, she's a grandma. To me, she's the woman I fell for."

Her grandmother, a heartbreaker. Huh.

Skylar gaped like a proverbial fish out of water. Who could've expected this turn of events? "But... but... she didn't recognize you. I mean, she recognized you as a man who knocked on her door looking for Earl. But not as a..."

"A former suitor?" Terrence chuckled without mirth. "I admired her from afar. To her, I was one of many tourists who visited the pastry store where she worked."

"Your hair must be a wig and the beard is fake, right?" Dallas said.

"Yes. I knew I'd be the first suspect if something happened to Earl."

No kidding.

Still, wouldn't Grandma recognize the shape of the nose or lips? Oh right. The shape of the nose could be fake, too. It did look a bit different in her portrait.

Skylar moved closer, resisting the urge to breathe into her sleeve. "Why didn't you try to talk to her? Ask her out?"

Terrence studied a stain on the carpet Skylar was reluctant to identify. "I never had the courage to ask her out. It didn't take long to discover her story from folks in town. She'd gone through a lot, and she still kept her head high. She's a remarkable woman." Tight lips turned into a hint of a smile. "Not to mention, a great baker." He must've visited the pastry store a lot when she still worked there.

Skylar nodded. "That she is. Both."

Maybe the way to some men's hearts was through their stomachs indeed. She stole a glance at Dallas. Then she'd have to give up all hope.

Terrence's expression soured again. "Then my vacation was over. I figured with us living in different locations and busy with our jobs it wasn't meant to be, anyway. I expected to forget about her soon."

"But you didn't," Skylar said slowly. "Some women are unforgettable."

"They truly are," Dallas echoed.

Her heart fluttered while she was flattered. Could he have meant her?

"I kept thinking about her. I decided I'd return here for my next vacation and ask her out. But years passed, and my start-up needed me so much I couldn't take a vacation. Then I got sick for a while. When I got better, I made the mistake of telling Earl about her. Showed him booklets of the pastry store that included a photo of her."

Huh. Skylar had designed those booklets. "I thought photos of the bakers would be a nice personal touch."

"It was. Then I was so busy with the launch of our new products. After I had to lay people off because of Earl's betrayal, I had to try to do their work, too. I couldn't afford sleep, much less a vacation. And once I lost the company, what did I have to offer her?" His shoulders sloped, and misery weighed down his features.

"My grandmother isn't materialistic." Skylar did her best to process this.

"Yet Earl's status impressed her." Terrence's eyes narrowed. "Two years after taking everything from me, he called me out of the blue and told me he was going to marry Dolores—*my* Dolores. Now he was taking away even what I didn't have but wished to—her love."

"It's a beautiful story. But you do realize this gives you a double motive, right?" Dallas said.

Good point. Skylar rubbed her forehead. Swept away with the romance that never happened, she'd forgotten it could all be just that—a beautiful story. Were Terrence's words the truth, or was he playing them?

"Where were you..." Dallas named the date Earl had presumably disappeared.

Terrence rolled his eyes. "I was drinking in this hotel. By myself. So there's no one to verify my alibi."

That might be a good sign. If he'd done something to Earl, wouldn't the guy make an effort to organize an alibi first? Unless he'd acted out of anger. Maybe fueled by alcohol.

Time to bluff again. "Someone saw you near the cottage where Earl was staying. How do you explain that?"

"I went to talk it out with him."

Dallas raised an eyebrow. "Talk it out?"

"Fine." The guy groaned. "I had a gun with me. But the cottage was empty."

Dallas's stance shifted. "Did you discharge the gun in the air?"

"Yes." But there was no way to verify it. Terrence's gaze sharpened. "I suspect Earl's new dealings aren't all legal ones."

She tensed. "Why do you think so?"

"The new products created some waves. He told me we should take the investors' funds, put them in offshore accounts, and disappear. I–I kind of hope he's done that."

Was Terrence trying to throw shade on the person who'd allegedly betrayed him? Or did this have some merit? Or had someone made sure Earl disappeared?

"We have to tell everything to the police. And it would be better for you if you went with us." She softened her voice. He did mention a gun, and she didn't want him to reach for it.

"Yeah. I know." He hid his face in his hands, then finally, raised his chin. "Let me clean up and take off the disguise, and I'll go with you."

Would he try to bolt while "cleaning up"? She exchanged glances with Dallas.

But before she could say anything, Terrence added, "After all this is over and—and it's proven I'm right—do you think your grandmother would give me a chance?"

Oh boy.

"I DON'T KNOW WHAT TO make of that conversation," Dallas muttered as Skylar drove them to her grandmother's cottage. She'd asked to check on her grandmother before dropping him off at the ranch, and of course, he'd agreed.

She made a turn to the narrow street leading to the sea cottage. "Me neither. I hope that, between the police and maybe with the help of your PI brother, it'll get sorted out. Grandma deserves better than a missing fiancé and a secret suitor who might've killed him."

Well, one thing he had no doubts about. He was falling further and further for Skylar. He took in her beautiful profile—the sweep of her lashes over the curve of her cheeks and the cute quirk of her lips never failed to make his heartbeat go faster.

He wanted to tell her many things, but he had no clue where to even start. He needed to use this chance alone with her before the opportunity slipped like water through his fingers. He reached for her hand. "Skylar—"

"What is he doing here?" Her eyes widened.

He followed her gaze and suppressed a grimace. Dressed in an immaculate black suit and shiny leather shoes again, unusual attire for their small town, Grant was leaning on the hood of his swanky car, parked at the curb near her grandmother's cottage. A ridiculously gigantic bouquet of burgundy roses blossomed in his hands.

Just great.

"I'd love to know, as well," Dallas grumbled.

"I guess we're about to find out." At least, she didn't look excited to see the guy, so that was something.

She pulled up to the driveway. Grant's face split into a wide grin when she leaped out of the car. His grin became a bit strained when Dallas unfolded his frame from her tight passenger seat.

"Skylar! You look gorgeous. These flowers are for you." Grant didn't pay any attention to Dallas.

Dallas would've been fine with it if all the smarmy guy's attention wasn't directed at her. His gut tightened. What could he say? Yes, he was officially jealous.

"Thank you." Skylar moved forward, her expression neutral. "I believe you've met Dallas."

"Hello, Grant." Dallas didn't offer his hand.

"Hello." Grant looked at him as if he were an obstacle to circumvent.

Skylar continued, "I appreciate the flowers, but you shouldn't have."

Undeterred, Grant handed her the bouquet that emanated a sweet aroma. "They pale compared to your beauty."

Seriously? Dallas cringed as he followed her to the porch. How exactly could burgundy roses pale?

She hesitated, then accepted the flowers. "According to that logic, I'd be the color of beetroot then."

Bingo. Dallas attempted to suppress a grin but didn't try too much. And roses weren't her favorite flowers.

"I just meant to say how exquisitely beautiful you are." Okay, so the guy just didn't give up. He didn't even ask whether there was any news about his father.

She climbed the porch and then turned around, her hazel eyes as unreadable as before. "I'm sorry. But Dallas and I are stopping by only for a moment, and then we have to leave."

Huh. She didn't reveal any new information. Was she cautious around Grant? Maybe even immune to his charm? Dallas perked up. A man could hope.

"Some other time, then." Meanwhile, Grant was laying it on thick. "You're too outstanding for this small town. You deserve to be in a much better setting. I wish I could take you to some place worthy of you. But they do have great restaurants in Charleston. How about a rain check?"

"Thank you." Skylar's lips curved up a tad. "I appreciate the offer, but I like my hometown just fine. Especially my aunt's restaurant which I consider *great*." With that, she disappeared inside the house.

Grant wasn't invited. Ha! Dallas hurried up the steps.

"Where are you going?" Grant muttered.

"I have an open invitation to be here at any time." Dallas closed the door from the inside.

He still wished Grant were a suspect, but they seemed to have a more valid one. And his brother Barrett had confirmed Grant had been in LA when Earl had disappeared.

It still didn't mean Grant couldn't have hired someone, right?

Chapter Thirteen

The next day, Skylar stared at the ocean sparkling like a myriad of diamonds under the generous sun.

She didn't just want to keep it in her heart forever—she wanted to keep it on a canvas. Her hands itched to bring out the easel and paints Dallas had gifted her.

"It's such an incredible, rare beauty," she whispered. Then she petted Breeze who trudged nearby.

"Yes, you are," Dallas said near her. How did he even hear her over the ocean's roar?

Though deeply pleased, she waved him off. "Oh please."

"I don't say empty words. You know I mean every one of them." His tone was serious, and his gaze intense.

He truly did. She knew him well enough to be sure. She knew him better than she knew herself. She could understand him better than she could understand herself. What did that say about her?

"I know. And thank you." And she didn't just want to keep him in her heart—she wanted to keep him in her life. A longing, as large as the ocean and just as impossible to bottle down, grew in her chest.

Breeze trudged along with them.

Then Skylar winced. She probably shouldn't even be with Dallas like this, out in the open. It was shocking *that man*—she refused to call him the name she'd called him before—hadn't contacted her yet.

Because now she'd done what she shouldn't do, according to him. Being in her hometown. Communicating with Dallas. And with Grandma's wedding up in the air—even Grandma had stopped preparations now—Skylar had no excuse for staying.

Of course, she needed to provide emotional comfort to her grandmother, and she did, when her aunt or Dallas's mother weren't with Grandma. But a man like that wouldn't understand.

She snatched up a pebble and sent it skipping over the water like she'd done with Dallas as children. *That man* had a rock instead of a heart.

Then she froze. But what if...

Breeze barked as if sensing Skylar's distress.

"Are you okay?" Concern glossed Dallas's baby blues.

"Yes. Why are you asking?" She did her best to keep her voice neutral and schooled her features the same way.

"You paled as if you'd seen a ghost."

She flinched again. He had no idea how right he was. "Do you ever wish you could go back and change your life?"

"No. Except for you leaving, of course." Then his eyes darkened like the ocean in a storm. "And I wish I could've stopped Dad from hitting Mom."

Maybe someone had. Skylar didn't believe his father had committed suicide in *that* cottage. But it was too-painful a topic. Yet she was glad Dallas had an alibi. He'd been with her at the time.

"You were just a teen then. It wasn't your fault. And you stood up to your father plenty of times." Which had gotten him beaten up. Just like his brothers. Could one of them...? No, she didn't even want to think that. "But you couldn't change him."

His jaw set in a tight line. "I should've done something... something more."

Compassion tightened around her heart like a vise, and she shifted toward him. "We can't change other people or the way they act. Like I couldn't stop Mom from leaving. Or... or..." Tears prickled behind her eyes, but she blinked fast, preventing them from spilling and becoming like diamonds on her cheeks, sparkling in the sun. "Or my father's reaction to it."

"It wasn't your fault, either." He cupped her chin.

"But some things I did later were my fault." She gazed into his eyes, channeling that compassion—not pity, never pity—and understanding. "While you only paid for other people's mistakes, including mine."

"I told you. You were worth it. You still are." His thumb traced her jaw as his voice turned husky.

She placed her hand on his bare forearm. She meant it as a gesture of support, or so she told herself. But it quickly became so much more.

Touching him sent a new surge of longing, a tide ready to swallow her, ready to erase her determination as if it had been written in sand. She removed her hand and stepped back. Then she turned away and rubbed Breeze's back.

Partly because it comforted her and partly because she couldn't bear to see his disappointment. She was sending him mixed messages, and it was all her fault. Guilt stung. She was sending *herself* mixed messages, but that mattered much less.

Then she picked up a stick and threw it for Breeze to catch, but the golden retriever just looked at it with sad eyes and stayed in one place. "That's strange."

Dallas's eyes narrowed. "She's not chasing seagulls, either. Not that the seagulls are complaining about her lack of attention."

Her stomach clenched. She leaned to Breeze. "What's wrong, darling?"

Breeze raised her snout, but of course, couldn't say anything. She just whined.

Argh. "Maybe we should take her to a vet?"

Dallas pulled out his phone. "Hopefully, she's just tired. But I'll text Austin and get an appointment."

"Thank you. And, um, if you could ask that there's no one with a pet tarantula before or after it, I'd appreciate it."

He nodded. "Already on it."

"Thanks." Life was easier and better when Dallas was near her, but she shouldn't get used to it.

He sent a text, then studied something on his phone, and frowned. He shrugged apologetically. "Sorry, it's from Barrett."

She tensed. "It's okay."

Based on his frown, it wasn't something pleasant. But then, what could be pleasant about a missing person investigation? Everything in her became taut, and Breeze must've felt Skylar's tension because the dog whined again. Or was something wrong with Breeze?

The golden retriever was usually a fireball of energy, and Skylar never had an issue encouraging her to move or cheer up. Rather the opposite, Skylar often had difficulty keeping up with the dog.

Finally, he slid his phone away. "I emailed it to you."

Her mouth went dry despite the humid air, and she dropped herself onto the warm sand beside Breeze. "Can you sum it up?"

He sat down near them, giving her a wave of reassurance, which mixed with her usual longing in his presence. "Barrett checked Earl's friends and associates. Earl didn't have much in the sense of friends. But he did meet up with one in a few travels, Wyatt Newman. And more importantly, Wyatt moved with Earl from his previous company to the current one. They didn't seem to associate at work, though. When Barrett dug deeper, he found Wyatt also worked at another company where Earl used to work."

A frisson, an alarm, tingled along her skin. "In what capacity?"

"As an accountant." His eyes narrowed, but then he shook his head as if to shake off the thought they both had. "I know. What a weird coincidence."

"There are lots of accountants in the world. It's a much-needed profession," she said, disliking her defensive tone.

But the alarm became an annoying fly that would take off every time before Skylar could catch it. Something about the new information bothered her, and not only an accountant's honor. Maybe she'd been spending too much time with her pet, but this just smelled right. As if they were on the right track.

A hermit crab scooted near Breeze, but she didn't even move her head. Normally, she'd chase anything that moved in a mile radius. The ignored seagulls cried out as if in confirmation. Skylar hugged Breeze, feeling her warmth, as conflicting thoughts appeared in her mind. Worries churned rising bile inside her.

It was all circumstantial, though.

Then she swallowed hard. "One of those lunches on travels... Did it happen to be in our hometown?"

Dallas found her hand. "Yes."

"Another interesting coincidence. How many times?" She stared at their intertwined hands, her desire for a future with this man pulsing at her wrist.

"Just once."

She didn't want to let his hand go, couldn't interrupt the connection between them, but she nearly jumped to her feet. "We need to talk to this Wyatt."

He cleared his throat. "That's going to be difficult. Wyatt took a leave of absence at work." He named the day Earl had told her grandmother he was going on a trip. "He put his mail on hold for a month at the post office. He paid a company to mow his lawn for a month in advance."

She grimaced. One promising lead, and it took them nowhere. "Any way to track down the geolocation of his phone?"

Dallas shook his head. "Barrett doesn't have that capacity. And since nobody is going to file a missing person report because the guy just went traveling, the police aren't involved yet."

"How about road cameras to show where he left the city and in what direction?"

"Good question." Dallas's eyebrows rose. "I didn't think of that. Barrett probably has, but he didn't say anything to me."

Skylar averted her gaze. She'd tried to conduct her own mini-investigation fifteen years ago. But the technology wasn't as developed then, and she'd had very few resources, anyway, especially when she'd been terrified even a single inquiry could hurt the people she loved. "Did he tell anyone where he was going?"

"No. But then neighbors said Wyatt always keeps to himself, and his coworkers said the same. Plus, he lives in a cul-de-sac lot, and he bought the two lots beside him, so he doesn't have any close neighbors to start with."

She wanted to place her head on his shoulder, but even having her hand in his was a luxury she didn't deserve. Especially when he squeezed her fingers, sending appreciation through her. "That might be intentional." She petted Breeze with her free hand. "What did Barrett find out about this mysterious Wyatt?"

"Mysterious is the right word because frankly, not much. Unlike most people these days, Wyatt has very little online footprint. No social media accounts at all. He moved to Texas from Nebraska, and before then, he lived in California and other states. He moved to South Carolina about the same time Earl started his new company. Wyatt doesn't seem to have any family. Never been married, no children. His former neighbors didn't see anyone visiting him. Didn't frequent any local bars. He didn't even have any pets."

Breeze lifted her head and barked as if to say that wasn't right.

Dallas continued, "Earl was the only person Wyatt seemed to socialize with. Wyatt was polite with people at work but rarely took part in office parties. When he did, it was clear he was making an effort instead of wanting to be there. When asked, he said he was an only child and didn't have any relatives left. People felt too uncomfortable to prod more."

Her throat constricted her airways. Although blessed with extended family, of her direct family she only had her grandmother left, so in some ways, she could relate to this guy. And hadn't she become a recluse until Dallas had drawn her out of her shell again?

Compassion unraveled in her, but something more was there. A part of her could guess what that something was and didn't want to. "Anything about who his parents were? About the way he grew up?"

"Nope, but Barrett is working on it."

"Please thank him for me. Do you think Wyatt might've come here?"

"Barrett is already on it. He's combing through hotels and any nearby inns. So far, nobody seems to have seen Wyatt here, so his destination could be any other place on earth."

While neither Dallas nor she had an investigative mind, they each had a pair of legs and should use them. "Still, let's show photos of this guy at the gas stations and restaurants, including my aunt's. Just humor me. I feel Wyatt—if that's his real name—and Earl's disappearance are connected somehow."

He got up and pulled her up. She stared into his ocean-blue eyes, aching for a new chance. He was so close she could count every tiny gray speck in those eyes, could feel his every breath caress her skin. Like the moon caused the tides to ebb and move away, he caused her entire being to shift toward him with his mere presence.

One more moment, and she'd say things she'd regret. She forced herself to pull away and remove her hands from his. Disappointment flashed in his eyes. Yup, she was a walking disappointment to him and herself. She'd failed him.

But she couldn't fail her grandmother and Breeze. Skylar glanced at Breeze, who got up, but with visible reluctance. "I'd still like to take her to the vet."

"Let's see if Austin texted me back." He checked his phone. "He said he can see her in an hour."

The tension gripping her throat eased up a bit. "Great. Thank you."

Reluctantly, she left Breeze with her grandmother at the cottage. The dog didn't seem to be up to much walking, and Skylar didn't want to force her.

At the first gas station, Skylar let him do the talking. He knew people here, while she didn't any longer. At least, not the teenager at the counter. But when

Dallas pulled up Wyatt's photo on his phone, it was like a sucker punch to Skylar. Her breath dragged in sharply.

She didn't recognize the features exactly. But she still couldn't get enough air in her lungs. It was more a feeling than a conscious thought, but a feeling so overpowering she nearly jumped back.

"Are you okay?" Dallas touched her hand.

It took all her willpower not to flinch. Words failed her, but she managed a shaky nod.

Analyze. Be rational about it. Well, as soon as she could breathe again.

The lanky teen with acne and spiky blond hair sent her a curious glance, then shook his head. "Never seen this guy."

Dallas's gaze stayed on her. "Thanks. Skylar, do you need anything? Water, maybe? Or something else?"

For you to love me again.

But she couldn't get that at a gas station convenience store. Or anywhere ever. It was still easier to move her head than her tongue, so she just gave a head shake and hurried out the glass doors. She needed fresh air. Lots of it.

Outside, she gulped for air, probably looking like a proverbial fish out of water. No, she wasn't even that. She was a gutted fish, and all that from an unclear suspicion.

"Are you sure you're okay?" Worry tightened his voice.

Finally, she was able to make coherent words out loud. "Yes. Let's go. But let me see the photo again in the vehicle."

"Sure." He opened the door for her once they reached his truck.

Heart pounding in her temples, she climbed inside and snatched his phone the instant he handed it to her. "Thanks."

"You're welcome." His brow furrowed. He didn't say another word, only walked around the vehicle, slipped inside, and revved the engine.

She vaguely realized they took off but didn't hear a single sound afterward. She stared at the photo, a sickening feeling knotting her stomach. Maybe she should've asked for something at the store, so she'd have a paper bag handy.

The thick salt-and-pepper hair with way more salt than pepper fell on the man's forehead, and the matching mustache and beard were unfamiliar. Men could hide most of their face with facial hair, though that thought shouldn't have jumped to mind. After all, even Dallas had a beard and mustache and he had nothing to hide.

The eye color could be changed with colored contacts, and the hair could be dyed. But not the chin and the nose, unless plastic surgery was involved. Okay, or prosthetics or putty used—but it was different to put that on for a disguise than to live in it. Was plastic surgery involved in this case?

Something was painfully familiar in the tilt of his head and in his gaze, only because it was singed into her brain as she'd stared at the photos for many years. Until she'd tried to force herself to stop remembering. It only made the image more vivid.

While she favored landscapes, she'd done her fair share of portraits, mostly on commission. She'd learned different techniques, and she'd learned to pay attention to faces. All in all, she didn't recognize the features exactly but something had set her off, and it couldn't just be the tilt of the head or the slant and expression of the eyes.

But then, he'd aged twenty-six years since the last time she'd seen him. Her judgment here couldn't be trusted.

She flipped through more photos. Dallas's brother was thorough, and she was grateful for it, as well as for the fact that Wyatt did go to at least some office parties. And his coworkers didn't have qualms about sharing them on social media, so she had a bit more than Wyatt's driver's license photo to work with. He probably didn't realize he'd been photographed at the office parties.

Too bad she couldn't see if he still had that tattoo, but of course, his shirt hid that area. And if someone had gone through the trouble of switching identities, wearing colored eye contacts, and getting plastic surgery, there was a high probability of a laser tattoo removal or at least a cover-up tattoo. She kept swiping at photos, the few that they were.

Shouldn't she recognize him at once? Shouldn't she feel something? Some call of the blood? *Shouldn't she?*

She bit into her lower lip until it hurt, until she tasted that metallic flavor of blood.

"Is he someone you might've known?" Dallas's voice filtered through her mental fog.

"Not sure yet." Finally, she found what she'd been looking for and was speechless again. Her mouth went dry. She should've agreed to that bottle of water.

One of the office parties was outside, and the wind lifted Wyatt's hair a tad. Just enough to reveal a birthmark above his right eyebrow.

Skylar had an identical one above hers.

DALLAS PULLED INTO the parking lot behind the convenience store of the next gas station.

Then he turned off the engine and waited. Skylar was going through some inner struggle, and he wished he could help her. But he couldn't rush her. The previous Skylar couldn't stop talking. The new Skylar could clam up fast.

Lord, whatever she's going through, please help her.

No matter their past, or maybe because of it, she mattered to him. She mattered a lot. Then she turned to him, her eyes hollow once again.

He tensed. "What happened? And how can I help?"

"Any way your brother can find out if Wyatt has a tattoo on his left shoulder blade?"

O–okay. Although the request surprised him and he couldn't imagine it was going to be easy, he nodded. "I'll ask." Then he leaned to her, the question in his mind slipping from his tongue. "What kind of tattoo?"

She visibly swallowed hard. "A spider. With a web. For sailors, the web signifies missing home. And yes, my fear of spiders wasn't because of being bitten. It was because an image was connected so deeply with my trauma it sent me into panic. Even if it was irrational."

"I'm sorry." His chest tightened, the tension so thick in the air the humid stuff was hard to breathe. "A sailor? You mean that this person is…" He could guess it, but he couldn't believe it.

"Yes." She ducked her chin. "My father."

"What?" Dallas's whole body jerked as he flinched as if from a slap. "Are you sure?" His recollection of the man was blurry at best, but he needed to trust hers. And wasn't her father presumed dead? For over a quarter of a century? He struggled as if a strong wind tried to knock him off his feet. "Could it just be someone with similar features?"

"I'm sure he *doesn't* look much like my father." She grimaced.

"Then why do you say..." He stared at her. She couldn't see the tattoo in the photos because the guy's shirt covered that area.

"A feeling, but there's more." She pointed at her forehead. "Do you see that?"

"I see a beautiful face, but what else am I looking at?" he asked carefully.

Her lips twitched in a hint of a smile, and some color returned to her cheeks. "Thank you, but I meant the birthmark. My father has the same birthmark in the same place. I might not remember many things about him now, but I remember that."

He did his best to wrap his mind around this development.

How was this possible? Why hadn't her father come back if he was alive? Didn't even try to contact her? Not to mention it was a shocker he could be alive in the first place.

"But... but everyone assumed he died." Including Dallas.

Her expression turned bitter. "No, he didn't," she spoke with more conviction than he'd expected.

What?

One could knock him out with a feather right now. If he felt like that, he could only imagine what this did to her. Without thinking, he drew her into his arms as much as the truck seats allowed and held her close. He meant the gesture to offer support, but soon blood surged in his veins. She fit in his arms perfectly even if *he* didn't fit in her life.

His breathing went shallow, and he cherished the moment. He didn't want to let her go. But after a few minutes of leaning into him, she eased out of his embrace. Just like he knew she would.

"I know this can't be easy for you..." His voice trailed off as he studied her.

She didn't seem to be glad her father might turn out to be alive. What he'd attributed to shock was something else. She looked frightened out of her mind. On guard, like a suppressed metal spring in an old couch, ready to uncoil if let go. And she'd mentioned trauma so deep the live embodiment of her father's tattoo sent her into a panic.

"You *already* knew your father might be alive." He should've said it as a question. Instead, it sounded like a statement. "Was it because you held onto hope? Because you needed him so badly?"

She shook her head, then sighed. "I might be able to tell you soon. But we need to take Breeze to her appointment. Let's check this gas station first and drive to Grandma's."

Was she shutting him out again? No, then she'd have slipped away and gone to the vet clinic by herself. Instead, she'd said, "we." It might be a small consolation, but it was something.

He hopped from his seat, jogged around to the passenger side, and opened the truck door for her. "Have you seen your father since he disappeared?"

"No." She dashed toward the convenience store in an obvious hurry to get there. And in an even more obvious hurry to get away from the questions.

He stiffened as he followed and caught up. He'd better not prod more, or she'd clam up completely.

As he opened the glass front door, she glanced back, and her gaze softened. "This is where I found Breeze."

Maybe she'd cut off his questions because she worried about her dog, after all. But apprehension rippled along his skin. A twenty-six-year-old mystery might be about to be cracked open. Skylar could be the key to it. Worry how it might affect her tightened his rib cage.

Cool air-conditioning greeted them in the store, together with the scents of coffee and an overpowering perfume of a blonde tourist who seemed to believe in bathing in it.

"I'll have that water now," Skylar said.

He picked up a water bottle, a peach-scented air freshener, and a bag of her favorite candies. Her lips twitched in a half smile, rewarding him amply.

He joined the four people already lined up at the counter and suppressed a grimace. But then this was a public place with no hope for privacy. He paid for his purchases, then showed Wyatt's photo to the clerk. The result was the same as at the first gas station, and Skylar's shoulders sagged.

"We'll figure it out." Dallas sent her an encouraging glance when they were outside, met by tender sun and warm fresh air tinged with a gasoline odor. He handed her the water and chewy candies.

She took an apricot-flavored one from its orange wrapper and popped the candy in her mouth. "Yes. And I hope I'll be proven wrong." Then she took a swig of water on her brisk walk to the car. "Thank you."

Huh. He waved to two people he knew at the pump, then rushed after her. It didn't look like Skylar wanted her father back in her life—on the minuscule chance Wyatt could be her father. But she clearly wanted answers, first for her grandmother's sake and now for her own.

Once in the truck, he revved the engine, then hung the peach-scented air freshener on the mirror before pulling out of the parking lot.

"Hmm. I thought you didn't particularly care for a peach scent." She crumpled the wrapper from another candy.

He shrugged. "I don't. But you do."

"You were always a balm to my soul." She was the one to reach for his hand this time. The gesture and her words reached deep within *his* soul. Her hand disappeared fast, and he told himself it was because she didn't want to distract him while driving.

At Austin's office, Dallas was in for a surprise, and Skylar probably more so.

Austin smiled, which hopefully meant Breeze was okay. "Breeze is fine. She's expecting puppies."

The proud future mama barked as if to confirm it.

"Puppies?" Skylar's jaw slackened. "But when we were here the previous time, you didn't mention that."

"It was too early to determine it," Austin said, somewhat defensively.

"Sorry. I understand. Right. Wow. I mean... Wow." Skylar blinked. "I need to think about what to do with the puppies. I'll have to place them all in good hands."

"I can ask my brothers and Mom." Though Dallas imagined his brothers wouldn't exactly consider a golden retriever a ranch dog. He would have to lead by example, so he'd be getting a puppy soon. A golden retriever mix, huh?

Not so bad considering some people he knew had pet rats. Even leading by example wouldn't help place—what did one call rat babies?—in the hands of his brothers or especially his mother. Which would mean Dallas would've gotten the whole bunch of rats. He swallowed hard. Yup, a golden retriever puppy sounded fantastic.

Skylar's phone rang. She glanced at the screen. "It's my grandma. I have to answer to make sure she's okay. My apologies."

A few minutes later, they had learned the news Mrs. Rafferty received from the local police over some spectacular homemade donuts. The blood recovered from weeds outside Earl's house was human. But whoever the person was, he wasn't related to Grant, so it couldn't be Earl.

Skylar frowned. "We should stop by the police station. I think we asked the wrong person to volunteer a blood sample."

Dallas's heart sank to the green tile. He didn't want to think about who she thought the right person was.

Chapter Fourteen

"Grandma, would you like to stay with Mrs. Lawrence for a few days?" Skylar asked the next day while washing dishes after breakfast.

Grandma still didn't allow her to install a dishwasher at the cottage. The golden specks on one of the saucers caught the sunlight filtering through the small kitchen window and sparkled. The elegant porcelain saucer boasted a gorgeous cobalt pattern and was made by a factory that existed since the eighteenth century.

This, like Grandma's many treasures, would one day pass to Skylar. She'd rather have Grandma, though.

Not hearing an answer, Skylar wiped her hands on a kitchen towel, an anchor printed on its wavy blue background, and turned around. On the floor, Breeze stretched on a sunspot that filtered through the window, a chew toy nearby.

Her grandmother, the reigning queen in her teapot kingdom, blinked at her from the breakfast nook, sipping the second cup of tea, this time raspberry. "Why would I stay with her?"

Good question.

Skylar put fresh water in Breeze's bowl, then sat on the oak chair next to Grandma to be on the same level. "Well, I need to do a few things, and I'd love for you to have company in the interim." More importantly, Skylar wanted her grandmother to be safe in case Skylar's search took her too far.

Or should she stop what she was doing?

Alarms sounded loud and clear inside her, but she raised her chin. She needed to do what she should've done fifteen years ago. She'd take her punishment for keeping silent. But before she could go to the police, she needed more information. Because how much would they be able to do with the fuzzy memories of a traumatized child for events from over a quarter of a century ago?

And the only place Skylar knew where Grandma could be safe was the ranch with a family of grown-up, muscular cowboy brothers—all well-trained to shoot. "Please?"

Breeze lifted her head as if asking how Skylar could forget about her. Breeze was a great dog, but she wasn't a guard dog. And she was expecting puppies. Not that Skylar would ever put Breeze in danger to start with. Tenderness spreading inside, Skylar bent to stroke Breeze's soft fur, and the golden retriever's tail thumped on the tile floor.

"Okay. I understand if you're busy." Grandma's eyes dimmed. "And with Earl still missing, I guess I'd better put the wedding plans on hold."

Skylar hated causing Grandma distress, and her stomach twisted. But if she told her grandmother the truth, Grandma would never let her only granddaughter get into any kind of peril. And what if Skylar's suspicions were wrong? She could bring Grandma lots of heartache for nothing.

Skylar moved to her favorite woman in the world, sank before her chair, and grasped her wrinkled hands. "Sorry. It's just for a few days." She hoped.

Grandma nodded, her eyes warming up. "I understand. But shouldn't we ask Amelia first if she's okay with me dropping on her head?"

"I'll do it."

While her grandmother started packing, Skylar changed her silk cream pajamas to jeans and a T-shirt for convenience, then pulled on sneakers, ditching her ironed slacks and flats.

Then she stepped out to the terrace and found the familiar number. Breeze followed her, and Skylar tensed, afraid the dog would run to the beach. Instead, Breeze stretched on the terrace, soaking up the sun.

"Hello, Mrs. Lawrence. I have a huge favor to ask. Can my grandmother stay with you for a few days?"

Mrs. Lawrence laughed. "It's not a huge favor at all. We'd love to have her. I have a guest room she's welcome to use any time. You're welcome here anytime, too, you know."

"I know." Skylar's heart warmed as she stared at turquoise waters wearing white foam like a blue dress with lace cuffs and collar. Her grandmother still had such a dress in the attic, the lace yellowed by now, but the velvet fabric soft and dreamy. "You have no idea how much that means to me. But here's why it's a huge favor. And why I'll need some of your sons on guard. Remember Grandma told you the reason I couldn't stay in Port Sunshine?"

"Yes, but not details." A note of indignation raised Mrs. Lawrence's voice.

Skylar squatted to pet Breeze, then straightened out. "I'm here now anyway. And I need some answers. I'm doing an investigation someone might not like, and I want to continue it. For that, I need my hands untied."

Mrs. Lawrence fell silent, and Skylar's heart squeezed painfully. Would she take her hospitable offer back? Without knowing it, Grandma could bring danger to the Lawrence family by her mere presence.

"Maybe it wasn't a good idea," Skylar whispered.

Finally, Mrs. Lawrence said, "Does Dallas know?"

"No."

"Don't you think he should?"

Another good question. Skylar stroked the wooden railing's uneven surface. "You see, he still cares about me."

Mrs. Lawrence chuckled. "You say that like it's a problem."

Great. Skylar sounded ungrateful. "No, I'm thrilled he cares about me. Delighted. But he won't let me do something even remotely dangerous."

"Again, you say it as if it's a bad thing."

Skylar sighed as she leaned into the railing's support. If only she could lean into Dallas's support. "It's a *wonderful* thing. But I need closure. And I need to tell the truth. The person who concealed a crime needs to be caught."

"Are you sure this is what you want?"

Skylar didn't hesitate to answer. "No. *Not at all.* But I feel this is what I have to do."

"Will you promise me you'll be careful? And keep in contact?"

Skylar nodded, then remembered Mrs. Lawrence couldn't see her. "Yes. I wouldn't want to leave Grandma alone."

Breeze got up and barked as if upset Skylar hadn't mentioned her. Skylar corrected herself. "And Breeze, of course. Especially with future puppies. But if anything, um, well, will you... will you take care of them?"

"You're scaring me."

A lump formed in Skylar's throat as Breeze bumped Skylar's hand. Breeze's nose felt cold and wet. "I don't think it'll ever come to that. I'm just being proactive. Would... would that be a yes?"

"You know it's a yes. Dallas isn't among my sons I need to put on guard, is he?"

Skylar swallowed hard as she rubbed Breeze's back while the dog stretched on the warm painted patio stones again, her pink tongue lolling. "No. Please."

He'd be angry with her. But she had to do this if she could hope for any future with him. And she deeply and thoroughly wanted a future with him.

A sigh traveled down the line. "I'm going to regret this. I'm going to regret this very much."

"Yes!" Skylar raised her fist in the air, accompanied by Breeze's bark, then corrected herself. "I didn't mean yes to you regretting this. Thank you so much. Means a lot to me."

"I'm going to regret this," Mrs. Lawrence said again before disconnecting.

Skylar stared at the horizon, breathing deeply the salty air while a breeze tap-danced on her skin. "Was this the right choice?" she whispered.

Breeze barked, perhaps asking how she was supposed to know.

Skylar had stepped on a slippery slope since she'd set foot in her hometown again, intending to stay for weeks. She'd traveled further along that slippery slope when she'd seen Wyatt's photo, and she slid deeper when she had Dallas's PI brother poke into Wyatt's life.

It was too late to stop now, wasn't it?

"Would you like a short run on the beach to walk off your energy?" Skylar tumbled down the path, but Breeze didn't follow her.

Instead, the golden retriever just looked at her as if to ask, "What energy?"

"Huh. All right then." Skylar returned to the terrace.

Her fingers itched to call Dallas. She needed him now more than ever, and that was saying something because she'd always needed him, even when she didn't admit it.

She pulled her shoulders back and went inside the cottage to help her grandmother pack. Her tail wagging, Breeze followed her.

"Let's make sure you're well fed." She put kibble into Breeze's bowl.

Then she called Grant's sister to try to set up a meeting with her, but the call went to voicemail. Skylar left a message. If she didn't receive a callback, Grant would be her only option to talk about Earl's friends and hope Grant could remember Wyatt. She grimaced. Calling Grant didn't sit well with her. It would sit even worse with Dallas.

But she dialed Grant's number. They'd exchanged numbers to keep in touch about any developments in Earl's case, but there had been a bit of a predatory gleam in Grant's eyes when he'd put her number in his phone.

He answered on the second ring. "I'm so glad you called, darling."

She cringed at the endearment. Still, she needed the information, so she didn't call him out on that. "Did your father ever mention anyone by the name of Wyatt Newman, by any chance?"

"Why don't we discuss it over dinner?"

"Why don't you just tell me now." Okay, she shouldn't have snapped.

In the following pause, she almost thought he hung up on her.

Finally, he said, "I believe it was Dad's accountant."

"Anything else you can tell me about that man?"

"Sorry." Then his voice turned suave again. "So how about that dinner?"

"Sorry." And she shouldn't have mimicked his words. There might go his collaboration. "I have someone in my life."

"That's a pity." He did sound disappointed.

"Would you mind asking your sister to call me?" Skylar didn't hold her breath, but it was worth trying.

"Sure."

"Thank you, and... I should've said it already. I hope your father is all right."

Once she disconnected, she texted the photos and the request to her aunt. If Auntie didn't remember that man visiting, she'd still ask around among her staff. Sociable and friendly, she might ask her colleagues at other eating establishments, as well.

Then her heart skipped a beat when her phone rang and Dallas's name flashed on the screen. "Hi, Dallas."

"Hi. Would you like to talk to the clerk at the remaining gas station? If the owner is there, we could ask to watch camera recordings. Politely. And then we could talk to cashiers at the grocery store. And..." He hesitated. "I have a little surprise for you for later, if you have time."

Her heart jumped, then settled. "Of course. I'm bringing Grandma to the ranch, so I'll meet you there."

"Can't wait to see you."

Her heart jumped again. "Ditto."

She went through her strict wardrobe, for the first time in years allowing herself to wish for a flowery summer dress. She didn't have a single pretty dress. Not any longer. She frowned at her black and gray suits and decided to stay in jeans and sneakers, only she changed the white T-shirt for a ballerina-slipper-hued one.

About an hour later, she followed Grandma to the ranch and helped her out of the car. Kai met them and picked up the suitcase before Skylar had a chance to.

After getting her grandmother settled, Skylar hugged her. "Please call me if you need anything."

"I'll be all right, Little Miss." Her grandmother patted Skylar's hand, then chuckled. "Your date is here."

Dallas entered the living room, and her heartbeat increased like always in his presence. Her cheeks flamed up. "It's not a date."

"Hello, Mrs. Rafferty and Skylar." His gaze bore into her. "Why not?"

There were supposed to be a million reasons, but with him looking at her like that, she couldn't recall even one.

Grandma gave Skylar a little nudge. "Go."

He shifted from one foot to the other, some awkwardness still between them, though not as much as several days ago. They used to meet up with her running into his arms and him lifting her and whirling around, making her head spin for more reasons than one.

"Would you be okay going in my truck?" he asked. "No sense in taking two vehicles."

She opened her mouth, intending to assert her independence. "Sure."

The ride back to town was awkward until he took her hand. Then the years seemed to slip away, and she could imagine she was still a young, carefree girl, overflowing with her first love. Delighted it was mutual. Confident it would last forever.

She knew better now, but why not allow herself to imagine it for a few precious heartbeats?

Anticipation tingled along her skin. "What's the surprise you talked about?"

He chuckled. "You'll have to wait to see it. You were always impatient."

"Not any longer. I learned to be patient." She paused, remembering something. "Thank you for fixing the cottage's railing and the porch and patching the roof. I was going to hire someone, but Grandma said it was taken care of. I don't need to be a PI like your brother to figure out who did it."

He shrugged like it was no big deal. "Mom would want me to help. And I did, too."

Even if he didn't do it for her, it still mattered a lot to her. The words escaped before she could stop them. Maybe she hadn't learned to think before she spoke as much as she'd thought she had. "You mean a lot to me. And... and I missed you."

"I missed you, too. More than you can imagine."

The words reached her heart, and she locked them there as if it were her aunt's antique trunk. "I have a great imagination if you don't remember."

"I do remember." He sent her a long glance before returning his attention to the road. "Everything."

When they'd dated, she'd been the chatty one, but now she discovered a comfortable silence with him. She was content just to sit there and have him hold her hand. Just have him beside her. That was all. So simple and yet so complicated.

Her phone playing a classic melody made her reach into her purse. Her aunt answered her text, but so far, nobody in her restaurant had seen this man. She promised to ask her friend, the owner of another restaurant. Of course, Auntie wanted to know why Skylar was searching for the guy, but answering that would have to wait.

"Aunt said nobody saw Wyatt at her restaurant." Disappointment clenched Skylar's stomach at the lack of results, but there was something else there. A bit of relief? She wasn't ready to find out if the man was her father. But she couldn't wait any longer, either. She'd waited twenty-six years already. Way too long.

Once in town, Dallas pulled up to the gas station.

"Could you please check your phone to see whether Barrett sent any new information?" She clicked her seat belt open.

"Let's see." He pulled his phone out of his pocket. "He says nobody saw Wyatt at the local hotels, either. He's checking inns now." He rushed around the truck, then opened the door for her.

At this point, she didn't want to get her hopes—or fears—up, and she was right not to because they returned to the truck empty-handed. Even after Dallas had met the owner and sweet-talked his way into watching the camera recordings.

But at the grocery store, they hit pay dirt when one of the cashiers recalled seeing Wyatt.

"That man wore a cap drawn low and sunglasses. He bent to pick up a credit card he dropped. A boy was running through the store and bumped into this guy, knocked off the sunglasses and the cap," the teen cashier with indigo hair and with a ring in his nose said. "The guy grunted something and put the cap and sunglasses back."

Huh. That bump wasn't intentional, but useful nevertheless.

"What did he buy?" Skylar moved closer.

"Chips, beef jerky, sodas." The teen shrugged.

"Did anything stand out about him?" Dallas asked.

"Not really."

Skylar thought of the SUV with tinted windows that ran her off the road. Would her own father do that? "When he left, did you by any chance see what car he went to in the parking lot?"

The cashier shook his head. Then his gaze flicked to the couple approaching the conveyor belt. "No. We stay pretty busy here. I gotta work now."

Dallas pulled a chocolate bar and Skylar's favorite candies from the counter as if to give them a reason for being there, then nodded to the chip bags while the cashier scanned the candies. "Any of these you like?"

The teen pointed at an orange bag with flames drawn on it. "These ones. But I still didn't see his car." He quirked an eyebrow that had a ring in it, too.

"It's fine." Dallas paid for a couple of bags of chips and gave them to the cashier. "Your information was very useful. Thank you so much."

They retreated to the parking lot. As they took off, he adjusted the rearview mirror, likely keeping watch for a tail. "Barrett sent more information about Wyatt. It doesn't look like the guy stayed in any local hotels or the inn."

"He could've rented a cottage." She spoke with even less conviction than she felt.

"Or maybe he was just passing through to meet with Earl?"

She was afraid of that. Her fingers wrapped around the cold door handle. "Anything else your brother said?"

"Yes. I'll email it to you. But the short version is, he talked to one of Wyatt's former employers. A small business owner. He didn't provide any details, but my brother had an impression that, when Wyatt left the company, it wasn't because he wanted to. But the business owner had no proof of wrongdoing to take to the police. My brother is reaching out to any other employers of Wyatt he can find. He'll keep us posted."

"Interesting." It fit with what she'd learned already. Then she glanced around. "Where are we going now?"

"To our cove. Remember? If you don't mind interrupting the investigation for a bit?" His expression turned eager and a bit inquisitive.

Nostalgia unraveled inside her, and she repeated his words to him. "I do remember. Everything." Guilt at pausing the search even for a few minutes stung her. But she'd hurt him so much already. How could she refuse his kind gesture?

His expression softened.

As he pulled up to the beach, she called Hart again, but the call went to voicemail for the second time. Then the second text from Auntie made Skylar narrow her eyes. "Nobody at Auntie's friend's restaurant has seen the guy, either," she said out loud.

"He could've left a long time ago."

"Or he could've worn that cap and glasses there." Premonition squeezed her heart. "There are some things that don't add up." But what she suspected was too scary to voice.

Wistfulness swelled her chest as minutes later they walked to the small cove hidden so well tourists still hadn't found it—which was a miracle, indeed.

Inside, it was slightly cooler and damper, but the tablecloth spread on the ground attracted her attention. It had bottles with lemonade and a cooler beside a stack of plates.

"I know it's rather simple, but..."

"I love it." She flung her arms around him before she could stop herself. She could tell herself all she wanted that she was no longer impulsive, that she was over him. But deep inside, she knew the truth. She didn't change as much as she'd tried to. And she was falling in love with him all over again.

He gaped. Then he lifted her and whirled around, filling her with fresh memories. Every cell in her body tingled with delight, and her laughter joined his.

"I love to hear you laugh again." He placed her on the ground, then touched the pins in her hair. "May I?"

She nodded as if it were a dream and she might spook it and wake up if she talked.

He removed the bobby pins, and her hair swished onto her shoulders. It was weird, but he didn't just set her hair free but also something inside her.

He slid his fingers through her hair. "I've dreamed of this moment for so long."

She blinked. "Really? That simple?"

"That simple." His lips brushed over her cheek, sending delicious ripples through her. "We humans often overcomplicate things."

But there were still secrets between them. There was hurt she'd inflicted on him. There was danger hanging over her head.

She didn't want to remember all that, but she had to. She found an easy distraction as she gestured to the tablecloth. "Let's eat before ants get to it. I'm surprised they haven't already."

"I asked Kai to put the things here right before we arrived." He threw his jacket on the ground for her to sit on.

"Thank him from me." She sat on the jacket, curious about what was in the cooler and guessing already.

He opened it and handed her ice cream. Peach flavor. Her favorite. Yes, he did remember everything. Just as he remembered the way they'd celebrated her first successes.

But he didn't *know* everything.

SKYLAR ASKED DALLAS to meet her at the cliff the next day, staying far from the edge, of course. She'd needed to face this place before sharing what she knew, but standing there, she shook so hard she couldn't speak. Instead, she wanted to run into his embrace and stay there forever, bury her face against his chest and hide from it all.

Her phone rang, and she reluctantly pulled away. She sent him an apologetic glance. "It might be Grandma."

"Of course. No problem." His gaze remained kind.

She fished out the phone from her jeans pocket, nodding to herself as her guess turned right, then swiped the screen to answer. "Hello, Grandma. I hope you're having a great time."

"I am, but I forgot a few things. I'm at my place right now, picking them up."

Her insides went cold. "Okay. Okay. Would you please do me a gigantic favor? Will you please lock the door and don't open it to anyone while getting your things? I have a key."

"Are y–you all right?" Grandma's voice trembled.

"I'm fine. Just please humor me." Skylar's pulse increased. She needed to warn her grandmother and take her back to the ranch immediately. And she needed time to think, to process everything, to see how all she now knew and all she only suspected fit together, like tiny strips of fabric on her grandmother's quilt.

"Okey dokey, but you owe me an explanation, missy."

"I'll see you soon." Skylar disconnected.

Her gaze locked with Dallas's, and her heart fluttered. She also wanted to tell him so many things. But she couldn't be so selfish. Her grandmother's safety had to be the priority. Skylar would explain everything later. But right now, she needed to hurry.

She should've told him already, even with the fifteen-year-old threat that if she told anyone about her memories of the day her father disappeared people she loved would pay for it. She should have, even if it felt more like an attempt to clear her conscience and justify her leaving. One more mistake to add to her long list.

Growing up, she'd told Dallas all her secrets, the few she'd had. Then she'd kept the biggest one from him. But not any longer. Once she was sure Grandma was okay, she'd call him and tell him everything. It was time.

"I'm sorry." She tore her gaze away from him. If she didn't, she'd stay. "I've got to go."

"Are you leaving already?" The depth of hurt in his voice made her flinch.

"Yes," she said, her thoughts with her grandmother already. How could she find the right words to spare the woman who'd raised her from this additional heartache?

After getting Grandma safe and talking to Dallas, Skylar was going to the police. Offer herself as bait if needed. Call Marina, too. Her friend was a lawyer, which would be handy in a situation like this.

"Bye, Dallas."

"Bye." His jaw hardened, throwing off her resolve.

But minutes later, Skylar floored the gas pedal all the way to the canary-yellow sea cottage and called her grandmother on the hands-free phone. Grandma didn't answer. Worry knotted Skylar's gut. Then regret tightened it further. She should've asked Dallas to go with her and explained everything on the way. What was she thinking?

She'd thought she'd changed, but sometimes her head was still in the clouds and she didn't make the right decisions. Far from it. She took a corner at a high speed, and the tires squealed.

To think about it, Dallas would never let her offer herself as bait. She nibbled on her lower lip. But was there any other way to guarantee her grandmother's safety? Fifteen years ago, Skylar had fled the danger, and it had only made the current situation worse.

She parked, leaped out of her sedan, and dashed to the house, taking the porch steps two at a time.

The door was locked, so she rang the bell. Then remembering she'd told Grandma not to answer, she snatched the keys from her purse, turned the key in the lock, and hurried inside.

And met the barrel of a gun.

Chapter Fifteen

Dallas picked up a pebble and threw it into the ocean, standing near the little cove he and Skylar used to frequent as children. Sometimes her cousins and his brothers had joined them.

The pebble skipped a few times, then drowned. And he was drowning in his sorrows, his heart heavy like not just a pebble, but a boulder.

Why had he imagined she'd stay this time? With her grandmother's wedding postponed, Skylar didn't have to spend another minute in their hometown. It seemed he wasn't a good enough reason for her to stick around.

But how could she be so nonchalant about it? Say she was leaving like that, and that was it? Break his heart all over again?

"I thought I might find you here." Kai's voice made Dallas turn around. "What happened?"

"Why do you ask?" Dallas grumbled.

"You look like a storm cloud." Kai strode to him. "No, I'm wrong. A storm cloud looks brighter than you do right now."

"Gee, thanks."

Kai scooped up a few pebbles and jiggled them in his palm. Then, for some time, they just tossed them into the water like in childhood. Dallas had usually won those competitions, and his pebbles still skipped further than Kai's did now. But there was no satisfaction in it. Kai kept quiet, which was never easy for him.

Finally, Dallas said, "Skylar said she's leaving."

His brother frowned. "She might come back."

"What if she doesn't?"

"Then go after her. She's your lifelong dream. She's worth going the extra mile—or fifty—for. And even if she rejects you, which I doubt, at least you'll know you've done everything you could."

Could there still be hope for him and Skylar? He gave his brother a sidelong glance. "Of all our brothers, I didn't expect words of wisdom from you."

Kai chuckled, unoffended. "I'm surprised myself."

Dallas selected another pebble. He'd known Kai his entire life but apparently hadn't known him enough. "Why don't you take your advice?"

"With Marina?" Kai visibly swallowed. "I told you. I didn't want to weigh her down. I'd never cut her wings. And when I nearly risked it all, she fell in love with someone else."

"What about now?"

After a long pause, Kai shrugged. "I'd rather have her in my life as a friend than not at all." Another pause ensued before Kai clapped him on the back. "But your situation is different. You love Skylar, and she loves you back. Geographic distance won't matter if you admit that simple truth."

Huh, more words of wisdom from his easygoing brother with a short attention span.

Dallas might as well admit that *simple truth*. "I love her. But I don't think she loves me back. Or she wouldn't be leaving."

"Not necessarily." Kai rolled his eyes. "For example, she might be running away from her feelings. Or, you know, she needs to get back to her work. That should be reasonable, right? Maybe she wants to see if she can wrap up things in Charleston and come back here. Difficult to say. I've dated lots in my life, and if I learned one thing from it—*it's that I haven't learned anything.*"

When his brother put a special emphasis on the last sentence, Dallas chuckled despite his gloomy mood. "I guess that's one way to put it."

"Trying to understand women is like trying to empty this ocean with a spoon." Kai gestured at the endless waters. "I don't think we're supposed to understand them. We just need to love and admire them."

No wonder Kai was so popular with women.

Dallas made a decision. "I'm going to Mrs. Rafferty's place. I hope Skylar hasn't left yet."

"I'll be praying." Kai nodded.

Dallas ran to his truck but paused near the door to answer a call. Skylar's contact flashed on the screen, and he swiped to accept. "Skylar?"

She spoke, but the voice was distant as if she didn't hold the phone close.

The words chilled the blood in Dallas's veins. "You don't have to kill us, you know."

FIFTEEN MINUTES EARLIER...

Skylar suppressed a shudder.

She'd made a grave mistake. She should've gone to the police *first*. It was too late now. She moved her hand close to her purse. Could she pull the gun fast enough?

Her grandmother was in the line of fire, and it set Skylar's teeth on edge. She shifted to the side. Breeze was barking frantically behind the bedroom door.

Her grandmother's eyes were huge as she slumped on a chair, and Skylar's heart went out to her. "I'm sorry," Grandma whispered. "I–I don't understand what's going on. This is my fiancé, Earl." She turned to the man with the gun. "Earl, why are you threatening my granddaughter?"

"Because she put her nose where it didn't belong!" he bellowed.

"My nose and the rest of my body were dragged into this... this mess." *Mess* wasn't an adequate word. Tragedy? Well, she didn't care for adequate words right now. Her hand started unzipping her purse.

Breeze kept barking. Maybe someone would hear her and call the police? The sea cottage was far from neighbors, but one could hope.

He must've had the same thought. "Shut up, Breeze!"

Waaaaait a minute. Skylar had brought Breeze to the sea cottage after Earl had already disappeared. How did he guess her name?

"I don't know how you got my dog. But you'd better tell her to shut up before I shoot her," he growled.

Skylar shuddered at the prospect. And the puppies! "Breeze, quiet, please. Your dog, huh?" A moment more, and she'd be able to slip her hand inside her purse. She was no sharpshooter by any means, but she wouldn't miss from close range. Unless he pulled the trigger first.

"I only had Breeze for a few days, but it doesn't matter." His eyes narrowed. "Put your purse on the floor and send it to me. Or your grandma is dead. I know you have a gun in there. When Hart and Grant came chasing up here, worried about their inheritance, I asked them to keep an eye on you."

Skylar's heart dropped onto the beige tile. Without the weapon, she and Grandma would die. But if she didn't obey, Grandma would die *immediately*.

"Now!" he yelled.

Skylar winced and placed the purse on the floor, then sent it toward him. Could she tackle him when he bent to pick it up? But he *didn't* pick it up, just kicked it far out of her reach.

Her mind whirled while her heart thundered in her temples. How to make sure she and her grandmother escaped alive? Could she use anything in the room to strike him? A teapot? Not heavy enough. If only she were by herself, she could take such a risk. She couldn't risk dashing to the kitchen to snatch a kitchen knife.

She needed time, and she needed to keep him talking.

"Let's try to find a solution to this situation." She softened her tone because arguing wouldn't get her anywhere. She wished Breeze were still here instead of locked in the bedroom. No, that wasn't true. She wouldn't want Breeze and her puppies to suffer.

Earl sneered. "There's only one solution."

"What... what's going on?" Grandma blinked and wrapped her tawny-hued shawl tighter around her shoulders as if cold. "You said you loved me. You proposed. Then you disappeared. What on earth is happening now?"

He exhaled, his shoulders sloping, but the gun remained firm in his grip. "I did fall in love with you. I–I just couldn't change anything."

Could he have tiny bits of remorse? Then there could be hope for stalling. He wouldn't let them out of here alive, but maybe Skylar could buy some time. But one wrong move, and it was over.

Skylar searched his face, hoping to see it in his eyes. His white hair was disheveled, and wrinkles dug deep into his face. His movements were jerky, his eyes frantic and cold. Not a good sign.

Breeze started barking again, and as much as Skylar wanted the dog to make noise, she asked her to stop.

"Help us understand then. Why don't we sit down and you tell us?" She did her best to mimic his vocal inflections.

He frowned. "Nobody can understand."

She moved closer, also doing her best to shield her grandmother. "Of all people, I'm the only one who can. I know why you did what you did. I know my father could be a horrible person."

Grandma gasped, her pale eyes going huge. "I thought we were never going to speak of *that*."

Now, Skylar sighed. She didn't want to hurt her grandmother. But the two of them had kept this secret since Skylar had started remembering things while in the first semester of college, and it was the wrong thing to do. It was time to voice it. "Because I saw him kill my mom."

Chapter Sixteen

Skylar reassessed the situation, pulling on her analytical brain and not her creative one. Earl didn't sit down to talk, but he didn't pull the trigger yet, either.

Hopefully, he needed someone to relate to him, to understand his reasons.

She could be that person—or rather pretend to be. "I grew up thinking my father died, thinking my mother left me. But that's not what happened."

"Why are you telling my fiancé this?" Grandma's voice trembled.

"Because we've kept silent too long. I'm not going to die without us talking about it." Skylar shifted to Earl. "And after what you've put her through, Grandma deserves to understand why. Don't you think?"

"I don't have time for this." His brown eyes narrowed.

Well, at least it wasn't an outright no.

Skylar faced her grandmother. "You know I began remembering small things after I started college. Just fragments. Like a shadow on a cliff. Then familiar-sounding voices. Later, seeing Dad leaving. Rain on my skin as I sneaked out. The scent of wet soil."

Earl didn't stop her yet. Good.

"Then there was an image in my mind of a woman in a red raincoat standing on a cliff, her hood covering her head. Since it was so vivid and striking, I decided to paint it. It was my best work, even if it gave me a feeling of unease. I didn't realize yet who the woman was. In that memory, I only saw her from the back. But it looked painfully familiar." Skylar's heart shifted with an equally painful wrench.

"I remember that painting," Grandma whispered.

"Hurry up. I don't have all day," Earl waved the gun at her.

Goosebumps erupted over Skylar's skin, both from the current danger and her dangerous memories. If only Dallas were here. She'd never stopped loving him. Why hadn't she told him the truth upon returning to Port Sunshine? Because of a threat years ago? Or was it because subconsciously she'd been afraid he'd turn out like her father? Like his father, for that matter? She was wrong, of course.

But maybe she could still tell him that story, even if it was the last thing she did. She slipped her hand into her pocket and hoped she pressed the right button to speed-dial him on her cell phone. Would he understand to call the police? She just hoped he wouldn't try to remedy the situation himself.

She grasped at straws as she drowned in the ocean of despair. "You can say you killed my father in self-defense. The police will believe you. You don't have to kill us, you know."

His gaze became pensive as if he considered that option. "They might, just might have believed me when it happened weeks ago. But they certainly won't now after I concealed the crime. Besides, I can't trust you'll keep quiet."

"I kept what my father did quiet, for all these years."

Earl's lip curled, and his clutch tightened on the gun. "That was for your father. Not the stranger who killed him."

Well, it was worth a try. Concealing a death seemed to be a habit where her father was concerned. Strange irony to have *his* murder concealed.

She drew a deep breath and refocused to show Dallas what was happening, if by some miracle he was listening. "Back to my story. On my visit here to see Grandma and Dallas, I left the painting of the woman in the red raincoat for sale at Dallas's uncle's store. Then I went back to Charleston. Later, more memories about the night my dad disappeared came back, as if the floodgates had opened. I called to take the painting back. But Kai told me it was already sold. I hoped it was a coincidence. It wasn't."

Tears washed Grandma's pale eyes. She blinked rapidly behind her thick glasses. "That woman in the painting... She was your mother, right?"

"Yes." Skylar leaned against the wall, her legs weak. She could make a dash to the kitchen for a knife, but once again, that would leave her grandmother in danger. And even if she tackled Earl and screamed for her grandmother to run, Grandma couldn't, well, run.

At a thump on the bedroom door, Skylar and Grandma glanced in its direction, but Earl's gaze didn't waver as he shouted, "Breeze, stop it!"

Breeze whined but stopped jumping at the door. Claws against tile echoed faintly as if she tried to dig under the wall and escape. Too bad they didn't have a mud floor.

Meanwhile, Skylar moved to the past again. "I had a new memory of when she turned around, her face streaked with rain or tears or both. Following Dad, I ran from tree to tree until we made it to the cliff. I hid behind a tree trunk, and I was small enough that Dad didn't notice me when he glanced back. He met my mother on the cliff."

Skylar swallowed hard, the memory clogging her throat. "She begged him to let her take me with her. But he yelled back at her."

Those screams still rang in her ears.

"I'll never forgive you! You were my entire world. I can't live without you. Why did you leave me? Betray me like that?" Tears ran down his face, mixing with the rain.

"I'm sorry. I'm so sorry. I just felt... felt suffocated." Her mother's tears were mixing with the rain, as well.

Now, Skylar couldn't speak around the huge lump in her throat. But she had to. She couldn't let Earl's attention waver long enough for him to remember to kill them. "I–I didn't understand at first why she'd wanted to meet at such a dangerous place. But then I realized my father told her to meet him there."

"This was going to be it for him." Earl's expression was gloomy.

It reflected Skylar's mood. For many years, she pushed the memories away. She still had difficulty reconciling the belligerent man on the cliff with the caring one who'd carried her on his shoulders, bought her ice cream, brushed her hair. "She must've known it was a dangerous place to meet, but she still had to try. For me."

"He was going to commit suicide in front of her. She was his world." Earl's lips thinned.

And Skylar wasn't enough? Didn't she matter even a little? Besides, she wasn't sure she believed Earl—or rather whatever story her father had told him.

"He was going to jump off the cliff. He ran to the edge. But your mother tried to stop him," Earl said gloomily. "They struggled. He told me he didn't mean to push her off the cliff, but she slipped off the wet surface." Then he said again, "She was his world."

The image of her father rushing to the edge, and her mother stepping in front of him, appeared in front of Skylar's eyes. But that memory was blurry. "I only remember the red splotch falling off the cliff. It took me several moments to realize it was my mother. I ran away. Thunder covered my footfalls, and rain covered my footprints. I didn't look where I ran. I just ran."

"He never would've realized you'd seen it if not for that painting." Earl scoffed.

She cringed. She'd thought her paintings were popular among tourists, but her father must've bought them all. Out of guilt? Remnants of affection? She'd never know. But he'd surely bought that painting with her mother not because he still loved her, but because he needed to erase the evidence.

Earl cleared his throat. "He said he found her down there later, her body mangled from smashing on the rocks below the shallow waters, but already floating out to sea. Something broke in him. But he didn't think people would believe it was an accident. It's why he got his boat out that night despite the storm—so he could retrieve her body and dispose of it. But he was seen going out on the boat. He thought he saw a shadow at the beach. That's when he came up with the idea to fake his death. To have a fresh start somewhere far away where nothing would remind him of your mother."

Skylar almost held her breath, digesting this bit she'd wondered about since the memories came back. She'd been to the spot. She'd seen the steep drop straight into the waters, nothing to stop her mother's fall or catch blood or clothing on the way down. Nothing a search party would've noticed being disturbed when they looked for little Skylar the next day. Just churning waters over jagged boulders, the tides eager to wash away blood and evidence.

"He didn't die that night." She didn't know why she repeated the obvious.

"The man he used to be did." Earl's eyes narrowed. His hand shook slightly, but he didn't put the weapon down.

"True." She nodded. The father she'd once loved so much had died that night. The man he'd become sent ripples of fear through her.

In the silence, Breeze jumped at the bedroom door again, but at Skylar's command, she stopped. A low growl rumbled through the door.

Lord, please save my grandmother and Breeze. I'm sorry I've blamed You for what happened that stormy night, but please, please don't let them die.

Could God hear her?

Could Dallas hear her? She couldn't know that either. "Your turn." Hands clasped in her lap, posture entreating and nonthreatening, she faced Earl. "What do you know about Wyatt Newman—the name my dad chose after disappearing? His new identity?"

Earl shook his head, but the gun in his hands remained steady. "Why don't you give us your version?"

"My dad sent his boat into the sea to create the suspicion that he'd drowned, then started a new life under a stolen identity. His house was remortgaged twice, so that should've clued me in on something. And someone must've helped him in the beginning."

"I don't know anything about that." Earl shrugged. "It was years later when I met him. I just know he got his accounting degree again in his new identity, this time online, but first, he worked on oil rigs."

"You and my father worked together at a few companies, right? Was it you or him who made the threatening call after he bought that painting and realized I was at the cliff?" The mechanically distorted voice still sent a shudder through her.

Earl shook his head. "I don't know anything about any threats, or any painting."

Skylar doubted it. Or maybe she just didn't want to believe her father would threaten to harm his mother or his daughter. Back then, however, she couldn't take the risk. She'd stayed away from her hometown like the caller had said and had kept quiet about her resurfaced memories.

The biggest mistake of her life. An unforgettable one.

Aching to have brought Grandma through all this, Skylar made eye contact with Earl again. "I'm surprised my father told you about this."

"We became good friends over the years. We made several businesses successful. And he was integral to my latest one. One day, we both got drunk. And he told me too much."

"And you found a way to control him. But why kill him now?" She regretted her words when Grandma gasped again. But Skylar needed to keep this going. The moment she stopped engaging him in the conversation would be the moment he pulled the trigger. She moved to her grandmother and gently wiped her tears. "If he was so essential to you? Oh, wait. Had he started to have pangs of conscience, after all?"

Or was that her wishful thinking?

"He was thinking about going to the police, confessing everything, and then asking for your forgiveness." Earl said slowly.

It still didn't all make sense. She hugged her grandmother, wishing she could spare the kind woman all this. "Even if my father did that, it only meant you'd lose a valuable business partner. Big loss, but not worth drastic measures." Unless... She nearly slapped herself on the forehead. "Unless you two had dishonest dealings, and he also wanted to confess those?"

"I couldn't let that happen. But I didn't want to kill him. I needed him. I just needed him to keep quiet, too."

Skylar nodded thoughtfully. "Of course, you couldn't let that happen. So that's why you traveled here and courted my grandmother. Dad left Grandma, but he still loved her." Skylar hoped. "You used that. Either he'd keep quiet, or you'd hurt Grandma."

"So all this was a lie!" Grandma screamed and shoved free from Skylar's embrace.

Earl sighed and faced his former fiancée. "It started that way, but I fell in love with you for real."

Skylar frowned as more fragments fell into place. "You hid away from my father in *that* cottage. When you suspected he figured that out, you wanted to leave. But he found you. What happened next?"

"I couldn't make him see reason." Earl's shoulders slumped further forward. "He got it into his head that I was going to harm his mother for real. Anyway, he came at me, waving a gun. He didn't care that he could have an affluent life somewhere far away. He regretted what he'd done and wanted to do what he could to set things right. I—you can see I had no choice!"

The words replayed in Skylar's head.

He regretted what he'd done.

Was it true? And could she ever forgive her father? Well, she might not have time for that, anyway.

It was remarkable how in the instant when life could be over, all the unimportant parts fell away and revealed what mattered like grains of sand revealing a hidden treasure. Clarity could be sharpened by adrenaline.

Her treasure was under her nose all the time. Dallas. She'd never stopped loving him, no matter how hard she'd tried. And another treasure, the one she'd buried in the sand for years was her artistic talent. The two passions she'd left behind.

Would she have the chance to come back to them?

Her gaze slid to the easel with the paints Dallas had given her. Her throat closed up. Somehow, even after she'd hurt him, he'd managed to give her back *herself.*

She wouldn't forget it for the rest of her life, even if the rest of her life would be only a few minutes. Deep longing unfurled inside her. She longed for him to know she loved him even more than she needed to stay alive.

Staying alive would help, though.

And for that, she needed Earl to keep talking. She nodded to him. "I get it. We fall in love when we least expect it."

Would Dallas hear her over the phone in her pocket? Would he be able to help? She wanted him to, but not at the cost of his life. And he should know what she should've told him a long time ago.

She raised her voice. "I didn't want to fall in love with Dallas again, either. I did my best not to. I tried so, so hard. But I couldn't help it. He's the most remarkable man I've ever met. Or ever will meet." And the latter wasn't just because she probably wouldn't be walking out of here alive. "And knowing my grandma, she's the most remarkable woman you've ever met."

"Thank you, my Little Miss," Grandma whispered.

Earl's expression softened, and guilt settled in his eyes as he glanced his fiancée's way, but only for a minute. "True. You're a remarkable woman." But then he frowned again. "If only your son had let sleeping dogs lie."

If only you didn't blackmail my father or get him mixed up in your wrongdoings to start with.

Of course, Skylar kept the thought to herself. Aggravating Earl wasn't in her best interests. "It's not too late to walk away from it all."

"Right." He sneered. "The moment I let you go will be the moment you run to the police."

He had a point there.

"You shouldn't have put your nose where it didn't belong," he said again, his tone weary. "But he told me you knew what he'd done, so I tried scaring you off. You should have gone. Then it wouldn't have come to this. I didn't want to hurt you, either of you. Now I have to." A whiny, not-fair tone filled his voice.

So it wasn't Dad who'd run her off the road. Relief loosened something tight in Skylar. She couldn't help feeling glad for that.

Earl turned to his fiancée. "We could've been happy."

"How could you?" Tears ran down Grandma's face, making Skylar suffer for her.

Skylar sensed the instant Earl changed. He looked dejected but determined, and his grip on the gun tightened. A shiver ran down her spine. He'd made a decision, and it wasn't a favorable one.

Then she had an idea as she edged closer to the easel. While she still wanted to shield her grandmother, she had no choice. Skylar was a bigger threat. Earl would take her out first.

He'd also expect her to go for her gun in the purse on the floor. So she might have an element of surprise. But for her and Grandma to have even a minuscule chance of survival, Skylar would need much more. She'd need a distraction.

She silently begged her grandmother to keep talking. Skylar had inherited her chatterbox character from her grandmother, but one wouldn't guess it now.

Finally, Grandma let it out, shrieking, "I loved you! I loved you so much! We were going to get married! Did all that mean nothing to you? Did it?"

You go, Grandma!

Would that be enough of a distraction? Skylar wasn't close to the easel yet when the front door flung open and she had no time to decide. As Earl spun toward the door and the new threat, she lunged for the heavy easel and smashed it at him with all her might. Shots thundered in the air.

Hot pain erupted inside her, blinding her. Voices and movements around her barely filtered through the crimson fog. She slipped to the floor.

Was it Dallas calling her name, or was she only imagining it? She tried to answer, but no words came out.

Then the world went black.

Chapter Seventeen

For two days, Dallas alternated between hope and despair and back many times and now clung to hope like a lifesaving buoy.

Skylar was sleeping in a hospital room, pale and surrounded by machines, but alive.

Alive.

The word tasted like spring water, refreshing and promising.

Thank You, Lord.

Then worry constricted his rib cage. While by some miracle the bullet didn't damage any organs or major arteries, so many things could still go wrong with a gunshot wound.

Lord, please give her a speedy recovery.

"It could've been worse," Austin whispered as he took a chair nearby. He moved so silently Dallas didn't hear his brother's footsteps.

Skylar's grandmother and Dallas's mom had been here, too, but Kai and their other brothers had dragged them to the cafeteria to have a snack.

Dallas winced. "I was afraid I lost her forever." The sheer volume of pain had been unbearable. He couldn't imagine living in a world where Skylar didn't exist.

"But you didn't. And hopefully, she'll make a full recovery."

"I'm praying so." He paused. "I just love her so much."

"Everyone knew it for a while." Austin rolled his eyes. "Well, maybe except Skylar. And she's the one who needs to know. Have you prayed for guidance?"

"Yes. But I still don't know what that guidance is."

"You will with time. Have you told her yet?"

Dallas shook his head. "What's the point? Her feelings toward me changed." The words he'd overheard on the phone sent his heartbeat into overdrive. Did she truly love him? If she hadn't been in danger at the time, he'd have been ecstatic to hear those three words. Until he realized she might've said them to show Earl she could relate to him. What if she didn't mean them?

"Maybe those feelings became stronger than ever." Austin winked. Could he be right?

"Or not. Besides, I don't want to tie her down to this place." No matter how difficult it was going to be to let her go again. Dallas's gut twisted as he took in her beautiful, peaceful features to remember them forever. "To stay out of guilt. She's finally becoming herself again. She's like a bird in the sky or a fish in the ocean. I want her to spread her wings." Well, fish didn't have wings.

Austin raised a reddish eyebrow. "Or fins?"

"You know what I mean."

His expression turned pensive. "Yes, I do."

What was that about?

A WEEK AFTER BEING discharged from the hospital, Skylar placed another stroke on the canvas and stepped back.

Worry clenched her stomach. It had been such a long time since she'd painted. Had she lost her skills? The sunset evoked a sense of awe, but could she evoke the same in others with her work?

Then her heart started beating faster as Dallas walked toward her in the sand.

"The doctor told you to take it easy for some time. Are you taking it easy?"

Right. Very romantic. Not! She didn't want him to see her as someone weak who needed looking after. "I sure am," she grunted, about to pack up the easel.

"Don't lift it. I'll carry it home for you."

"I can carry it." She stroked the smooth surface lovingly. "And remember, it saved my life."

"The worst day of mine." His eyes widened as if he realized what he'd said. "Not because your life was saved but because it could've been lost."

That was also the day she'd told him—in a way—that she loved him. In the hospital, he'd told her he'd heard the conversation and called the police. And he'd just called it the worst day of his life. But he'd declared her love for him, and yet he hadn't said that he loved her too.

Her heart fell into the sand. Was it too late for them, after all? Had she done such irreparable damage to their relationship that he'd—understandably—given up on her? He still obviously cared about her, or he wouldn't be here right now, fussing over her. But maybe not to the degree of loving her, and her loss felt overwhelming.

"Wow." He touched the edge of the painting. "It's striking. I don't even know what's more striking, you or the painting."

Secretly pleased, she playfully slapped his bare forearm exposed from his T-shirt. "Yeah, sure. Kai must be giving you lessons on how to give compliments."

"I don't need those kinds of lessons to see how amazing you are." Yet he didn't say he loved her.

A gigantic lump formed in her throat, but she muttered, "Thank you." Then she frowned. "I'll have to do lots of community service for not reporting my father when I remembered what he did. But it's much better than the alternative. Marina came through for us, and will make sure Grandma and I both get much lighter punishments than I expected." She dragged the toe of her sneaker through the sand, digging deep. If only she hadn't buried her memories so deep. If only she and Grandma had gone to the police when she began remembering them. "I'm sorry I didn't tell you about my memories. I'm sorry I broke off our engagement."

"I understand you had your reasons." His voice was gentle.

"I wanted to keep you and Grandma safe. But I went about it the wrong way." Guilt still needled her. She shouldn't have told Grandma. At least then, she could have spared her from having to share in the punishment. But it was over now.

"It's in the past," Dallas said as if confirming her thoughts. "And I'm sorry you went through so much."

"Thank you. By the way, I'm keeping Breeze." She lifted her chin. She couldn't imagine her life without the goofy dog. But then, she couldn't imagine her life without Dallas, either, and she didn't know where they were standing now. "I don't care if she used to be Earl's dog. She's mine now."

"Good. And I'll be glad to get a puppy. Mom, too. My brothers are still undecided, though."

They kept silent for a few moments. Earl had confessed to shooting Wyatt and told the police where he'd buried him in the sand. Skylar had given her father a proper burial when the remains were released to her. She'd even visited the grave with her grandmother and Dallas, more for Grandma's sake than her own. But she hadn't put flowers there.

Instead, she'd let a wreath float in the ocean. For Mom.

She'd let her past consume her before, even when she'd avoided it. Or maybe precisely because she'd avoided it. She needed to live in her present. And she ached for Dallas to be her present and her future.

While she'd been painting again, she'd allowed herself to dream they'd be together again. Was it only a dream? "I've decided to stay in Port Sunshine."

His face lit up. "Are you sure?"

"Yes." She smoothed out the line she'd dug in the sand with her toes. If only she could so easily smooth away the barriers between them. "I need to comfort Grandma after her double heartache. The seaside cottage needs renovations and a paint-over. My aunt could use some help at the restaurant. And this place... It calls to my heart."

You. You call to my heart.

"What about your job?" he asked.

Huh. She'd expected him to be more ecstatic. "I can do some bookkeeping jobs remotely. And if a client insists on meeting in person once in a while, I can drive to Charleston."

"Great. And you could sell your watercolors and paintings again." He lifted her up and whirled her around, making her head spin.

"If not, I'll enjoy them in my spare time," she said when she could talk again because he took her breath away. Every cell in her body went ecstatic at being in his arms.

"I think my mind needed a paint-over." She started packing her art supplies when he put her down.

"Excuse me? A paint-over?"

"My life doesn't need to go from one swing of the pendulum to the other. It doesn't have to be either-or. I don't have to be either a serious accountant or a goofy chatterbox artist. We have so many sides of us, and we don't need to suppress some of them to fit into a new mold."

"You've put it beautifully."

"And we shouldn't judge ourselves or judge others based on our parents or theirs. We are our own people." Subconsciously, once she'd realized what her father had done, once she'd focused on what *his* father had done, she'd been scared there was a chance Dallas might turn out the same. "Instead of finding myself in a big city, I ran away from myself and my memories."

"And me."

"And you."

But he *still* didn't say he loved her. Her heart sank into the sand. Was it too late for them, after all?

AS HE LED SKYLAR TO their special little cove, Dallas didn't remember the last time he'd been this nervous. What would her answer be?

His stomach clenched. He hadn't been this much on the edge the first time he'd proposed. An overconfident teenager, he'd been sure she'd say yes.

"Okay, when can I open my eyes?" She giggled.

"Just a little more." He held her hand, guiding her.

"What if I stumble?"

"I'll make sure you stay standing." He hoped he'd get to do that for the rest of his life. Not that he'd want her to stumble, of course.

She stopped. "Is Breeze still running along?"

Breeze barked as if to show that yes, she sure was. And she was going to play an important role in all this, too.

Kai, who'd guarded the cove entrance until Dallas got there, waved at them. Dallas waved back and gestured that Kai could leave. "Thanks, bro."

"Thanks, bro? Dallas, can you at least give me a hint?" Skylar demonstratively sighed.

He shook his head but then remembered she couldn't see him. "Nope. Sorry."

Then, when they were close enough, Breeze took off and ran inside the cove.

"Oh no! Breeze, wait!" Dallas shouted. She'd better not set her coat on fire.

"I guess I can open my eyes now?"

"Yes." He ran after the dog before Breeze could get into any mischief. "But I wanted it to be a surprise."

Skylar gasped behind his back. "It sure is."

Dallas caught up with Breeze and leashed her before she could get close to any candles. "Stay. I really need you to stay."

He'd thought the same thoughts before Skylar had left for college. He winced as he straightened. History wasn't going to repeat itself, was it?

But now that Skylar had decided to stay in their small town for good, he'd never forgive himself if he didn't try for the second time. The third time, if needed, but he hoped it wouldn't come to that.

Her eyes were huge. "You did... all that?"

"My brothers helped. Marina, too. And your grandmother by keeping you busy."

He did his best to see it through her eyes. Peach-scented candles on the ground, a little picnic with her favorite foods on a makeshift table, and the words he'd constructed from seashells on the sand. It had taken a lot of time to gather those seashells, but he'd had a lot of patience and brothers with eagle eyes. Even if some of them had groaned when he suggested he should spell her name with seashells.

He'd thought to write those words on the sand at first but had been afraid the tide would wash them away.

Then he noticed Breeze messed up one letter in her frantic run. "Oh, oops, the *Y* got moved."

Skylar blinked. "I don't know what got moved, much less why."

"The *Y* in 'marry me.'" His pulse skyrocketed, and his mouth went dry. All thoughts flew out of his brain, except one. What was she going to answer?

She stared at him. "Do you mean it?"

Breeze nudged his hand as if to give a gentle reminder. He slapped himself on the forehead. "Oh no!"

Skylar's lips trembled. "You... you don't mean it? You didn't mean to propose?"

Breeze stretched on the ground and covered her head with her paw.

"I'm messing it up, aren't I?" he whispered.

Breeze barked as if to say, "Welcome to the club."

"I mean, of course, I mean it." He dropped to one knee.

"But you never said you loved me. Well, not after I came back. Even after I said I loved you," she whispered.

"Of course, I love you! I thought it was clear."

Skylar laughed and rolled her eyes. "You're supposed to say it, as well. Spell it out, if you will." She gestured at the seashells.

Oh. "I loved you long before I realized it. I loved you my entire life. And even when I wanted to stop loving you, I just... couldn't. I'll love you till my last breath. Skylar, you're the very air I breathe. You're my sunshine in the sky. You're the breeze from the ocean."

Breeze barked again at the sound of her name.

"Maybe that didn't sound right," he added fast.

Tears appeared in Skylar's eyes, and he swallowed hard. Did he upset her? "No," she whispered.

No? He'd never been great with words. And he'd never been a creative type. He didn't know how to show how he felt.

"No, you're wrong." She wiped her tears and took his hands in hers. "That sounded right. And perfect. And more than I ever could wish for."

Was there a *but* coming? He went cold. "But?"

"There's no *but*. I love you. I never stopped loving you. If you can forgive me for leaving you—"

"I already have. I want to spend the rest of my life with you."

The golden retriever whined.

Dallas chuckled. "And with you, too, of course. I know it now says 'marr me,' but will you marry me?"

The dog barked again. Her exasperated look clearly said, "These humans!"

"Oh right. Thanks for the reminder. Or several reminders." He carefully untied the pink ribbon on Breeze's collar, and the ring plopped into his palm.

"Are you for real?" Skylar's eyes still stayed huge.

His heart dropped near the candles. Maybe the proposal wasn't such a great idea. Was he moving too fast for her? "You're my dream and my reality, and I want it to be this way for the rest of my life. But if you don't feel that way or if you need time—"

"Yes! Yes! Yes!" Skylar squealed, jumped, and clapped. "I mean, yes to marrying you. I don't need more time. We've waited waaaay too long already."

She leaned to hug him, then bent to hug Breeze. The golden retriever rose on her hind paws, and she and Skylar did some weird dance, both squealing.

He laughed, deliriously happy. His girl was definitely back. Or rather his forever woman. Her smile was open and bright, just like before.

Ecstatic, he placed the ring on her finger and got up to catch her in his embrace. He loved the sound of her laughter and the confidence that returned to her. He loved the new pensive and practical side of her. He loved *everything* about her.

Her gaze lingered on the ring, and her smile slipped a bit.

He froze. "You don't like it?" He'd enlisted help from Marina and Skylar's grandma, but one never knew.

"I love it! I absolutely love it! But... it's not the same ring you proposed with the first time. You didn't... didn't need to get an upgrade. I'd happily marry you even if you put a rubber band on my finger."

"I, well, I threw that ring into the ocean after you returned it to me. I was angry then. Okay, I dove after it afterward but couldn't find it."

"I'm sorry for everything I put you through."

He didn't want her to be sad. Ever. "It's in the past. And you had your reasons. But you're here now. My love and my bride."

"I'm here now," she echoed, her eyes warm again. "With you, my love and my future husband."

The tender way she said those words gave him a jolt of joy even more than the words themselves. "It's not just about giving you a more expensive ring now. I want the ocean to wash away past hurts and take that ring. This is a second chance, but it's also a new beginning for us."

"Yes, it is." She drew him to her and brushed her lips against his, sending a delicious shiver through him. "It truly is."

Chapter Eighteen

Skylar breathed in a lungful of salty air, her veil floating in the breeze. That fresh air mixed with the flower aroma from her bouquet.

Warm sand caressed her bare toes as she walked between rows of white chairs on the beach, her grandmother leaning on her but looking ten years younger. Skylar had taken over several arrangements and even the bouquet her grandmother was supposed to carry while walking down the aisle. Now, she slowed and whispered to Grandma. "I'm so sorry. I feel like I'm stealing your wedding."

"Nonsense!" Grandma waved her off and pressed on with surprising agility. "There'll be other men in my life. But you know there's only one man for you. And he's waited long enough."

He sure had.

Skylar's heart swelled as she gazed at Dallas waiting for her now, dashingly handsome in his tuxedo even if he felt out of place in it. He beamed at her the instant their gazes met, and she basked in the love lighting up his eyes, feeling its warm glow no matter the distance.

She'd dreamed of this day since she'd fallen in love with him nearly two decades ago. It wasn't exactly like she'd dreamed up or drawn on paper that had later become a wedding invitation card for many. Because it was better. Because this wasn't an idyllic wedding invitation card with a glossy surface and overused words but an invitation to a new life together.

All the seats, decorated with white ribbons and white flowers, were occupied. She was an only child, but her cousins made it here for her wedding, sitting beside her aunt, and Dallas had a large family who'd thankfully forgiven her. Even Terrence Hirst sat in a far seat, though Skylar wasn't sure how she felt about that yet. Many townspeople showed up. People here supported each other, and it warmed her heart.

Breeze barked and tried to jump into the aisle, but Mrs. Lawrence held the dog in place. Skylar sent her golden retriever an apologetic glance and nearly stopped to pet her. Dallas had told her he'd help with the puppies. There were positive things to be said for solitude, but she was glad she wasn't in this alone.

How would it have worked out if they'd gotten married the first time? Would it have worked at all?

Now she knew she'd subconsciously tried to escape the tragedy of what she'd seen that stormy night. She'd put on gigantic glasses as pink as the sunrises she'd loved to paint. And when she'd had to confront those memories, she'd run the opposite way—away to the big city to find comfort in the certainty of numbers and spreadsheets and clear lines instead of blurred ones like in her watercolors.

Neither version of her then had been ready for marriage or a long-term commitment. Dallas deserved better.

She smiled at him as she took her place near him. He deserved the woman she was now, the woman who'd combined both sides and finally found herself.

The best man, Kai, gave her a thumbs-up with his usual mischievous grin, but his eyes turned wistful any time he looked at her maid of honor, Marina. And he sent lots of glances Marina's way.

Skylar hid a smile as the ceremony began. Kai and Marina had been best friends, but clearly, Kai had a thing for her now. And conversations with her childhood friend revealed that Marina had a soft spot for the flirtatious and laid-back Kai but had always put her studies and career—and fine, getting away from her demanding father—first.

Could there be much more between these best friends? And could Skylar nudge them toward each other?

All the bridesmaids wore turquoise silk off-the-shoulder dresses, the slippery fabric flowing to their ankles. And all of them wore the seashell bracelets Skylar had made when they'd been fourteen. Skylar's chest expanded. They'd all kept those friendship bracelets. Several bracelets were missing a seashell or two, and a few other seashells were chipped. Some of the women wore them on their wrist, some on an ankle, and one as a decoration in her beautifully styled updo.

But the seashell bracelets were there. And that represented their friendship and lives.

Her gaze flicked back to Dallas, and her heart started beating faster. What an incredible day. What an incredible man.

In her teens, she'd already known where she belonged and whom she belonged with. But at the time, she hadn't been the person Dallas should belong with. They got their second chance, and gratitude lifted her spirit the same way he now lifted her veil.

Once she'd remembered that horrible night, she started seeing him through the fabric of her trauma, thin but not transparent like this veil. More than the phone call demanding she stay away from her grandmother and Dallas or the people she loved would suffer had made her break off the engagement, though there was that.

No matter how well she knew him, a small subconscious part of her had been terrified he'd do the same thing her father had done to her mother. After all, Dallas's father was abusive, and anger issues could be hereditary. Plus, Dallas had years of suppressed anger due to his upbringing. So what if he hadn't exhibited violent tendencies toward her? Skylar's father had treated her mother well until that stormy night.

But Skylar could see him clearly now in the bright sun, just as he was. Not perfect, but yet the kind, caring man of her dreams and of her reality. And she knew he saw her clearly, just as she was. He always had, and he always would.

"I love you so much," she mouthed to him. She'd had to keep those words deep inside for so long, and now she could let them soar in the sky again.

"I love you, too," he whispered back.

As she looked up at the sky, a whiff of her mother's favorite floral perfume traveled to her. Her heart contracted. Must be her imagination. She could allow herself to miss her mother now. She didn't know whether she'd ever be able to forgive her father, but eventually, she'd be able to move on. To keep on loving Dallas and living her dream in this beautiful coastal town.

One mystery had been resolved, but *that* cottage seemed to have many more, including the one about Dallas's father. But that wasn't Skylar's story.

The moment the priest announced Dallas and Skylar husband and wife, her heart soared.

And it soared even further when Dallas kissed her.

Epilogue

Marina Helms winced as something clattered in the restaurant kitchen's opposite corner. How exactly had she gotten herself into this situation? She was used to things being organized and everything in order. This was chaos.

"What happened?" she yelled.

"I dropped a pan," her only remaining sous-chef yelled back.

Hopefully, not with the food in it. They were behind on the orders already.

She breathed in the scents of baked fish, garlic, and spices, doing her best to smooth her raw nerves. She was no cook, but how difficult could it be to flip a few steaks? Easy-peasy, right?

Minutes later, she was looking at charred steak. Apparently, not easy at all.

Her sister, Saylor, who was chopping a salad right now, grimaced, then turned up the air-conditioning, sending a wave of cool air through the kitchen. "Yes, the customer wanted their steak well-done, but not burned."

"What an astute observation." Marina groaned and started a new one with a jolt of envy toward her childhood friend, Skylar.

Skylar was on her honeymoon now, in bliss with the guy she'd always loved. No matter the years apart, Marina had reconnected with her friend recently and was happy for her. She really was.

Skylar had found her passion again in many senses, and she'd deserved it, especially after everything she'd gone through. Marina didn't intend to get married again. One heartache and failed marriage was enough. More than enough.

She glanced with longing at the beautiful cerulean sky beyond the window and the calm waves touching the sand, then returned her attention to the skillet. Hopefully, the steak was good enough.

Her mother was on a cruise, and this was Marina's first day working the restaurant without her. She could handle it fine. But for various reasons, several staff members had called in, unable to come to work today.

At least, the day couldn't get any worse, right?

One of her remaining waitresses, Jan, rushed into the kitchen. "I'm so sorry, but my babysitter just called. My daughter is unwell. I have to go."

Marina sighed. She stood corrected. It just got worse. Still, she nodded. "Of course. I hope your daughter feels better."

Then she placed the steak on the plate with rice and green beans. She'd have to deliver it herself. And while she didn't like asking for help, she was in too deep now.

"Thanks, Sis." She did her best to stifle the resentment souring her stomach like acid as she hurried to the dining hall carrying the tray with the plate, a bowl of the salad Saylor had made, and a basket with biscuits emitting a mouthwatering aroma.

Saylor had stayed to help and was much better at cooking than Marina had ever been. But the rest of their sisters had returned to their busy lives in the city after Skylar's wedding. So unfair.

Yes, Mom had only asked Marina to help in her absence because Marina was the eldest and therefore the most responsible one. Why did the firstborn child always have to be punished for arriving first?

The buzz of voices in the dining room met her together with a few curious glances. One of those glances sent a jolt of awareness charging through her.

Kai. Her secret crush. So secret it had taken her years to realize it herself. Her heartbeat increased from his mere presence.

Distracted, she stumbled, and her arms flailed in her desperate attempt to catch herself. Food flew in different directions. One of the biscuits landed in someone's tea.

Oh no!

She held onto the plate and the basket.

Kai rushed to her and steadied her. He wore a white pirate shirt with long sleeves, and now he also wore a steak, a few rice grains, and green beans with long pods. One of those beans even ended up in the loop of his earring.

The steak skidded on the floor, and the rice and green beans plopped behind it. Except for the pod that stayed in the earring as a statement to her clumsiness.

"I'm... I'm so sorry." She gave out a sound close to a hiccup but not quite.

"Hello, Marina." He smelled of something musky and exciting, sending her pulse into overdrive. "It's okay. Are you all right?"

"Hi. Yes. No. Yes. Of course, I'm all right." Even if she realized she wore some rice, too, and probably had a green pod stuck in her hair.

She stepped back from the enticing heat of his arms. Because now he wasn't the flirtatious boy with twinkles in his brown eyes she'd become best friends with. He was a man with a broad chest and muscles chiseled by outdoor labor. But just as before, he was off-limits. Even more so now.

She tore her glance away from him and surveyed the damage. "We'll get that tea replaced right away," she said to the woman who now had a biscuit in her iced tea.

A few biscuits landed in a corner and one on a man's lap. But nobody was wearing the salad. Whew!

Overall, Kai had endured the biggest damage. She gasped at the large grease stain spreading on his shirt. "I... I'll pay for dry cleaning. Or... or I can try to remove it now."

"Yeah, why doesn't he take off that shirt?" A woman in a bright marmalade-hued dress with a wide white belt called out.

Heat crept up Marina's neck.

Thankfully, Kai didn't pay attention to the comment. "It's no problem." Then he stooped to gather the mess on the floor with napkins. "Don't worry. I'll clean this up."

"No, I'll take care of it." She placed the juicy steak back on the tray, which was far from a good idea, but she couldn't think straight in his presence.

Why was this happening again? She was supposed to get over her ridiculous crush many years ago. She had. She'd even fallen in love with someone else. Someone who'd felt safe. Who'd been his total opposite.

Well, the joke was on her, wasn't it?

"I'm so sorry about the steak, sir," she apologized to a bald sixtysomething man in gray slacks. "I'll get another one ready immediately." She didn't know how, but she'd have to figure it out.

She'd helped at her mother's restaurant before, but mostly by waiting on tables. She'd never made anyone wear food then.

"You're understaffed today, aren't you?" Kai's tone turned unusually serious.

She nodded. "Yes." And she needed to get back into the kitchen instead of staring into his eyes. Oh, and mop up the floor before anyone slipped.

"You're doing great. Looking great, too." He winked.

Yeah right. He'd paid compliments to everything in sight, one of the secrets of his popularity. Usually, she was well-put together, but today, her apron was stained and crooked, her hair probably a mess—or did she forget to take off her hairnet? She'd be grateful if she didn't have sweat stains under her armpits from all the heat in the kitchen.

"Any day now." The woman pointed at her tall glass of iced tea with a floating biscuit in it. Then she gestured to the biscuits near the wall. "And you're just inviting roaches with bread on the floor. Not to mention, I've been waiting *forever* for my order."

Now Marina would have those stains from all the heat she was getting *here*.

"Right. Sorry about that." Her stomach clenched while she picked up the biscuits. She didn't like apologizing, either.

Twin boys at a nearby table started fighting, so their screams mostly drowned her words.

She squared her shoulders as she marched back into the kitchen. She was a confident, successful woman now. Not a shy geek who'd been mercilessly teased until Kai found out and put a stop to it.

She could do this.

"Help! My daughter fell into the water!" The cry from the patio made her run there.

Just in time to see Kai dive into the ocean.

THE END

From Alexa: Thank you so much for reading! Did you enjoy Skylar and Dallas's story? I hope you'll also want to read the next book in the series and see Marina and Kai get their chance at happiness. If so, please click here[1] to purchase their story, *Seaside Cowboy's Best Friend.*

---

1. https://books2read.com/u/bQAYOe

Other books by Alexa Verde

TO SEE AN UPDATED LIST of all my other books or subscribe to my weekly reader newsletter (and get a free ebook as your welcome gift!) click here[2].

---

2. https://www.subscribepage.com/alexaverdepublishedbooks

Acknowledgments

First of all, thank You to God for putting up with me, and for all the blessings!

A million thanks to you, my readers, for reading my books, for sending me encouragement, and for supporting me.

Many thanks to my street team, Alexa's Amazing Readers, and to my beta readers, whom I love to pieces. Special thanks to Terry, Patricia, MaryEllen, Carol W., Michaela, Trudy, Margaret, Mary Jane, Susan, Louise, and Debbie for their feedback and help with typo-spotting!

Thanks to Linda Klager for suggesting the town name; to Teresa Kirk, Denise Chrisman Ward, Lois Medders, MJ Lockey, Michelle Bauer, Lisa Stillman Barret, Sylvia Vann, Carol Fritz, and Patricia Oaks for suggesting character names; and to Jan C Stetson for naming the dog.

Heartfelt thanks to author Jessie Gussman for helping me so much on the way. Jessie, you make me laugh, you make me smile, and you make the world a better place.

I also thank my wonderful editor, Deirdre, for coming through for me every time.